THE MAN WITH THE HAT

ESMEE OTTER

TRANSLATED BY
ESMEE OTTER

DUTCH OTTER

Thanks to my grandfather, Erick Filemon,

for his inspiring insights and enthusiasm,

as well as for modelling for the cover of this book!

1 HAPPY PILLS

My new mom calls them *happy pills*. But despite the brightly coloured shapes that scrape my throat every day, I see him standing in the corner of the room. The man with the hat.

He has one single eye, the white of which contrasts sharply with his complexion, watching me closely from under the brim of his fedora. On the other side, he has a steak cheek. I don't know how else to call it, it's hard to describe. Reddish, mangled, with bulges and collapsed grooves. And above it, a tawdry grey fedora.

I look at him. I still find it hard to realise he's not there. Not for real, at least. According to my psychiatrist, Jack Reed, he exists solely in my mind. A manifestation of trauma, he calls it. You'd think I'd be able to remember such trauma, right? But I really don't know which crevices of my memory I would have to delve into. There's a lot I don't remember. Who are my real parents? Are they still alive? Where are they? Why was I separated from them? And when was the last time I saw them?

I vaguely remember my sixth birthday. Although, I think it was my birthday, because I recall something about a present. In that memory I am splashing my arms in the water and my mother is with me. I can only partially picture her face as she wraps her arms around me. She has a certain look in her eyes - one I don't fully understand.

That image is one of the remaining few from my younger years, pre adoption. Jack says that is quite normal. Suffering can hide and lurk in the shadow for years and present itself in different ways - masquerading and shapeshifting. So the man with the hat doesn't have to be a literal interpretation, according to him. He has been trying to bring the actual suffering to the surface for months, ever since the man with the hat first appeared, with lengthy conversations, memory training and sleep hypnosis.

One vision emerged, last Friday, of a long hallway with snow-white walls and an unblemished carpet with a lily pattern. Since the day before yesterday, that carpet has even gained color: lilac. The lilac lily carpet. Why this memory? And not one that can tell me more?

Jack calls it a breakthrough in a conversation with my foster parents. The therapy is working, he claims with his usual smug attitude. Well, that's what they pay you big money for, after all. I myself am not so convinced. We have been plodding along for nearly ten months, on the one hand trying to uncover my trauma and on the other hand burying its manifestation with the yellow happy pills.

But I obediently keep attending the therapy sessions. I don't want Kyra and Danny to worry. They have a hard enough time with their real daughter, Reina. She needs special attention and measured living rules, like a strict daily routine. My nightly screeching doesn't fit in with that, Kyra has made that more than clear to me.

And Danny... He already had his hands full with one daughter he hadn't counted on. And now the daughter, whom he had chosen, has become a mental wreck who can barely make it through college. I had everything going for me. My studies were going well and I had been living in a dorm for a few months; it gave Kyra more peace of mind, which she needed for Reina. She's not that happy to have me back - which I don't find surprising, given the circumstances, but it is difficult.

Danny takes care of me. At night, he will come to hold and reassure me, telling me I'm safe and rocking back and forth until I am calm again. He keeps repeating Jack's words to Kyra: "A stable home environment is of utmost important for the progress of therapy."

"And that's important for Reina too," Kyra then says, "but *she* doesn't get that either."

"And she's your real daughter," I finish her sentence in my head. I sigh deeply.

"What are you thinking about?"

I look up.

Jack is hunched over his desk, leaning on his elbows. That iconic, barely perceptible grin peeps out from under his knuckles. "You know I'm always on to you. There's nowhere to hide, Amber." He puts his chin on top of his hands.

I'd really like to shake my head right now. Sometimes I really dislike him. Not because of who he is, but because of the fact that he can see right through me. He's right. I have nowhere to hide. Not with him.

"And that's just the thing you're so good at," he adds. "Who really knows what's hiding behind you? Behind the mask you wear every day?" He is silent for a moment - and I know he is waiting for my response. I feel his eyes pierce mine. Deep and incisive. It feels oppressive. I swallow and wipe my sticky forehead with my sleeve.

"You can take off your jumper, you know."

I shake my head and reach for the cup of tea in front of me, just so my hands have something to do. I take a big sip, followed by another. I put the cup back on its saucer.

"What are you thinking about?"

I look at my hands. My thumbnail presses into my skin; all the lines meet under the pressure point.

"Are you still uncomfortable with him in the room?"

I shrug.

He stands up and slides his desk chair back. He looks around the room. "Where is he now?"

I look up. My uncertain gaze meets his determined one. My eyes turn carefully to the left corner of the room, to the empty spot next to the huge houseplant. Empty in the eyes of Jack, that is.

He walks towards the corner and lifts his arm. "Here?"

"Slightly to the left."

He takes a step to the side. "Is he standing here?"

I bob my head.

Jack takes another small step to the side. His fingers disappear into the right half of the man with the hat's face.

I nod.

Jack stretches his arm. His wrist disappears and his fingers protrude from the steak cheek. He fidgets them back and forth.

I grimace. I just can't get used to it, no matter how many times he does that.

Jack stands in front of the man now, his back turned towards him. He looks at me sternly. "How do you feel now?"

I shrug. "It's not like he's always there."

"But when he is, you feel uncomfortable. Why is that, do you think?"

"Because he looks at me."

"Does it bother you when people look at you?"

I let out a deep sigh. "Yes, it annoys me."

"And what if I look at you?"

The corner of my mouth twitches. "I find that even more annoying."

He chuckles. "Why?"

I look at him for a moment before replying. "Because you see through me."

He purses his lips and averts his gaze. "That comes with the job, I'm afraid."

I look at the nail mark in my hand. "Is he ever going to leave?"

It remains silent for a moment.

I look up. My breath catches in my throat. One eye, pressing through Jack's right eye. His cheek, discoloured. Deep furrows pushing through the skin. I clutch the chair arms. The dark lips forcing through Jack's. His whole face contorts as the man with the hat makes his way forward. My eyes roll in their sockets. Before I know it, my forehead hits the cherry wood top in front of me.

Circles form in the remaining layer of tea in the white mug.

"Amber?"

I blink my eyes. A sharp pain jolts through my head like a needle. I reach for it.

"Does it hurt?"

I blink again and look at Jack's sweaty face, hovering over me. His hand feels cool on my forehead. I swallow effortfully. "I think it's ebbing away."

"I'll get you some water. Just stay down for a while." He gently lays my head on the pillow. It takes me a while to realise I'm lying on the sofa. Normally I lie here only when I am under his hypnosis, with him sitting two arm lengths away in the brown leather armchair.

"Here you go." He holds a glass of water in front of me.

I slowly rise and grasp it with both hands.

"Careful," he murmurs.

I want to listen, but I drink voraciously. It's like I haven't drunk anything for hours. Perhaps that's true. "How long-?" I utter.

He smiles compassionately. "Not long." He pulls the armchair towards him and sits down opposite me.

I look at the clock on his wall and then at him.

He's biting his lip. "I don't have another client anyway, so just sit quietly for a while. When you feel better, you can get up. If that goes well, I'll let you go home. O—" he fumbles in his pocket, "but not without eating something first." He pulls out an *Oat To Enjoy This* breakfast bar. I always see him eating a bar like that before our session. "Oatmeal-" he starts.

"-is good for your energy," I complement him.

He chuckles. "See, you've learned something from me after all."

I nod as I tear off the wrapper. "I do listen to you."

He purses his lips. "So long as you listen to your own body too."

I look up at him as I take a bite.

"Are you eating properly?"

I chew slowly and hold the bar up in front of his face.

"You know what I mean, Amber. You've gotten skinnier again."

"I'm surprised you can see that," I respond with a half-full mouth, tugging at my oversized sweater.

He's silent for a moment and frowns deeply. "Are you hiding it from your parents?"

I chew at length on a piece of oatmeal.

"From Kyra?.... From Danny?"

Finally, I swallow my bite. "I think I feel better already."

He grins. "One answer," he urges. "You haven't been very, um, talkative this session."

"And whose fault is that?"

He bites his lip. "What happened?"

My eyes dart to the corner of the room, which is now empty for me too. The man with the hat is not there. "He came through you," I start, "with his face, I mean. First his eye, then that cheek of his, then his lips. And your whole..." I gasp and wave my hand in front of my face. "...your whole face distorted."

He nods slowly. "Are they becoming more frequent, the delusions?"

"It's not that I see him more often. But he does seem to be getting closer. A little bit each time."

"Does that scare you?"

I raise my eyebrows. "I already find it fucked up to see him from a distance." I eat the last piece of the bar as Jack's eyes watch me closely.

"We still need to find out why you're seeing him. And why it started after the fire. Was it the fire itself? Was it your roommate's face? The fear?"

I stare silently out of the window. They're good questions, but I don't have the answers. And when I try to find the answers, my head turns into one big haze. It feels like an impenetrable fog in which nothing is clear. Every vague memory I have vanishes completely into the background. While pondering, I heave a sigh. "My bus is about to depart," I remark.

I get up from the sofa and start to walk towards the door, but he grabs me by the wrist.

"Not so fast, Amber."

I look back. My chest feels heavy and tense.

"You know what I mean."

"I just don't believe in it," I respond gruffly.

"Do you think the dose is too low?"

I shake my head unintentionally. "I just thought... it would be more effective. But I still see him. Clearer every day and closer and closer."

"Try it for a while longer. If it doesn't improve after this round, we'll see if we need to increase the dose. But give it a little more time. Allow yourself that."

My fingertips glide over the unblemished white box on his desk, on the spot that previously had an unfortunate encounter with my forehead.

"And try to stick to it this time. Three times a day, at the same time as much as you can. And I'll see you the day after tomorrow."

I turn to him, but my gaze does not meet his. The man with the hat is here again. He is now standing by the sofa. His fingertips stroke the dark brown leather of the armrest.

"Amber." Jack snaps his fingers.

"Yes," I respond instinctively. I walk towards the door of his office and place my hand on the latch.

"Aren't you forgetting something?"

I remain still. My empty hand balls into a fist and then relaxes. I feel the cool cardboard press gently against my palm, as Jack's warm breath rolls down my neck. I grasp the box and clasp it firmly in my hand. "See you Friday," I mutter. I pull open the door and step outside. As I close the door behind me, I see him walking back to his desk. Before he disappears from sight, he reaches for the white mug.

2 HAILSTONES

My eyes follow the joints of the tiles as I walk along the pavement. Occasionally, I see shoes passing by. Black lacquered shoes with wide noses. I imagine a man in a grey suit walking by, holding a brown leather briefcase in one hand and a mobile phone in the other, pressed firmly to his ear. I look up and catch a glimpse of the man through the shop window beside me. His suit is blue and his bag is black. He holds his mobile phone in front of him while peering at it with an arched neck. He walks right through the man with the hat.

I turn around and look at both men. They are wearing the same glossy black shoes, although the shine is duller on the one pair. Could the man with the hat perhaps be a businessman, I wonder randomly. I turn towards the bus shelter, which is still about fifty metres away from me, and walk along slowly, fixated on the reflection in the windows.

Across the street walks a woman with a pram and a young girl, who is maybe about four years old, by her hand. The girl clutches a large ice cream cone in her other hand, which she voraciously munches. The ice cream melts too quickly, though, and it drips over her hand, down her arm and via her elbow onto her bright yellow dress.

A dull ache shoots through my left hand. I look at the iron rack I almost knocked over, containing a number of different newspapers. My gaze falls on The Pay Per, the daily paper made right here in the centre of Vassen. On the front page are three images. A photo of some couple celebrating 50 years of marriage, covering almost half the page, an image of an offer at the swimming pool and a landscape photograph of a large building partly surrounded by scaffolding. For a moment, the image of the lilac lily carpet flickers before my eyes.

I pick up the paper and turn the pages until I reach the page number belonging to the picture of the building. It is a mini article on the renovation of an extravagant but run-down-looking hotel. The information takes up less than a quarter of a page. My fingers slide along the edge of the page, my nail pinches the edge and rips a tear in the page.

"Are you going to buy that or just stand there and read it?" a barbed voice chimes.

I abruptly slam the paper shut and look up.

A burly bald man leans against the window frame in the doorway of the tobacco shop.

"Um, I—" I start to stutter.

He grins. His gaze slides down my body and slowly creeps upwards until it lingers on my breasts.

I see his Adam's apple move as he swallows. Small drops of sweat form on my forehead.

"Or did you forget your wallet?" he continues. It is only then that he looks at my face again. My breath falters.

"I could lend it to you. I see you pass by here three times a week anyway."

He steps outside, towards the rack and closer to me. "Or you can work for it. I could use someone at the back of the shop." His spotted, wrinkled hand now rests on the edge of the rack, less than twenty centimetres away from my own hand. His other hand caresses his stomach before tucking his thumb behind his belt. He lets out a groaning sigh. "How old are you?"

My eyes tremble in their sockets.

"I'll pay you well."

At that moment, I see the reflection of the bus in the window. I throw the newspaper down on the rack, turn around and stand in front of the doors within a few steps. The slight hiss strokes my eardrums as I watch the doors open in front of me. I get in, show the driver my multi-use ticket and walk with a brisk stride to the back seats of the bus. With a heavy sigh, I sink down on the window seat on the highway side, as far away from the scruffy old man from the tobacco shop as humanly possible.

The bus starts moving and I invariably watch the traffic in the road next to me. Cars slide in and out of my field of vision. We turn a corner. I look at the screen for the next stop and see that the stops are different from the ones I'm supposed to see. It's the wrong bus. But I don't care about that now. I slip in my earbuds and put on my favourite music. The type of music people never expect from me, seemingly. Because I look *so innocent* and *well-behaved*. I rest my head against the window and close my eyes. I mentally prepare myself for the walk later on, and for the altercation with Kyra because, once again, I will be coming home late. I sigh again. I just want to crawl into my bed, pull my blanket over my head, listen to music and then sleep, as though it's raining cats and dogs outside. But the sun is shining in full and it is too hot for a thick blanket to provide me comfort and solace.

With a light squeak, the bus comes to a halt and the doors slide open, hissing. Through my music, I hear footsteps approaching. They stop close to me. I open my eyes and my gaze instantly meets hers: my former college roommate, Denise. Of all the people who could have taken this particular bus at this time of day... when I'm not even supposed to be on this bus.

Her eyes spit fire. She turns briskly and walks back to the front of the bus, where she perches on a seat.

I put my hand against my sternum and feel a frantic pounding. As if things aren't bad enough, I think with dismay. My teeth imprint dents into my lower lip. I take a deep breath, stroking my arm with my hand. It's not my fault. Not my responsibility. It's not my fault. It's not my fault. It's not...

. . .

CRACKLE, CRACKLE.

Flames swirl around the bed. Smoke billows across the walls.

"HIIIIIRAAAAAAAAAAAAAUUUUHHHHH!"

My eardrums clatter.

Her eyes roll in their sockets as the flames whip around her head.

SMACK!

I rub my cheek after hitting it hard.

An older woman, sitting two rows in front of me, looks back, with a confused look on her face. Her eyes squeeze into slits as she grimaces.

Preferably I would stick my tongue out at her, but that won't get me anywhere, according to Jack's sage advice.

Before I know it, my thoughts wander back to the raging fire. The vision in my head is more extreme than the actual event, seemingly. Jack calls it an interpretation.

Denise's hair did catch fire. One moment, her copper strands were still flowing over her sheets; the next, the fire snatched the neatly trimmed ends and rolled over the lengths. She managed to put it out just in time to prevent her scalp from burning. Her scream was for real, though; it still echoes between my bedroom walls sometimes in the dead of night, when I am overwhelmed by distressing thoughts. It makes me revisit the whole incident. That night. The fire. And the aftermath.

The next day, we had gathered in the dean's office, where Denise had insisted, with a whole lot of shouting and stomping, that I could have prevented the incident or at least stopped it. But it had all happened so fast. She had lit the candle herself and had also forgotten to blow it out. I had insisted that she should not have put the candle so close to her bed, that I had still been half asleep and that I had only really realised what was happening when she was screaming at the top of her lungs.

That night - when I slept back home, at Kyra and Danny's, considering Denise no longer wanted to bunk with me and there was no free room left on campus - I couldn't catch any sleep. Every time I closed my eyes, I saw the fire in front of me, in a powerful and destructive rage. The following night, I didn't sleep either. I fell asleep occasionally, but jolted awake immediately each time. The day after, I was like a zombie. I experienced everything, but it all registered late or only halfway. The next night I didn't sleep again.

After the fourth night, there was some kind of habituation. Heavily tired, but with eyes open. Slow, but moving. Flat and vague. This was now my new life. The line between fantasy and reality blurred more and more. It started with black spots, globs, smudges. Colours danced through my field of vision. A large object on the road as I cycled to the shop, and as soon as I looked at it, it was gone.

Later, I heard my name being said. Determined and clear. As if someone was standing right next to me, trying to get my attention. But when I turned my head, nobody was there. My heartbeat quickened. My hands turned clammy. My breathing shortened. What was happening to me?

On the sixth day, I walked down the alley behind our house, clutching a dripping trash bag. I shuffled to the local dumpster, where I dumped the bag. Nothing was in focus and yet everything was. I went back to the shed door. My hand was already on the latch when my attention was drawn. There was something on my left, further down the alley. I tried to focus on it without looking at it. I saw it really clearly, right there, out of the corner of my eye. I turned my head and looked at it.

It was looking back at me.

I ran back inside, screaming. Kyra jumped up with eyes as big as breakfast plates. Danny rushed towards me and grabbed me by my shoulders. Both went to investigate the alley. Both saw nothing at all. Danny inquired further. Kyra sat back down on the sofa and turned up the sound on the TV. I cried in Danny's arms until Reina returned from day care. Kyra sent us to the annexe so we wouldn't upset her, not expecting me to once again make their eardrums ring at what I found in my room. Or rather, who. You guessed it: cheek, eye, hat.

I can't remember how long Danny pressed me against him or how soaked his shirt got. I can only remember finally sleeping again for the first time that night. I closed my eyes without the vision of the fire. And I owed that, in my mind, to Danny.

My pocket vibrates. I whip out a pink mobile phone and flip it open. There's a message from Danny.

Hey honey, were you on your way home already? X

I type back a message.

Caught the wrong bus. Passes station. Can I come to you? Are you still at work? Xx

I rest my head against the window and look at the screen in the bus. Two more stops before Vassen Central. From there, Danny's office is about a ten-minute walk.

Yes, for a little while. Come to me. We'll go home together. See you soon. X

I put my phone back in my pocket with a smile. My eyes follow the cars passing the bus as it comes to a stop. Then, my hand slips into my other pocket and takes out a crumpled piece of paper. I fold it open silently and look at it. It's the article about the hotel renovation, which I had secretly torn out of The Pay Per, without that pervert from the tobacco shop noticing. With the article is a small photograph of the hotel lobby. I stare at it and feel a strange sense of recognition wash over me, just like I noticed when I first looked at the picture of the hotel's exterior on the front page. I start reading the article.

Betting on former glory

The renovation of Hotel Lethalis has resumed. The hotel that experienced its glory years in the early 1980s. Famous for its extravagant dance parties and notorious for illegal gaming. Golden Ten was not a silver lining, but a grey stain on the hotel's immaculate legacy.

The owner hopes to restore the hotel to its former glory to revive the tourism of Midsberg. Without the gambling, she stresses with a twinkling smile.

My fingertips smooth the newsprint after folding it. I put it back in my pocket and hear the sound of my earbuds crackling. I grab my mp3-player and twist the plug a little. More crackles and squeaks. My right hand probes the cord, bending and swirling, until I find the culprit. I fold the cord in half, on the spot causing the interference, and secure it with a hair tie. This is yet another broken pair, but it usually lasts another month or two like this. I would love higher-quality earplugs, but they are expensive. If I want them, I have to work for them myself, Kyra says. I wonder if I can combine that with my therapy.

"Hey, lady!"

I startle and yank out an earbud. At the front of the empty bus, the driver looks at me with a dead face.

"This is the last stop."

"S-sorry," I respond as I hastily jump up and run to the door. I hadn't at all realised that the bus has come to a halt. Even the engine is already off. "Thanks," I mutter as I get out. I look around the large car park, half of which is filled with cars of all shapes and sizes. This is not Vassen Central.

The driver also gets out and closes the doors. He reaches into his pocket and pulls out a packet of cigarettes. He pops one into his mouth and holds out his lighter.

I watch the flame as I approach him.

He takes a deep drag and blows the smoke upwards. "Did you need something?"

"Um, yes. Vassen Central. Where's that?"

"You just missed that stop. One back." He takes another puff as he looks at me from head to toe.

"How do I get there?" I ask softly. My index finger hooks around the thumb of my other hand and I turn with my one foot.

He points in a direction. "Just walk that way. It's straightforward. But a good twenty minutes' walk."

Twenty!? Shit.

"If you wait a bit, you can ride with me. I'll pass there on my way home anyway."

I bite my lip and shake my head. "No thanks."

"Are you sure? It's a small effort."

"Thanks, but I'll walk." I smile as warmly as I can and start to turn around.

"You'll get blisters that way. It's really not a problem."

"Walking is good for me." I tap my stomach for a moment. "Keeps me in shape."

He chuckles and throws the cigarette on the ground. "You don't need that." He tramples the smouldering cigarette with his foot. "Come with me, I'll start the car." He walks towards me.

My heart skips a beat. "Oh, no, you really don't need to. I-"

"Don't be silly." He walks past me. "Come."

I look around me. There are cars here and there, but not another person in sight. If Danny finds out I got in the car with a stranger, I'll never hear the end of it. I have to get out of this, I think, panicked.

The man stops at a small red car and opens the passenger door. "I can have you there in two minutes," he shouts.

With lead in my shoes, I shuffle backwards.

Trrrrr! Trrrrrrr!

I grab my pink phone from my pocket and hold it up. "My father!" I yell at the bus driver. I flip my phone open and hold it to my ear. "Hey dad," I say cheerfully, briefly raising my hand to the man for a half-wave.

The bus driver slams the door shut and walks around his car.

"Yes, the stop after Vassen Central, in the car park," I say loudly.

The man casts another glance at me, then disappears into his car and starts the engine.

I start walking while still pressing the mobile phone to my ear. "Yes, thank you, I'll see you in a minute. I am already walking towards you." My heart pounds against my ribcage.

The red car drives out of the car park, towards Vassen.

"I'm doing alright, what about you? How's your day?" My eyes follow the car as it disappears from my sight. With a deep sigh, I lower my phone and glance at the screen.

What's the hold-up? X

My fingers slide frantically over the keypad.

I missed the stop. I don't know where I am. Xx

I glance at the send icon on my screen and less than three seconds later my phone actually rings.

"Where are you? What do you see around you? Stay there, I'm coming to you." Danny's voice sounds steady yet agitated.

My heart rate immediately lowers.

I close my eyes as I feel his arms around me.

"Well done, darling," Danny assures me. He gently kisses me on the crown.

"He did seem honest. He really went to Va-"

"Never trust 'em." He grabs me by my shoulders and looks deep into my eyes. "Never. Trust. Anyone. You did really well. No matter how nice and how honest they may seem. It need only be that one person." He holds a finger in front of my face. "Just one who means harm. And then..." He bites his lip and holds me tight. "That's why you have to stay safe. Don't go with strangers. Don't accept drinks. Don't exchange numbers. Stay away from suspicious vehicles. If one keeps following you, call me right away and tell me where you are. And don't-"

"And don't just help strangers," I complement him.

He lets go of me and looks me sternly in the eye. His grey eyes gleam. "I'm serious, Amber."

"I know," I say softly.

"I know what this world can be like." He swallows and wipes his mouth.

I study his expression.

"You can't trust anyone. Not even acquaintances."

I tilt my head slightly and grin. "What about you? Should I not trust you either?"

He emits a sound that could be either a laugh or a sob. "Me, you can trust, but above all, trust yourself. Always yourself and your own feelings first." He takes my hand and lays it on my gut. "This is where you should be able to feel it."

"That's indeed where I felt it." I look at the spot where the red car had been just a while ago. "My feet felt heavy and my heart pounded harder, but I still felt kind of calm."

He nods. "Alertness."

"But my feet... I felt like I wouldn't be able to run even if I tried."

"You remember what I taught you, right?"

I nod. "Knees, eyes, crotch." I follow the points right in front of him with a clenched fist. "A head-butt if they grab me from behind." I depict it. "The nose or the Adam's apple."

He grabs my wrist firmly and pulls me towards him.

My knee brushes against his groin.

"Great response." He lets go of me and sighs. "But you have to do it really hard."

"I know," I respond with a small smile. "Do you want to feel it?"

He chuckles. "We'll do that at home on the pillow. Come." He turns and pulls open the door of his dark blue station wagon.

I get in and wait until he has also sat down. "Danny?"

He looks at me questioningly as he fastens his belt.

"What happened?"

"What do you mean?" He turns the key in the ignition. The engine hums.

"You said you know what the world can be like. You seemed so serious."

"Oh." He raises his eyebrows. His hands squeeze the steering wheel. The skin around the ring on his right ring finger turns white. His eyes dart from side to side, his lips stick together.

"You don't have to tell me if you don't want to. But maybe it'll help."

His lower lip disappears into his mouth. He leans back, pondering. Then, he flips the car key a quarter turn and idles the engine. It takes a moment for him to make eye contact again. And when he does, he starts talking.

My lower lip trembles. "I'm sorry."

Danny shakes his head for a moment. "That's how the world is. Or can be, that's how I prefer to see it."

"Why did she kill herself?"

His eyes grow dull. "Shame, guilt... I don't really know. We could always understand and relate to each other so well. We often didn't even need to say a word. But after the incident, she seemed like a totally different person. She put up a huge wall around her. Even I couldn't get through that." He sighs deeply.

I gulp. "And your uncle, what happened to him?"

"He moved to the countryside with his family."

"Did they stay with him!? But-"

"Aunt Margot never wanted to believe it. And Jason, well... what can I say. He wasn't in a position to make a choice. He was still a minor. And because his mother stayed with him, so did he." Danny remains silent for a moment.

"Did you ever see him again?"

He shakes his head. "At the police station, that... that was the last time."

We silently gaze forward.

There is a tapping on the roof of the car. First softly, then louder and louder.

"I didn't know you had a sister. A twin, at that."

He casts a gloomy glance at me, "I never talk about it. It's been so long." He stares silently ahead and heaves a deep sigh. "I don't even remember what she was really like. And whether my memories of her are accurate. Especially those last two years have stuck with me." He taps his temple for a moment. "And that's not how I want to remember her." He swallows.

I shift and stare at my knees.

He directs his gaze out the window, at the bleak sky turning from light grey to a menacingly dark hue. "We'd better get going," he says as he restarts the engine. He takes a deep breath and releases his handbrake.

I put my hand on his, resting on the handbrake. I look into his eyes. "Thank you," I say softly. "For sharing that with me." I look at my hand. My fingers feel cold and warm at the same time.

He nods slowly. "Promise me you'll always put your own safety first."

I gaze into his eyes. "I promise." My breath falters.

He withdraws his hand and holds it to my cheek. His thumb gently strokes up and down. His mouth opens for a moment, but he quickly closes it again. He lowers his hand to the gear lever and shifts it before driving off the car park.

The sound of the engine is drowned out by the rumbling hailstones, crashing into the roof like galloping horses.

3 THE LADY IN RED

Cutlery clangs as the hail taps against the living room windows.

Kyra sits with folded hands watching Reina, who is sitting in her raised chair next to me. She scoops some applesauce onto her special plastic spoon and brings it to her mouth. She loses half of what she scoops up along the way. She quickly straightens Reina's bib and watches her guzzle the morsel.

Danny rests his chin on his fist, staring at his plate, as he absent-mindedly prods beans onto his fork. He moves the fork up and down, without bringing it to his mouth.

My thumbs caress my cutlery for a moment. I am hungry, but it feels like there is some sort of gelatine in my throat, trying to prevent anything from entering my mouth. My gaze keeps shifting to Danny, like a magnet. I've never seen him like this before. "Therapy went well," I begin cautiously, trying to break the icy silence.

"Stop it." Kyra grabs Reina's hand and pulls away the plastic knife.

Reina starts moaning. *Naaahuhhhuhe!*

I look at Reina as she throws her head into her neck and waves her arms. "I think we are almost at the heart of it," I continue.

Danny looks up and raises his eyebrows for a moment.

"I should hope so," Kyra says. She looks at me with her piercing brown eyes. "It costs us plenty of time and money."

Danny casts a quick glance at her. "Glad to hear it, Amber." He smiles faintly.

I look at him, open my mouth for a moment and then stare at my plate.

"You only have two months left before you have to resume your studies," Kyra says. "You haven't forgotten about that, I hope? Because they *will* kick you out if you don't do well and that's not an empty threat. Do you still submit your homework?"

I nod silently.

"Good," she responds, "You should be grateful that the faculty is being so considerate of you. They don't need to be so lenient, yet they are willing to make an exception for you. That's very decent of them."

Danny finally brings his fork towards his mouth. He chews with a listless look.

"You need your degree, because you won't get anywhere in this world without it," she continues.

This world? I look from her to Danny, who has stopped chewing. I gulp.

"And it's time f-" She grabs Reina by her wrist. "Don't play with your food!"

Reina smears applesauce on her face with her free hand.

"I said, NO playing with your food."

Mnaaahhh.

"Reina!"

The wailing continues.

My fork pricks through a bean on my plate. "Reina. Food cargo." I lean forward and extend the bean to her.

She gasps. Her intense gaze fixates on the impaled white bean.

"*Bvvvuuhhh,*" I mimic the sound of an aeroplane as I bob the fork up and down.

She opens her mouth.

"Careful with that fork." The wrinkles in Kyra's forehead deepen.

I watch as Reina bites the bean off the iron. A blob of applesauce falls from her face.

Kyra turns to Danny. "I really do need some support. Someone to help with the housework. Cleaning, cooking, shopping. It's too hard for one person to do all that besides caring for Reina. Someone needs to take over from Amber, now that she doesn't help out around the house anymore."

Danny finally swallows his bite. "We've discussed this." He lays down his fork. "Reina can stay overnight at the care home. Every other weekend or on a few weekdays."

An icy silence falls.

"She is *not* going to stay overnight at that place. She is our daughter, Danny. We have a duty to look after her."

He rubs his eyes for a moment. "We'll look after her that way as well."

"No, because then she'll be all alone. She should be able to be with her parents, like any other child. She has a right to that. She gets the care and attention she needs, right here, at her home. For me, it's a matter of getting household help. *Here.*"

"Right now, we have to make choices."

"And what choice is that exactly? Because you are not sending my daughter away. She feels safe here. She gets all the love and care that she needs here and you know she can't get that anywhere else. That so-called care home will lock her up when she's being difficult."

Danny frowns and rubs his forehead.

"You know structure is very important to her. She needs help getting dressed in the morning. Oats with milk and fruit for breakfast.

Beans, applesauce and sausage in the evening. Then a bath. And a story, before she goes to sleep. That one is very important to her. She can't sleep if she isn't read her bed time story."

"They can do that too," he responds with a sharp tongue.

They look at each other silently.

The hairs on the back of my neck stand up.

Niiiaaaaaaaahh.

"I'm not going to argue about this. I want to get help here."

"You can pick a cleaning lady on the notice board in the supermarket."

"You're not listening. A cleaner only cleans. Who does the shopping? Who cooks?"

Hmmmmna! Haaaanngg.

"We don't have the money for such help right now, so please take advantage of the support offered by the municipality."

Kyra raises an eyebrow and shakes her head slightly.

"I'll do the shopping from tomorrow on, after work. If you give me a list or text it to me, I'll make sure to get it."

"After you finish work is way too late. Then I'd have to cook still and we wouldn't eat until nine o'clock. That doesn't work for Reina."

"Well, then go buy the *weekly* groceries while Reina is at daycare."

She looks at him piercingly.

I bite my lip. With my right hand, I reach into my pocket for the torn piece of newspaper. The paper feels warm and kind of soft to the touch. My heartbeat slows down right away. Why did I take this in the first place?, I wonder silently. I even went so far as to steal it. I think about the lilac lily carpet again and how that image popped into my head as soon as I saw the picture of Lethalis on the front page. That picture spoke to me in a strange way. But why? Why does the name *Lethalis* mean something to me in a very vague way? It's like that large building rises up from the mist in my mind.

"Reina, no!" Kyra's eyes grow as big as ping-pong balls.

Reina's plate clatters on the laminate, splattering the table legs with splotches of applesauce. Beans escape in all directions, bouncing and rolling and overtaking each other. The sausage flees from under her chair, like a dog on the loose. Reina starts bellowing loudly.

"Now look what you've done." Kyra picks up her plate and walks to the kitchen, directly adjacent to the dining room. When she returns, she pulls Reina out of her chair. "I'm going to wash her. Clean this up." She disappears from the room, pulling the door shut behind her. Reina's wailing immediately softens.

At least the soundproofing is on-point since the last dispute with our neighbours.

Danny and I are left in silence. We look at each other for a while.

I stand up and lift my plate, which is still half full, off the table. With a questioning glance, I look at Danny. He nods. I grab his plate, which is even fuller than mine, and walk to the kitchen. I slide the beans and sausages into a silicone container, which I then put in the fridge. I turn on the tap and rinse both plates. The leftover applesauce slithers through the sink. I put the plates in the dishwasher, rinse out a dishcloth and start wiping the blobs of apple sauce from the table legs.

He slides his chair back and kneels on the floor beside me. He bends down and picks up the sausage from the floor. His fingers grope for every bean he can find.

Moments later, we sit silently at the table again.

Trrrr trrrr.

My pocket starts to vibrate. I take out my phone and look at the alarm. With a slight sigh, I turn it off. I look up when I hear a flat thump. There is a glass of water on the table in front of me.

Danny looks at me meaningfully.

I snatch the white cardboard box from my pocket, which is crushed considerably. I pull out a strip and push a pill through the foil. The coloured shape falls onto my palm, and I look at it before putting it in my mouth. The happy pill grazes my throat as I take it with water.

"How are you?" he asks in a soft voice.

I stare at my thumbs. They circle each other. "I'm alright," I say coyly.

"Was it too much? What I told you this afternoon?"

I look up and shake my head.

His lips form into thin lines.

"I just..." I sigh and rest my head on my hand, "I've never seen you like this."

He lifts one corner of his mouth, but there is no joy in his eyes. "Are you worried?"

I nod.

"That's sweet, but there's no need. I can bear it." He sighs. "With some time, this too will pass. And your mother doesn't mean it badly, either. I hope you can understand that. She has a lot on her mind and she's under a lot of stress, trying to manage everything as well as she can. It's a lot and it's... it's difficult. But that's just the way things are right now."

I stare into his grey eyes. "Do you miss her?"

He raises his eyebrows.

"Your sister, I mean," I clarify.

"Oh, um..." His Adam's apple moves up and down. He folds his hands and rests his elbows on the table. "Whenever I think of her, I miss her. And, as I said, I don't think of her often. Not anymore. Your mother and I, we... we never really talk about it, honestly. What's in the past, is in the past."

My fingers gently stroke my mouth and pick at my bottom lip. "But what if the past has an effect on the present?" I ask, pouting for a moment. "I don't even know what lies in the past."

His eyebrows draw together. "What you're doing, with your therapy, that's very brave of you. And very useful, too, even though it might not always seem like it." He bites his lip.

"Wouldn't you be better off using the money for Reina?" I continue softly. "If that child-care is s-"

"No."

"But if Reina, or Kyra rather, needs that care, then-"

"Right now, I have two daughters who need care. And it's tough for Kyra right now, but that too will pass. When you're feeling better again, we can have another look at things."

My incisor pushes into my thumbnail. "What if I don't get better?"

He looks straight at me.

I gulp. The sound of hail, tapping against the windows, hushes in my ears.

"We were just talking to Jack yesterday about your breakthrough with the carpet." He grabs my hand and pulls it away from my mouth. My nail slips from between my teeth. "It really will be fine." He strokes my hand with his thumb. "I promise you that."

There is a rumble on the stairs.

"I'm scared," I say cautiously.

He studies my face with a worried look.

"I'm scared of what I don't remember."

Footsteps sound muffled in the hall.

He gives a small squeeze and then lets go of my hand. He crosses his arms. "That too will be fine," he says as the dining room door flings open.

Kyra enters.

"Did you manage?" he asks her.

She nods and sits back on her chair. She sighs deeply and turns her head to me. "Coffee please, for me and your father."

I get up and walk to the kitchen. With my back to them, I fill the water reservoir of the coffee maker. I can't see Kyra from this angle, but I can feel her eyes burning into my back. I replace the water reservoir and slide a paper filter into the valve. My fingers slide over the cold iron of the coffee can that I pull towards me, still with a burning back. I rock the lid open and insert the scoop into the coffee. I pull it out with a hefty cup on it. I flip it over the filter and scoop a second time. I push the lid of the coffee maker shut and press the power button. My wrists rest on the kitchen worktop as I stare at the coffee pot. The machine makes a soft pulsing, almost smoky sound.

I breathe in, five seconds. Hold for three seconds. Out, five seconds. Hold for three seconds. I repeat the breath as I count. The sound of the coffee maker and the clattering hail fail to drown out the uncomfortable silence.

Sixteen seconds. Thirty-two seconds. One hundred and eight seconds.

My toes curl under the soles of my feet.

Two hundred and fourteen seconds.

Beep!

The ceramic cups clang against each other with chirpy little squeaks as I grab them from the cupboard. I pour one cup full to a centimetre below the rim, the other cup to two centimetres below the rim - this is where half a scoop of sugar and a dash of milk go in. I stir the coffee with a spoon and put the spoon in the sink, without leaving any drops on the kitchen top - just the way Kyra prefers it. My feet carefully tread the ground as I walk to the table with both cups, my gaze fixed on the coffee that swirls to the edges with every step. I set the cup with the black coffee down on the table for Danny and the cream-coloured one in front of Kyra.

"Thank you, Amber," I hear him say.

Kyra looks at the clock and then back at me. "You can go read to Reina now," she says, grabbing the cup with both hands.

I nod and walk out of the room, pulling the door shut behind me. I breathe in and out deeply. My shoulders slump. I walk down the hall to the stairs and continue my way up. My toes brush the dark blue high-pile rug of the hallway. It's not the best interior choice, in terms of cleaning, but Reina loves that fluffy fabric. It is very soft and pleasing to her sensitive senses. And she has only peed on it three times. The floors in the bathroom and her bedroom could learn a thing or two from that.

I playfully knock on her bedroom door four times, which is right opposite the stairs. "Reina, I'm here for your story," I announce myself softly. I push open the door and look at Reina sitting on her bed with half-dried hair. She flutters her hands.

I smile and join her on the bed. "Which story do you want to hear today?" I take the stack of booklets from her bedside table and put them on the bed one by one. "*The caterpillar with the fat belly, Kitty and Bear, Bird and her friends* or *The fish and the red coral*?"

I hear the muffled voices of Danny and Kyra through the ventilation shaft. Loose words creep into my ear canal. When I prick up my ears, I manage to hear more.

"...your work...I...tough..."

"...money for it! ...blame it on..."

"*Cappy*," Reina exclaims and she slaps the booklet about the caterpillar with her hand.

I put the other booklets away and sit cross-legged. My back leans against the wall. Reina joins me quietly. She leans her head on my shoulder and slowly rolls her little hands in and out of her lap, making soft, whirring sounds.

"...anything for her, ever! ...Amber, Amber, Amber..."

I gently bite my lower lip.

"You... YOU... off the pill... your choice!"

I flick open the booklet. "This is Caterpillar," I say in the warmest voice possible.

"...NOT Reina's fault!"

"Caterpillar has a really fat belly." I rub the soft fabric plastered on Caterpillar's belly. Reina's little fingers follow mine.

"...three times a week... not... your daughter too!"

My heart races. "That's because of all the flowers. Red, green, yellow and blue." My index finger follows the drawings of the coloured flowers. Reina's little finger slides along under mine on the thick glossy paper.

"...monster..."

I slink. "Shall we make a tent?" I ask with a smile.

Nyah! Reina giggles and turns her head wildly; her way of nodding.

I pull her duvet over us and grab the lamp from the bedside table to shed extra light on the book. "I'm in pain, says Caterpillar. And it doesn't feel good."

"Pain," Reina says softly.

My breath falters. Sometimes she pronounces a word perfectly, that's nothing new, but it's in the way she said this particular word... it makes my heart sting. I guide her little fingers to Beetle's smooth wings. Gently, I tell on, with as much joy in my voice as I can muster. "He visits Beetle, who knows a lot. Say Beetle, says Caterpillar, will you look at my gut?"

"Sweet dreams." I press a kiss to Reina's forehead and turn on her nightlight.

She pulls her blanket up to her chin. "Amma, seal."

"Thank you," I say soothingly, with my hand on the door handle. "I'll sleep well too." I turn off the ceiling lamp as I walk out of the room and pull the door shut behind me. To my left, I see Kyra and Danny's bedroom door, the bathroom door and the door leading to the attic. I walk down the stairs, down the hall and back into the dining room. The room is empty. I walk to the kitchen, pour myself a glass of water and walk back into the hall. From there, I open the door to the annex. I walk down a narrow corridor past Danny's home office. I hear the rattling of a keyboard and imagine Danny frantically typing. Though I doubt he's drafting contracts right now. I open the other door, at the end of the corridor, and step into my room.

Up against the left wall are my bed and my wardrobe, filled with oversized long-sleeved jumpers. Along the right wall is my desk, with a lamp and a monitor on it. The steak-cheeked man stands next to it, his skin and grey fedora sticking out against the white wall, which holds a large pinboard with my own drawings. There are so many drawings on there, that the ones in the back are hidden from view.

I take off my shirt, casually throwing it towards my bed, as I walk through my room. In the back is a door, which leads to my private bathroom. I enter and wash my face over the sink. The water feels wonderfully cool on my skin. I lift my head and look in the mirror. A water droplet falls from my chin onto the edge of the sink.

I stare into the green-coloured eyes in the reflective surface. Interspersed through the green are amber streaks and flecks. It's probably what I owe my name to.

"This is me," I say to myself, out loud. I turn my face and look at it from different angles. "This is my face." I raise my eyebrows and bring my face closer to the mirror. My eyelashes move up and down as I blink. My dark green eyes disappear from view for a moment with each blink. A deep sigh escapes from between my lips and forms a haze on the surface. I wipe it away. The figure in the mirror does exactly the same thing as I, but it feels like it could make a different move at any moment. One that I don't expect. One that I don't initiate.

I straighten up and look at the body beneath the face. Slender, somewhat muscular arms. A narrow waist with visible lower ribs. Firm contoured thighs. Legs like a horse's, as Kyra put it. My fingers push into the skin. I sigh again. My fingers feel my skin, but it doesn't seem quite real. As if there is a layer in between, made of a strange substance that desensitises my fingertips. I watch the pushed-in skin turn white; as if I'm watching it happen through someone else's eyes, as if I'm watching a movie and sympathising with the main character. But this main character doesn't get a pleasant ending. And there is no one to see or hear her. I twist my hips and look at the posture in the mirror. My spine pushes through my skin. I wonder if there was ever a time when I recognised myself in the mirror. A time when I could look into my eyes and think: *yes... here I am, hello!* Was there ever a time when I wasn't being governed?

Knock, knock.

"Yeah," I call out.

The bedroom door creaks open.

I walk away from the mirror, into my bedroom. I sit down on my bed and look at Danny, who is standing in the middle of my room.

His eyes shoot back and forth, scanning my room. He clears his throat and looks at the floor. "I didn't know you were already heading for bed."

I tap my hand on the bedspread next to me. "I'm not asleep yet."

He puts his hands in his pockets and sits down next to me, now looking at his feet.

"I read Reina her story. She must be asleep now."

"Oh yeah?"

"She wanted to read *The caterpillar with the fat belly* again. Maybe we can get the new book for her birthday. I heard it's pretty good."

Danny nods silently.

I watch his expression for a long time and put my hand on his knee. I open my mouth for a moment, before biting my lip, hesitantly. "Thank you," I finally say. "Thank you for sharing that with me. It must have been really hard for you." I swallow. "How the world could be so... I have no words for it." I look at his face. I see a drop slide down his cheek to his jaw; the tear takes a break on a stubble. My breath falters.

His back begins to jerk. He bends down and buries his face in his hands. His body shakes with every choked sob emerging from his throat.

I place my hand on his back and gently stroke up and down. A sharp pain stabs at the centre of my throat. It makes it difficult to swallow or speak; if it could say anything, it would probably just scream. I wrap both my arms around him and hold him, my chin resting high up on his back.

Eventually, his sobbing dissolves into the silence of the house.

I open my eyes and blink. My vision is blurred. On both my sides, I see white walls. Under my feet, I see carpet with graceful lines - the patterns make up lilies. I squint my eyes. I know this. I recognise this.

I look up and see a thick fog rolling towards me down the long corridor. I gasp for breath. My body twists and turns. My toes settle hard against the ground. My hair waves up and down against my back and neck as I run. My heart jolts and beats faster with every step. I glance behind me. The fog keeps coming towards me, getting closer and closer. My breath howls in my throat. My lungs contract with force, thrusting painful shocks through my side. I look back once more and see the thick cloud of fog right behind me.

When I look ahead, it's already too late. I crash into the white wall, squeezing all the air from my lungs. I collapse through my knees and falter to the ground. My body rolls, bending and twisting. Panting, I lie there, face down on the rough carpet, watching the lilies dance around each other.

My gaze slides upwards, over the white walls. With a pounding head, I scramble up to a sitting position and look out into the corridor.

The fog is gone.

I sigh deeply. The corridor is empty; I can see all the way to the end. But... I squint my eyes. It's not just a wall at the end. There's something... something else. A shape, a figure.

I seek support against the wall as I carefully lift myself up. I crane my neck, trying to make sense of the figure. The more I focus my gaze, the closer it seems to get - wall and all. I see sleek hair of a reddish hue waving over broad shoulders. Long slender arms hanging limply along a body. Fingertips extend halfway up the thighs. The legs are firm and rounded, leaning on two stiletto heels, one of which is broken. Shiny red fabric drapes to just over the knees. My gaze slides upwards slowly. To the hips. The belly. The chest. The neck…

KRRRHHHAAAAAAAAAHHHHYYAAAAAAAA!

Flames lash around the figure like wild whips, slamming against the walls; heat melting the red fabric.

I put my hands over my mouth as I watch the copper hairs smoulder; the skin turns red and begins to bubble. My chest jolts as I start to sob.

The arms remain limp along the body, making no attempt to knock out the fire, while she continues to screech deafeningly.

I sink to the ground, with my hands pressed firmly to my ears, but it is of little use: her screams cleave through flesh and bone, sending chills through my spine and spikes through my head. I rock back and forth with my face between my knees. I see the light of the fire creeping closer across the carpet. The lilies dance in the flames.

I squeeze my eyes shut. When I open them again, I see her face. Right in front of me.

Screaming, I trash around me, entangled in my blanket. My eyes are wide open, but I can't see my room. I know there are two strong arms wrapping around my body, but I don't feel them. My face is pressed against his chest as his arms hold me tighter. My breath escapes in a long gasp and turns to sobbing. It takes a while before I feel the warmth of Danny's body. My hands reach for his shoulders and squeeze gently.

"The woman in red?" he asks softly.

I nod, smothering my sobbing on his shoulder cap.

Orange light glides across my bedroom floor to the bed. The sun is rising.

4 SWEET BITTERNESS

I'm standing in front of the wide staircase that leads to the entrance of my school. This is where I stand every first Monday of the month, as I have agreed with the head of faculty. Every time we discuss my progress, such as the level of my submitted homework, and I listen to any feedback, plus we talk about whether personal adjustments are needed. We also talk about the things I need to work on harder in order to re-enter next year, for my final year of study.

I bitterly regret that my - what shall I call it, a nervous breakdown? - didn't happen at a later time. At least then I would have had my degree under my belt, and I could've just take some time off before starting a job. I was halfway through the school year before everything went up in flames. And now I have to do a lot of duplicate work and acquire knowledge that feels brand-new at times, even though I've already studied it. It feels like everything I take in wears off just as fast.

It makes me wonder how efficient this *gap year* is. That's what they call it: a gap year, under special circumstances. Other students take a gap year to work or travel the world. They gain experience, see beautiful sights, learn about different cultures and make lots of new connections, possibly for life. They don't have to meet monthly quotas, either, during their year off. I don't really understand why it has to be different for me. Wouldn't Danny have been better off lying about the reason for my gap year? Or perhaps I would've been better off if he had.

This is the tenth time I have stood here in front of the stairs with just a bag on my shoulder and earplugs in, in the middle of the day. I take a deep breath and stroke my hand gently through my hair. I can feel that my armpit is soaking wet. I hold my hand over my eyes and look at the sky. This is supposed to be a day to enjoy; to sit on the terrace with friends, swim in the sea or build a campfire until late at night. I lower my hand.

Summer break starts in a few days and then everyone will be doing fun and exciting things. But me? I will be sitting in Jack's musty office three times a week, where I always leave sweaty. In a few weeks, I should be done. Then, I'll be *better*, according to the current treatment plan. The closer that moment gets, the more anxious I feel. I don't know exactly how much progress we've made. In fact, it feels like I'm doing even worse now. The pills do help with most of the anxiety symptoms, but the man with the hat is still with me. Even now, he is looking down on me from up the stairs. Maybe this is the fate I have to accept. Maybe it won't get better than this and I just have to learn to deal with this; having him follow me around wherever and whenever, and scaring the living shit out of me at random times.

Two more months. Then, I will have to mingle among my peers again, be back in lectures every day and do projects, including collaborative ones. In my free hours, I'll need to make sure the house is clean and tidy and that we've got food in the house. Will I go back to working behind the till on the weekends? Or just on Thursday evenings? And what if I'll still be having panic attacks? What about the nightmares and hallucinations? Will the man with the hat join me behind the till? I wonder if we'd make a good team...

I swallow wearily. Don't think about it, I think to myself. Only think about right now, this very moment. I am now standing in front of these stairs. All I have to do is go inside. Lay my work on Ms Katen's desk, listen to her talk about all the things I need to do better. All I have to do is understand how great an exception they are making for me, nod and say thank you. Look happy. Walk out with my head down, catch the bus and head back home. And also clean the bathroom, because that's the least I can do, as Kyra told me this morning.

My heart jumps up and down in my chest. I raise my shoulders and twist them in circles. I stretch my neck on both sides. Yes, right now all I have to do is walk up those stairs and go inside.

I rummage through my bag for my medication and my bottle of water. The happy pill seems twice as big as it crawls down my throat, slowly and painfully.

The school bell rings merrily to signal the end of class. Students now have five minutes to get to their next lesson. But the lucky ones come through these doors and walk down the stairs because their school day is over or just because they want to have a nice drink on a terrace during their break. They walk along the stone path towards the road with a field on either side, full of blades of grass with dried-out tips.

I gaze at the grass as I follow closely behind my fellow students.

Amber, call me.

I look at the screen of my phone and my legs instantly turn to solid lead. I knew this was going to happen. I knew there would be consequences. I knew that, and still I did it. Why? Not so that Danny would get mad at me. Will he be very angry? Of course he's angry! Shit... What have I done!? Why didn't I go inside? What's going to happen now? Will I get kicked out of school? Will I get another chance? Do I have to go back and apologise?

Tears well up in my eyes as my head spins and the well-known brain fog begins to descend. My breathing is rushed and cuts sharply through my throat. I pull my knees up to my chest and inhale deeply. Four counts. Hold for two counts. Out, six counts. Hold for two counts.

My phone vibrates again.

Pick up.

Jack's breathing exercises bring no relief. I grab the white cardboard box from my bag. It's not yet time to take another happy pill. But it can't hurt, right? A double dose should make me... happy.

Amber, please pick up.

I pop a pill from the strip. The pill lies motionless on my hand. Innocuous. Harmless.

Where are you?

I place the pill on my tongue and take a swig from my water bottle. What would the effect be if I take one, or maybe even two, too many? It wouldn't be an instant overdose, would it? And it is meant to inhibit my anxiety symptoms. So maybe my current dose is not sufficient after all. Jack is right. Jack is always right.

I just want to know if you are okay. Can you call me?

I pop another pill from the strip and look at it. I don't want Danny to be mad at me. I don't want this. I don't want any of this. My hand closes around the pill. I feel the muscles tighten.

My phone continues to vibrate.

The pill touches my lower lip. I can taste the bitterness. A tear rolls down my cheek. What am I even brooding about? This might not do anything at all. It's probably not even as harmful as they say - they just have to state that on the label as a warning, so that they don't get sued. If you can have three to four of these in a day, why not take them at a single moment? Apparently your body can handle it just fine - especially if the dose might be too light as it is, as Jack had suggested. Yes, this is okay. This is just a test to see how a heavier dose suits me. Maybe I'll be able to function better. Maybe, with a heavier dose, I can just go back to school and do my tests and finally get my degree. Without panic attacks, anxiety and nocturnal terror. Maybe I can have a side job again and someday, one day, live on my own - even though I would miss Danny so much.

Amber, I beg you.

I look at the message and imagine him, typing on his phone. Is he worried? Am I worrying him? I bite my lip. I don't want to worry him at all. I don't want to bother him. The second pill slides down my tongue.

I love you. Call me.

The hairs on the back of my neck bristle and I stiffen. It's as if he knows. I gently take the pill off my tongue and close my mouth. I look at the man with the hat, standing silently next to a lamppost in the quiet park. He stares at me, but I can't read his face. He always shows that one expression and it is simply expressionless. He slowly raises a hand, as if to greet me.

I almost wave back.

He puts his right hand in the pocket of his tawdry trousers.

My heart makes a small jump. I reach for the piece of newspaper in my pocket and take it out. The piece of paper is now crumpled beyond smoothening, and some of the letters are faded in the folds. I stare at the picture of Lethalis, the old hotel building being renovated. My shoulders sag. What is this feeling? Why does it haunt me? How can a photograph have such a hold on a person? And why does that sprawling lily carpet traipse past my mind's eye again?

I grab my phone and send back a single sentence.

I'm okay.

I don't want him to worry about me, so I can't just take off and go to Lethalis. Not right now. I'd have to discuss it with him; ask if it's okay. He has the right to that.

But, that means I'd have to go home now. My stomach contracts. There is nothing to do but catch the bus and suffer the consequences. I take a deep breath and stand up. My fingers tingle and my insides feel paralysed. I can already feel the storm brewing.

If human ears could detect it, I would hear the tension crackling in the air. But clinking cutlery and heavy breathing is all my ears perceive, besides Reina's moans.

I scoop up small bits of food and force them down my throat with tremendous effort. My mouth feels dry and my throat seems to have cement poured down in it, as stiff and heavy as it feels. Until Reina has gone to bed, I am still safe, but I prefer to get it over with right now because this particular silence is unbearable.

Not much later, Kyra lifts Reina from her chair and silently leaves the room.

I feel my arms getting heavy. I stare straight at the table top in front of me. Tears begin to burn in my eyes and my face feels hot.

"Amber," Danny says in a compelling tone.

I twirl my thumbs around each other and look at the tabletop with increasing intent.

"Amber, look at me."

I blink my eyes wildly, but I can't hold back my tears. My gaze cautiously creeps upwards as the image becomes increasingly blurred. Through the blur, I can see the swollen vein on his forehead.

"What you did today, that can never happen again."

I nod, gulping, pressing my nails into my palms.

"You know the lengths we went to to arrange this for you. It took an incredible amount of effort and neither of us want that to have been in vain. You understand how important this is, right? So much depends on this, like you getting your degree, for one. And the radio silence? Don't you *ever* do that to me again. You do not ever just keep quiet without a damn good the reason."

I open my mouth.

"Me," he says loudly. He points to himself with his thumb. "You have to let *me* know what's going on. You can't just ignore me like that. I didn't hear from you for hours. I didn't know what happened—you could've been kidnapped or lying in a ditch somewhere." The vein in his forehead throbs. "Where do you get the guts to treat me like this!" He slaps his hand on the table. "When I call, you answer. That was the agreement." He looks at me piercingly. "If I text you, you text back. Did we agree on that, yes or no?"

I nod.

"I need to be able to trust you, Amber. I need to be able to trust you to keep your commitments."

I swallow and feel a stabbing pain in my throat. I want to say it wasn't my intention and that I didn't want to worry him. I want to say I'm sorry and that I will never do it again. But the lump in my throat prevents me from saying anything. I swallow again and again, but the feeling doesn't go away.

My pocket begins to vibrate. I grab my phone with heavy arms and look at the alarm clock.

Danny sighs deeply and looks at me silently. He gets up, grabs a glass of water and sets it down on the table in front of me. The ring on his finger taps against the glass, sending a piercing echo through the living room.

Should I tell him that I've already taken my third pill of the day? But then I'd have to explain why. Or perhaps, he won't believe me and he'll think I can't be trusted. I have to keep my commitments, like I promised. I take out the white cardboard box, pop a pill and knock back the glass of water. The way the pill scrapes the inside of my throat has never felt so pleasant.

He puts his hand on my head and strokes my hair. "Sorry for shouting at you sweetheart, but it affects me. Deeply. You're my responsibility and if I don't hear from you... I get worried sick." He presses a kiss to my crown. "I just want to..." He pauses. "I want you to be safe."

"S-sorry," I finally utter. I swallow the lump in my throat and look up at him with watery eyes.

He crouches beside me, puts his hand on my cheek and dries my tears with his thumb. "Promise me this won't happen again."

I nod wildly.

"And you're going to school tomorrow, after your session with Jack. I told ms. Katen you were bedridden with a migraine and that's why you couldn't come and didn't contact her. So when she asks you how you're doing, just say you're doing a lot better. Just a bit sensitive to light, still." He lowers his hand. "So make sure you bring your sunglasses," he adds, smiling.

I smile back and nod again as snot runs from my nose. I quickly wipe it away with my sleeve.

"Good." He looks at me for a long time.

I feel a warm, whole feeling well up in my chest as I stare into his grey eyes, still sobbing silently. His breath strokes my neck like a warm breeze, making my skin tingle. His hand feels hot on my knee.

Footsteps sound on the landing.

Danny lets go of my knee and returns to his seat. "Look sad," he says. He smiles for a brief moment.

I faintly smile back and bury my face in my crossed arms, slouching over the table.

The door flings open and Kyra enters. She joins the table and heaves a deep sigh. "Go read to Reina," she says. "I'll make the coffee."

I hear her walk towards the kitchen. I look up and meet Danny's gaze. He nods his head. I get up and disappear from the room. I walk up the stairs and stand there for a while, listening, as I wait for my tears to dry. It remains completely silent in the living room.

I heave a sigh and knock four times on Reina's door.

Hnnnyaa.

Reina is sitting on the bed, rocking her head. She normally sits fluttering her hands, but now she keeps her arms firmly pressed to her body.

"Reina?" I ask softly.

CLINGGG!

The sound of porcelain shattering echoes through the ventilation shaft. I grab the reading books and pull Reina's blanket over us like a tent. "Which story do you want to read today?"

She shakes her head.

"None? Don't you want to hear about Caterpillar?"

She keeps shaking her head.

I put the booklets on her bedside table and hear glass breaking from downstairs. My heart jumps in my chest. I tightly tug the blanket over us and use my phone to make a light. "Do you want to colour?"

No.

"Play a game? Or shall I braid your hair?"

Reina stops shaking her head and gently rocks back and forth.

I stroke my hand through her soft hair. I divide her hair into three strands and start braiding them, while I hear Reina humming quietly.

"She has to go!" Kyra's voice echoes between the cold walls of the ventilation shaft.

I prick up my ears.

"...not a good example... SHE is your real child. ...agreement! ...eighteen... her education..."

I swallow and keep braiding Reina's silky hair.

Rahhh yaaah mmhnnnn.

I finish the braid with a satin pink elastic. I take a quick look at the result. A few missed tufts of hair hang dishevelled along the braid. It's looked better before, but it'll have to do. I sigh and stroke Reina on her head.

Then, a heavy, dull clap sounds.

I startle and throw off the blanket.

Reina starts wailing, then crying, then screeching.

HAAAAAAARRRRRAAAAAAHHHH!

I try to hug her, but she flails her arms wildly. "Sweetheart," I try to soothe. I grab her arms and pull her towards me. I hug her as she pounds on my back and head, screaming and wailing. The throbbing in my ears alternates with sharp stabs.

The door flies open. A hand grabs my collar and pulls me back hard. I let go of Reina and fall backwards off the bed. My arm scrapes the bedside table. Dazed, I look up at the stature of Kyra, who is stooping over Reina. I scramble to my feet.

Kyra turns to me. Her eyebrows dip sharply to the bridge of her nose. Her jaw muscles tighten firmly. "*What* do you think you're doing?!"

My legs go numb.

"You can't clamp down on Reina like that!"

"B-but I wanted to comfort her," I stammer.

"GET OUT!"

I almost trip over my own feet as I hobble out of the room. I run down the stairs and freeze in the hallway, my eyes fixed on the living room door. Carefully, I put my hand on the latch and push it down. I step into the living room and see Danny on his knees on the kitchen floor. In his one hand, he's holding a can, in the other hand, a duster. The glass shards jingle gently as he sweeps them up.

RAAAAHHHHHH!

I walk up to him. "Can I help?"

He remains silent, with his eyes fixed on the tumbling shards.

I crouch beside him and reach for a large piece of glass, but before I can touch it, Danny grabs my wrist. I look into his grey eyes and feel miles away from him. I am so close to him; he is even touching me, but right now he seems completely absent. My gaze falls on the cut on his cheek. The blood around it stays in place, but still gleams with moisture.

"Go to your room," he says in a hoarse voice. He lets go of my wrist.

I look at my wrist and see a bloody imprint on my skin. "Danny," I exclaim. I put my hand on his shoulder and look deep into his eyes. I see the light and dark streaks in his eyes. The brown spot in his left iris. The reflection of the ball of light above our heads. But I don't see Danny.

"Your room," he repeats.

My hand slides off his shoulder as I stand up. With a limp in my legs, I make my way to the door. I walk down the hall, through the door towards the annexe, down the corridor past Danny's office and through my bedroom door into my own room. I close the door behind me and lower myself to the floor, my back resting against the door.

It will be another two hours before I hear Danny stumbling into his office. Three hours before I finally find the peace to head towards bed. And four hours before Danny sits down on the edge of my bed.

"Are you asleep?" Danny's warm voice sounds in the darkness.

I want to answer, but my mouth feels dry.

My blanket crackles under the weight of his hand. He leans over me and I feel his lips touch my forehead. "Goodnight," he says softly. The pressure on the blanket disappears as he gets up and starts walking away.

"Danny," I say with a soft sigh. Despite it being pitch dark, I know he turns around to me. I sit up and turn on my nightlight.

"Did I wake you up?" He sits back down on the edge of my bed.

I shake my head.

"Make sure you get some sleep."

"Danny..." I look at him and again see everything I am used to seeing. I look at the cut on his cheek, which is now neatly wiped clean.

"Don't worry," he says abruptly. "You know she doesn't mean any harm."

"What's going to happen to me?" I ask, sitting down next to him, shrugging off the blanket.

He frowns for a moment. "Nothing," he says after a brief silence. "You have nothing to worry about."

"But with my educ-"

"It will all be fine." He sits up.

"But Kyra," I begin.

He puts a hand on my crown and pulls me closer to him. "I promise you. You're staying with me."

I look into his glittering eyes and feel tears burning behind mine.

He smiles warmly.

I look at his lips. I bring my face closer to his and press a soft kiss on his mouth.

He widens his eyes and looks at me in surprise.

I press my lips to his again, more firmly now. For a moment, I feel the warmth of his face and taste a sweet bitterness. Then, I feel his hands on my shoulders, and I am slowly being pushed back. With red-hot cheeks, I look into his eyes.

"Amber, what are you doing?"

I see the confusion on his face. I feel his hands holding me at bay. I swallow. A warm wave floods my head. The energy drains from my arms and legs. Freezing cold wells up from my insides. "Um- I..." I stammer.

He releases my shoulders and slides over the edge of the bed, further away from me. He scratches the back of his head and silently looks around my bedroom. He looks at me again, opens his mouth and closes it again. He looks at his hands and at the ring on his finger. "This." He briefly points at himself and then at me. "Can't happen. I am your father. Maybe not biologically, but... I've watched you grow up. From the time you were this little." He extends his hand at the level of his chest as he sits. He is silent for a moment. His eyes flick from left to right. "I understand-" He clears his throat. "I understand if you might feel confused. And I'm sorry if..." he swallows, "if I might have done something to confuse you. But... you're my daughter." He strokes his forehead with his fingers and looks at me.

I dodge his gaze and stare at the floor, squinting. Tears begin to well up.

His hand touches my crown again, lightly and hesitantly. "Go to sleep," he whispers.

I hear my bed creaking and his footsteps shuffling across the floor, further and further away from me. The hinges of the door squeak softly. A soft pounding. And then silence. I look at the door. I know he is still behind it, because I didn't hear his footsteps disappear. I begin to sob silently and bury my face in my hands. I try to fight the tears so Danny doesn't hear me, but it's a lost battle.

Where did that kiss come from? What did I do? Did I screw up? What if he tells Kyra? Then she'll really want me out of the house. Maybe I *should* leave. Especially after what he had just told me about his twin sister... what was I thinking!?

My insides burn and squeeze together. My stomach turns over. I've ruined it. I've ruined everything. I bite my lip. I love him. I feel safe with him. He is everything to me. I become all warm when I see him, when he looks at me, when he touches me.... I fall backwards onto my bed and stare at the ceiling. Tears roll down my cheeks.

His footsteps move with a dull sound. The door to his office closes.

I look at my mobile phone. It's 1:30 in the morning. At ten o'clock I'll have to be at Jack's for my therapy session. Danny will be out the door by seven, so if I get up after that time, we won't need to see each other. Maybe that'd be for the best, to not see him for a while. But what if he sees Kyra before then? I need a chance to talk to him. Clear the air. I clutch at my rumbling belly and suppress the urge to gag. I can't face him yet. I'd rather hide under my blanket and not come out from under it. Even though I won't be able to hide from him forever. Kyra would start to wonder what's going on, too... Would he tell her? Of course, he would. She's going to jump out of her skin, absolutely livid; this'll be the last straw for her. I'll be thrown to the curb, with no home, no safety net. Nowhere to go. No safe haven. There's no place left for me.

I turn onto my side and look at the man with the hat staring motionless at me from the corner of the room. Couldn't you have stopped me!? I looked at him with annoyance and anger. You must have known what was going on, seeing how you've been observing me for months on end.

My mouth feels parched. Should I tell Jack what happened? But then he'll ask me all those burning questions. Why? What does Danny mean to me? What does a kiss mean to me? Where does this feeling come from? And then he'll start explaining to me the underlying psychological reason, peering at me with pinched eyes over his fingertips, silently condemning me with his gaze.

A deep sigh emerges from my lungs. I slide my hands under my head, in an effort to console myself, but then my heart makes a jump. My hand slides up further and reaches under my pillow for the crumpled piece of newspaper. I grab it and stare at the article about that familiar-feeling hotel called Lethalis.

"Amber," sounds a soft whisper in my room.

I shoot up and look around wildly. There's no-one in sight; well, except for the man with the hat, that is. I listen intently to the prolonged silence. Just when my muscles start to relax, I hear it again: a woozy high-pitched voice saying my name. I bring my ear closer to the newspaper clipping and listen intently.

"Amber," it sounds louder. With trembling eyelashes, I stare at the piece of paper.

The door to my room flies open with a loud bang, and I fall backwards onto my bed in terror.

Hhhmmmmnaah.

My heart pounds in my throat. I quickly tuck the newspaper snippet back under my pillow and look at the little girl with the tousled ash blonde hair, just as ash blonde as Danny's. His one and only daughter. I feel a stabbing pain in my chest.

Reina stumbles over to my bed and drops onto the comforter. She flails her arms.

"What happened to your braid?" I ask gently as I stroke through her hair. I don't get an answer, but I don't need one either; Kyra obviously untied it.

"What's going on?" Danny's voice sounds from the doorway.

I look at him and then quickly back at Reina. "I-" A lump forms in my throat. "I guess she can't sleep."

He walks over to my bed and picks her up. "Leave her to me."

I feel his eyes burning on my crown.

"Go to sleep." He turns and leaves the room with Reina in his arms.

I wait until I no longer hear his footsteps before I get up and close the door behind him. I sink to my knees and feel my stomach turn over again. Now I *know* I won't get a wink of sleep tonight. I grab my jeans, which I casually tossed next to my desk earlier this night, and snatch my medication from my pocket. I press another happy pill from the strip onto my hand. I take it between my fingers and look at it as I swirl it around. I let the pill slide onto my tongue and swallow. The pill scrapes my uvula and creeps down my throat. I swallow laboriously, trying to collect extra saliva in my mouth to be able to swallow once more. The happy pill slowly creeps deeper and deeper. I'm pretty sure I've swallowed it now, but it feels like it's still stuck in my throat.

I rest the back of my head against my cold door and close my eyes. I breathe in and out quietly, trying to clear my head. Meanwhile, I see the clock indicate three in the morning. I fervently wish for fatigue to overcome me and overpower my inner turmoil, like a thick blanket draping over my body and mind.

But slumber is a faraway dream.

5 THE BREATH

I sit on the sturdy oak chair in front of Jack's desk. My gaze is locked on him, but my attention is elsewhere. It's as if there's a haze sticking to my eyes.

"Amber," sounds a whispering voice. It's the same as before. That whispering female voice; sweet and luring. She repeats my name as if it were an invitation. It feels both familiar and uncomfortable.

In the distance, I do register Jack's voice, but it fails to break through the barrier. Before my mind's eye flash too many images. Danny. Reina with her loose hair. Danny. The newspaper snippet. Danny. Kyra and her piercing eyes. Danny. Danny. Danny. I can feel my tears welling up again.

I reach into my pocket and pop a happy pill from the strip. I bring the pill to my mouth and place it on my tongue. I grab the cup from the coaster on Jack's desk, taking a big sip of the tea, and feel the pill slither down my throat. I set the cup back down and feel Jack's hand wrap around mine. I blink slowly. All the images fade away, until all I see is the one in front of me: Jack, frowning at me, with his right hand resting on my left. I see it, but I don't feel it. I bring my other hand to my face and dry my cheeks.

"I don't know where you are, Amber," Jack remarks. "And that worries me. What is it that you aren't sharing with me?"

I stare at my knees.

A blackbird chirps from the largest branch of the oak tree outside the window.

"Why aren't you sharing it with me?"

I bite my lip.

"I can't help you if you don't talk to me, Amber."

A block of concrete rests on my diaphragm—I'm just glad I can breathe right now, let alone talk.

"Let me in, Amber."

"Amber," the whispering voice repeats.

I look around the room and scratch at the itchy scars on my forearms.

"Amber," Jack says again, in a stern voice. The voice follows.

A silence falls; so heavy it is almost palpable.

The man with the hat stands next to the large plant, in his usual spot. He bends forward slightly, staring at me from under the brim of his fedora.

"Okay, if you don't want to talk.... Then I'd like to try hypnosis again," Jack says.

I look into his eyes. Maybe hypnosis is for the best. It'll practically put me under, under water; that's how it feels—I'm there, yet I'm not. I feel, yet I don't. Time passes without my noticing, as I float silently about in the chilly water. Perhaps he could keep me under hypnosis permanently...

Jack squeezes my hand. "Are you okay with that?" he asks.

I nod compliantly. This is the first time he has asked me for permission for hypnosis, ever. Normally I just undergo it. He's the one who decides.

He taps the rim of the cup in front of me. "Drink your tea."

I grab the cup with both hands and pour the now lukewarm tea down my throat.

"Very good." He gets up and stands next to me.

I let myself be led to the couch. I sit down and feel the energy drain from my limbs.

"Get comfortable," he says as he grabs the large video camera from the corner of the room and sets it in place with the lens pointed at me. The red light turns on.

I follow Jack's directions.

The leather of his armchair crackles beneath him as he sits down across from me. "You can close your eyes. You're safe here," he says.

I close my eyes as that last word darts between my ears. Back and forth. Up and down. *Safe...*

"Focus your attention on your breathing. Just feel it, don't direct anything. Feel the air flowing in and out of your lungs. Feel how your chest gently rises with your inhale and sinks down with each exhale. Notice that you're breathing even more steadily, even more slowly, as you relax more and more." He gives the camera a little tap.

I gently breathe in and out.

"Feel how your muscles relax around your stomach, your spine. Let it sink down, through your knees, through your shins and your feet. Let all the tension go. Let yourself go. Let yourself be. Relaxed and ea-"

Jack's voice has faded away and it's dark before my eyes. I can only hear my own breathing. It's as if I'm in a dark room, all by myself. My familiar place. Apart from everything and everyone. Safely tucked away in the darkness. Protected from my own probing thoughts; relentless and invasive.

"Amber," sounds the whispering voice.

I automatically look around, but I can't see a thing in the pitch darkness. A stab of pain shoots through my head. I squeeze my eyes shut.

An image looms before my mind's eye. A bed with a white sheet. Blood-stained fingers hanging limply down the side. A person perches over the bed. Tangled, sallow rust-coloured hair undulates across the sheet. A shimmering bright red fabric envelops the slender figure.

A gurgling breath echoes around me.

My heart shrinks in my chest. My lungs contract and my breath stalls as I look at the bed with the bloodied fingers and the woman in red beside it.

The image fades away and then all I hear is that breathing. In and out. Louder and louder.

The hairs on my arms jump straight up. I want to open my eyes, but they remain closed; as if my eyelashes are glued together. The rasping breath is now right next to me; gurgling into my left ear. I feel a sigh on the back of my neck and the hairs bristle up there as well.

A wave of energy rushes through my body and I feel my limbs convulse.

I hear the breath louder and louder. Rasping and gurgling. I want to press my hands on my ears to block out the sound, but my arms won't come up. I want to scream, but no sound comes out of my throat. My lips separate; I manage but a sigh and a soft squeak. With all my might I try to open my eyes.

"Amber," the voice sounds gruff and out of breath. "Amber!"

A deafening screech vibrates my eardrums.

My eyes pop open.

I see Jack's face right above me; inches from my face. His eyes go wide. I taste the salt on my lips. I gasp for breath. "Help," I bring out softly. His sour breath brushes my face as my eyes fall shut. I'm back in the pitch darkness where I so desperately wanted to be, but it doesn't feel safe anymore. The emptiness presses down on me like lead and suffocates me.

I frantically look around me, desperate for a way out, and see a glimpse of light. The flickering flame of a candle. I go toward it without moving my legs. Underneath my feet, a strip of carpet appears. I look at it as I glide across it. The carpet's coloured lilac and graceful lilies bloom on it.

I look up and see a little girl walking in front of me, with her back turned to me. Her blond hair sways back and forth as she walks, as does the fabric of her blue dress, on which little flowers dance.

The gurgling breath rolls across the void like a cloud of dust, filling the silence. Louder and louder. The flickering light of the fire illuminates the darkness. It sets everything ablaze.

"Amber."

I open my eyes.

My heart pounds heavily in my chest. I put a hand on my chest to restrain my heart. Above me I see a white ceiling with dark wooden beams; the familiar ceiling of Jack's office. I turn my head and see Jack sitting in his leather chair. He has one hand in front of his mouth and is frowning deeply as he watches me intently. I look in front of me and sit up. My gaze slides over my body. Everything is exactly as it was when I laid down. I shake my head for a moment and look at Jack, who is still peering at me.

"How do you feel?" he asks reluctantly.

"D-dazed," I stammer.

He strokes his chin with two fingers. "Did something happen?"

My eyes flick from left to right and back again. "I saw.... I saw a girl. She was walking in front of me."

He lowers his hand.

"A girl?"

I nod.

"How old?"

I bite my lip. "About six years old, I think."

"Where?"

"On a carpet with... lilies."

He nods slowly. "And what else? What did you see?"

I recall his face hoovering over me and shake my head.

"Was there anything else you noticed?" he continues asking.

"I did hear *something*."

He leans forward and rests his elbows on his knees. "Tell me."

"It was a breath." The muscles in my eyebrows contract. "Like a gurgle, that's what it sounded like. Low and deep and intermittent. Rasping, if I explain it right."

He squeezes his eyes to slits.

"And my name, I heard my name a few times," I continue hesitantly. Should I tell him I heard my name being said even before the hypnosis? He'd probably think I'm going crazy - or crazier, so to say.

He slowly sits back in his chair and crosses one leg over the other. His shoe rests on his knee. "Are you taking your medication?"

"Yes," I reply quickly as I nod.

"Are you taking it like you're supposed to?"

I nod again.

"Are you being honest with me?"

I bite my tongue.

"You know I can tell when you're lying to me, Amber. Tell me the truth. Are you taking your medication like you're supposed to?"

I remain silent and avoid his gaze.

"I just saw you taking your medication right before hypnosis. That could mean three things. Either you forgot this morning and are taking it now. Or you took your afternoon dose too early, which also makes me wonder... why? Or you're taking more than you're supposed to take."

My fingernails press into my palms. "You said yourself that we might have to increase the dose."

"I did indeed say that. But you always increase or decrease a dose in consultation with me. In fact, I am the absolute lead in that. Is there a reason why you increased your dose yourself?"

My heart begins to beat faster. I gently shake my head.

"No ... complaints?" He looks at me intently. "I mean, you're taking extra all of a sudden. There must be a reason. You've been taking them exactly as I prescribed them, for nearly ten months. What makes today different? Or has this been going on for longer?" He leans forward. "Amber, you *have* to answer me. Since when have you been taking a higher dose?"

"Since yesterday," I respond.

He stares at me, opens his mouth, and closes it again. He bites his lip for a moment, still staring at me with those piercing eyes. "I'm going to trust you on that, Amber. Please don't make me regret that. Now, tell me. Did something happen yesterday?"

I've been dreading that question. I shift back and forth on my buttocks, restless and agitated. I feel like a cat in a corner. I wipe the sweat from my forehead and feel the moisture between my thighs. Today was not the best day to wear leather pants.

"Have you read the side effects of your medication?"

I think back to the first time I received my medication. The package insert folded out to two sheets full of information and warnings, which I'd thoroughly read. I nod silently.

"Then you should know that they can cause hallucinations if they're not used responsibly. Is that right?"

I think for a moment. "I guess I'd forgotten about that," I reluctantly admit.

"That's why you need to do as I tell you. If I prescribe you three pills a day, I do it for a reason. When we decrease or increase the dose, we do so gradually. First off, we would start with just a quarter extra and observe the effects for a prolonged period of time. We'd keep a close

eye on how it affects you and I'd also inform your parents so that
they can keep an eye on you at home. Increasing your dose is not a
decision made lightly and definitely not a decision made by *you*." He
frowns. "I'm responsible for you, Amber. In this regard, at least. If
you take your medication use into your own hands, it endangers the
both of us."

I avert my eyes. Yet another thing I've done wrong this week. I see
Danny's shocked look from last night flash before my eyes. I feel his
hands grabbing my shoulders and pushing me away. Then I see Jack's
face hovering over me, drops of sweat glistening on his forehead, and
I feel his breath rolling down my face. I shake my head in a vain
attempt to erase the image.

"Our time is up," he says abruptly. "But, Amber ... promise me one
thing." He looks at me sternly. "Three pills a day. We'll discuss your
current dose the day after tomorrow. And I can't stress this enough,
but do not trust *anything* you see, hear or feel since you took a higher
dose and for the next few days. It will take a while to disappear from
your system. Hallucinations can seem very, very real, and that can be
dangerous. Stay indoors as much as possible for now, just to be on
the safe side. Your safety comes first, after all."

I get up and walk past him to his desk. I grab my shoulder bag from
the floor and trudge to the door of his office.

"By the way, Amber..."

I turn and look at him.

"I'm obligated to inform your parents about this."

My heart sinks.

6 FORMER GLORY

With legs as spaghetti, I find myself standing beside the bus shelter. Everything goes past me, like the wind blowing. I don't see the man from the tobacco shop ogling. I don't smell the freshly baked bread the woman next to me is holding. I don't feel the burning sun on my skin. And I don't see the bus stopping right in front of me and driving off a little later.

I reach into my one pocket and feel the medicine box. I reach into my other pocket and feel the newspaper snippet. The air squeezes from my lungs and I withdraw both hands. I inhale deeply and try to sense my heartbeat. I feel my chest contract and expand with each breath. My hand reaches into my pocket again.

This. This is my only escape, I think warily as my fingers touch the contents of my pocket. I pull it out and look at the piece of paper between my fingers. My gaze lingers on the name of the hotel. I grab my phone and open the navigation app.

The bus shelter disappears into the background as I walk past the shops.

Wide buildings with small windows and large driveways slide in and out of my field of vision. There are only a few dozen cars in the various driveways. At almost every building are tall poles with vertically stretched flags. The road turns into a farmland lane and a while later into a neat street through a residential area.

My eyes scan the surroundings, searching for the bus stop indicated on my navigation app, but the supermarket next door catches my eye first. I start walking towards it when my pocket starts vibrating. I grab my phone and flip it open.

Ms Katen called. Let's talk when I finish work. See you soon.

My heart skips a beat. What should I answer? I don't want to go home yet—I want to go to Lethalis. And I am afraid of what Danny might say. I have failed to keep my appointment once again. I stand rooted to the ground and watch the time tick away. My finger slowly taps against the side of my phone as I try to think of a solution. My teeth knead my lower lip like clay.

Mom says you're not home yet. Where are you?

I stare at the display and see his name appear on the screen, with a ringing telephone icon above it. My heart's now beating in my throat and my ears feel hot. After a few seconds, the name disappears and I get a message confirming the missed call.

Pick up.

My finger pushes the button with a red phone on it and holds it down until my phone vibrates gently. For a moment I see Danny's name on the screen again. Then the screen goes black and the vibrating stops. I close the phone and put it back in my pocket with clammy hands. My limbs feel heavy.

There is no turning back now.

I walk into the supermarket and grab a basket. I walk through the aisles and grab a pack of four bottles of water, four packs of noodles, a pack of oatmeal biscuits, painkillers, a pack of wet wipes and a can of energy drink. I dump the contents at the till and add a pack of gum.

The woman behind the till looks up from her mobile phone and slides it to the side with a sigh. She starts scanning the items.

"Can I have a bag?" I ask.

Beep.

Without looking up, she scans the last items and pulls a white plastic bag from under the counter, stroking it flat and placing it on top of the groceries. "Twelve seventy-five," she says languidly.

I pull out my wallet and look at the contents. I see a fifty note, one of twenty, some spare change and my debit card and ID. I grab the fifty and place it on the counter in front of me.

She frowns at the note, rolls her eyes and taps loudly on some buttons in front of her. The till pops open. She crams the note in and takes the change out. She slams the drawer shut and smacks the change on the counter.

The plastic bag crackles as I stuff the groceries inside.

"Receipt?" the woman asks gruffly.

"No, thank you," I respond. "Have a nice day."

The woman grabs her phone again and the world disappears around her.

If only it were that easy for me, I think to myself. I raise my eyebrows as I grab the change from the counter and walk back outside. Which bus was I supposed to take? I think deeply as I put the money back into my wallet. Number 54, I hope. I walk to the bus shelter and look at the grid on the wall. It should come within a few minutes—provided I haven't been in the store for too long.

I grab my earbuds and put them in my ears. I turn on my mp3-player and hear the comforting sounds of my favourite punk rock band. I close my eyes.

Sheep bleat in the wind as the wheels of the bus roll over the tarmac, right past the meadow. A large lake glides past the windows. Sunlight refracts on the surface of the water, making it glisten like diamonds.

I keep a close eye on the screen showing the stops.

The sun has already weakened a little by the time Chestnut Avenue in Midsberg appears on the screen. I press the stop button. A few minutes later, the bus comes to a squeaking halt. I get out and hear the doors slide shut behind me with a hissing sound.

It should be about a 20-minute walk still, and I don't know which way to go. I look around me. My hand briefly strokes my pocket. If I'd turn on my phone, I'd see all the missed calls and messages from Danny. If I were to tell him where I was, he'd personally come and get me. And he'd be angry—even angrier than yesterday.

My legs feel weak. I recall his face in front of me as he pushes me away from him, as we sit on the edge of my bed. I see his eyes and that surprised expression surrounding them. Kyra is never going to let me set foot in that house again, I think gloomily. And Jack's added insult to injury.

I start walking aimlessly in a direction. I should probably ask someone for directions.

A drop of sweat rolls down my temple. It may be the middle of summer, but it seems to be exceptionally hot today. With the tip of my sleeve, I pat my forehead dry. Sweat itches on the scars under my sleeves and I scratch them frantically to stop the itching. Why did I have to wear my fake leather trousers today?

Sighing, sweating, and with a weary mind, I keep on walking. When the renovations are finished and Lethalis opens officially, they should put in an extra bus stop, I think irritably. For people without a car or without money for a taxi, this really isn't viable. Especially when you're carrying heavy suitcases.

I raise my bag on my shoulder and curse myself for not writing down the route to the hotel. I used to write down routes when I went to university, for the entire first week, and when I visited Jack's office for the first time. I had even printed out pictures of what the route looked like. But, now that there's a pretty handy app for it, which I can use on my mobile, I've gotten way too used to just looking up directions at any time, anywhere. Not that I often need to do so, as I rarely go out, but it would've worked great right now. I just can't risk the flood of missed calls and messages from Danny—they'd surely force me back home, and I have things to take care of first. Things to find out.

A white dog's wet nose brushes along my ankle. I look down at the creature. It has curly fur and small black beady eyes. I can read the eyes of most dogs pretty well, but these yapping little mutts leave me feeling clueless. I find them unpredictable as hell. And now, that thing starts barking at me!

"Stop it, Mukkie."

I look at the woman on the other side of the leash. She's a short stocky person with white curly hair—just like *Mukkie*—, deep wrinkles and a gaudy silver necklace. She looks at me and smiles. She makes no attempt to restrain the dog as it barks and bites into my pants and jumps up against my leg.

A hot fist forms behind my ribs and boils my blood. I sweep the beast aside with my shoe, but it keeps coming at me, while the woman pretends to be alive and present. I clench my molars and feel my jaw muscles contract. Before I truly get the urge to kick the yapping beast, I open my mouth. "Where can I find Hotel Lethalis?"

The woman purses her lips. "That dump?" She shakes her head slowly. "That one's closed, mind you. If you want to stay around here, you're better off going to Bullinger's B&B, which is just around the corner. Good breakfast they have there. They get their bread fresh every morning from Val's Bakery, the local one. Very tasty. And not expensive at all, a night there, let me tell you. It's—"

"That way, then?" I ask, still focused on her nod.

"No, round the corner here." She gestures behind her.

My molars grind. "Lethalis. It's that way?" I emphasise, pointing in the opposite direction to her gesture.

"You don't want to go there, my child. That's closed to guests, it has been for years and years. And it's for the best, trust me. They shouldn't even *think* of renovating it, if you ask me. Best to just let it go to waste. Lost and forgotten. The only ones that go there, or used to go there, I should say—mind you, you probably weren't even born back then—are the people wh-"

"Yeah, thanks," I cut her short, taking a step towards where Lethalis apparently is.

The dog squeals loudly.

"Oh dear, Mukkie, what's the matter, poor thing? Are you hungry?"

I imagine the woman bending over the animal and feeding it sweets as a reward for its conduct. The thought soon fades as I briskly walk down the street, determined to find the hotel—hopefully without any other yappers along the way. *Mukkie...* what the hell kind of a name is *Mukkie*?

With one bag over my shoulder and my other, plastic bag full of food and drinks in my hand, I stroll through a residential area, still hoping that I'm going the right way. According to that lady's general hand gesture, Lethalis must be in this direction.

I pass a house with a garden full of sunflowers and a large porch with a wooden bench on it. I imagine sipping my morning coffee there, enjoying the peace and quiet together with Danny, sitting next to me on the bench with the newspaper in his hands. With that daydream alive in my mind, I keep on walking.

It's quiet outside, considering how warm it is. There's no one in the shade watering their plants. No one walking to his or her car, with or without a shopping bag—having just returned from a trip to the grocery store. No one walking in or out of the huge church. I look at the church building in the middle of the residential area. It is disproportionately large, with colourful windows and majestic decorations on the facade. I have always liked the leaded glass. The images on it less so.

I pass a neatly laid-out garden with hedges of the same height, blooming pink roses and colourful flower beds. As I keep walking, the gardens become smaller and wilder—the one more unkept than the other. The houses grow smaller, rundown and more tawdry, and they soon transition into patches of meadow.

My armpits slosh as I drink the second bottle of water from the plastic bag.

To my left is a long row of trees, the motorway and a cycle path. Behind it is meadow with farms and fields full of sheep and cows, dryly munching on grass. To my right is even more meadow, as far as the eye can see. As I walk further and further, my feet throb and there seems to be no end in sight. Either I'm walking the wrong way, or my navigation app was too optimistic regarding pedestrianism.

I consider turning on my phone to check the route, as true doubt sets in. But that's when I see it, finally. A striking building at the end of a long driveway. With groups of trees on either side of the building and a large steel gate in front.

With a hurried pace, I approach the gate and look through the bars at the building. There it is. Lethalis. That strangely familiar feeling descends on my heart. I take in the building and its surroundings carefully, trying to remember something. It looks different from the picture in the paper, which must have been taken much earlier.

The grounds are remarkably empty. If renovation is in full swing, as the newspaper article states, I would have expected workmen. Instead of clanging hammers, I hear singing birds and the gentle summer breeze rustling through the trees. I grab my medication from my pocket and swallow the pill dry, staring at the building that seems to be growing bigger and bigger.

I rattle the latch of the gate for a moment, but it doesn't give way. It must be locked. My bemused gaze glides from right to left and spots a hole in the fence. I examine the damaged fence, look around nervously and stuff both my bags through the hole before wriggling through myself.

A burning sensation wells up in my chest as I approach the large stone steps in front of the building. I look at the closed door, my heart pounding in my throat. What if someone catches me, breaking and entering?

"Hello?" sounds a lilting voice.

I startle and turn around at lightning speed. A petite busty woman with fiery red hair walks towards me, wearing a petrol blue dress with a pattern of red cherries, which look hand-painted. Her eyes sparkle and she smiles broadly.

"Are you looking for something?" she asks.

"Ah, hello. S-sorry for coming here, but..." I frantically search for words and glance at the building behind me. "I was just really curious about Lethalis. I'm Amber and um..." The words stick in my throat.

"Amber?" The woman looks at me with an intensely joyful expression.

"Yeah, you see, I think I've been here before, when I was really young. I don't know how young exactly, but I... uhm... I don't remember much of that time," I stammer.

"You don't remember?"

I shake my head.

"You're here for a reason, aren't you? Something led you here," the woman responds briskly.

"Ehh, yes... yes, it did." I snatch the newspaper article from my pocket and give it to her.

The woman takes the paper and studies it intently. "The renovation of Hotel Lethalis has resumed," she reads out loud. She breathes a sigh. "It's about time too, isn't it? When the doors of Lethalis were still open, guests came from far and wide to stay here. It was a real hotspot in those days." She hands back the piece of paper and looks at me piercingly. "But if you were here when you were young... your *parents* can tell you more about it, right? Or an older sibling, maybe?"

I shake my head again. "That's the tricky thing. I don't know who my parents are or if they're still alive. I was adopted when I was seven."

She raises her eyebrow. "Oh..."

I look back at the hotel. The facade towers over me. "I was wondering if maybe I could look around inside? To see if I can remember more."

I dare not tell the woman about the voice that seemed to come from inside the newsprint, calling my name and luring me to this place. The man with the hat pointed it out to me in the park, groping in his pocket, knowing I had hidden the newsprint in that very pocket. And that lily carpet... that memory seems to be linked to this as well.

The woman nods slowly. "Well, seems like you are our first guest in over a decade, Amber." The woman smiles radiantly. She pushes open the double doors, revealing a spacious hall with a high ceiling.

At the end of the hall is a sparkling white counter about six metres wide, on which two familiar hands rest. I look the man with the hat in his eye and feel strangely relaxed. His shabby outfit and grey fedora don't look out of place here, somehow. To our right, I see white stone stairs leading up and down. To our left are large double doors, painted snow-white. To the left of the counter is a large glass door that seemingly leads to the garden.

"Welcome to Lethalis." The woman turns to face me, her dress twirling gracefully around her legs. "My name is Toke." She looks at me expectantly. "This beautiful hotel is mine. I call it my home," she adds, smiling brightly. "Lethalis may seem a bit run-down, but it is a beautiful, hidden gem that will ultimately shine again, as it once did." She takes a few steps backwards as she narrates liltingly. "Lethalis has a very rich history, which too few people remember. And I am going to change that. I will restore Lethalis to its former glory, with all the nostalgic features to those who used to admire it." She waves her hand at herself and then through the empty lobby. "This is the lounge. You can wait here to check in, while enjoying a nice drink; warm in the icy winter or cool in the sultry summer."

I imagine a set of large comfortable sofas on the white stone floor that Toke gestures to.

"You can relax and read the newspaper here in the morning and meet new people in the evening. Who knows, maybe even for life." She steps back a bit. "Here, you'll find the fireplace, where the fire is *always* burning."

I look at the empty fireplace and imagine the flames. For a moment, the woman in red skims past my mind's eye, screeching among the fiery whips.

Toke turns and walks through the double doors on the left side of the lobby.

I follow her.

"This is the dining room." She gestures through the huge empty hall. "Here are thirty tables for four, fifty tables for two, ten for six and another ten tables for more than eight people." She peers into the venue. "Mostly families come here," she adds.

I see it all before me with my vivid imagination. Giant chandeliers on the high ceiling, casting golden halos of light on the cherry wood tabletops. Families, friends and business partners telling bloated stories and listening intently to each other whilst enjoying a generous three-course meal.

"And there's the kitchen," Toke continues, gesturing towards the freshly plastered walls in the left-hand corner of the room. "The food here is very good." She chuckles warmly and leads me back into the hall towards the wide staircase. Next to the stairs are two doors, one of white wood and one of steel. "Here, on the left, you'll find the elevator. Nice and practical for those with limited mobility, carrying heavy suitcases, or for those who don't want to sweat unnecessarily." She winks at me boldly.

I wipe the drops of sweat from my forehead. Like the elevator, the air-conditioning is also out-of-order. I follow her up the stone stairs, my soles flopping on the steps. The stairs make an angular u-turn and, halfway up, a flat section connects the two stairs between a floor. I'm completely out of breath by the time we reach the top. I lean on my knees for a moment—white stars dance around my vision.

Toke watches me intently. "Low on stamina?"

I wipe my arm along my face and nod, "Apparently, but it's also... really hot."

She looks out the tall window next to the stairs. "It's *exceptionally* hot for the time of year. Make sure you drink enough. Dehydration is no picnic."

Looking down at my bag of drinks, I see the floor beneath me. It's carpet. Sallow and dusty, but unmistakably with a purple hue. Light-coloured lines trace across the carpet, forming graceful patterns of lilies. I gasp and look down the corridor. It's the lilac lily carpet!

My hands clutch at my chest as Toke looks at me in silence. My heart beats with such force that I fear it will jump out and run away.

"Do you remember anything?"

I shake my head. "No, not really, but this carpet... I recognise this."

She observes me for a moment. "You recognise the lilies?"

I nod slowly.

"Interesting." She resumes her stride, slightly slower now. "You'll find rooms 100 to 199 right here. One floor up are the rooms up to 299. And then we have the third floor, which goes up to room 398."

The words sink in slowly. I stare into the corridor. "It goes up to 398? Isn't there a room 399?"

"Room 399?" she repeats my words. "Why?"

I look at her non-comprehendingly. "It only seemed logical to me..." I utter.

She shakes her head wildly. "You are not allowed to go to room 399," she says sternly.

With an expectant look, I keep waiting for a further explanation.

Toke breathes a sigh. "I don't want any new accidents here."

"New ones? Why? What happened?"

Toke ignores my questions and pushes open one of the room doors. The light from outside is dimmed slightly by the plastic sheets hanging against the facade.

I poke my head into the room and see a door leading to the bathroom.

"Bleak, huh?" sounds Toke's voice from further down.

I pull my head back and follow her.

Toke pushes open one door after another in the corridor. Behind each door is the same room. Empty, freshly plastered and with plastic sheeting in front of the windows.

"All the doors are currently unlocked so there's no fuss with missing keys."

"Was there before?" I ask curiously.

She looks back at me. "In Lethalis' heyday, each room had its own key. But sometimes one got lost, and sometimes.... Well, not everyone has solely good intentions, unfortunately. A door could be locked at the worst possible time, more often than you liked. And what happens behind closed doors..."

"Are you going to use keycards now?" I ask curiously.

"Keycards? What are those?"

"Those smart cards, which you slide into one of these devices, which releases the lock. You see that a lot in hotels these days," I say, remembering the hotels I've stayed in with Danny during some of his business trips abroad.

"Interesting," Toke responds. "Who knows if there will be any..."

I saunter behind her. "How far along are you with the renovation, anyway?"

She looks at me and raises an eyebrow. "Hmmm. I heard the builders talking about insulation boards and grouting the facade again. But... construction is pretty much at a standstill at the moment."

"Huh?" I respond aloud.

"Didn't you know?"

I shake my head and take the crumpled piece of newspaper out of my pocket. I smooth the paper and stare at the article.

· · ·

Betting on former glory

VASSEN – WEDNESDAY, July 16, 2008

The renovation of Hotel Lethalis has resumed. The hotel that experienced its glory years in the early 1980s. Famous for its extravagant dance parties and notorious for illegal gaming. Golden Ten was not a silver lining, but a grey stain on the hotel's immaculate legacy.

The owner hopes to restore the hotel to its former glory to revive the tourism of Midsberg. Without the gambling, she stresses with a twinkling smile.

"It's not in there," Toke says stiffly. She waves her hand. "But it doesn't matter either way, because you found it. You're here now and that's what's important." She watches me silently for a while, until I turn my attention back to her. "Did you know they replaced all the window frames?" she continues. "And even the whole staircase... I don't think it's an improvement, frankly. They should have just left the stairs made of wood, it's part of the character of Lethalis. Just put up with the slow rot and replace the wood every once in a while. But turning it all to stone..." She sighs deeply. "How much can you change until something is no longer the same?" Her nostrils flare open. "And that smell of plaster doesn't belong here either," she grumbles.

"Will it stay white?" I ask as my fingertips stroke across the wall in the corridor.

She follows my fingers with her eyes. "Don't you like the daisies better?"

"Daisies?" I respond in surprise.

She smiles weakly. "There used to be very pretty daisies on here."

I nod thoughtfully. "Those are nice flowers."

"I know, right? They're *happy* flowers." She turns the corner abruptly, into a short corridor. On the right side of the corridor is just wall, on the left are windows. The plastic sheets sway in the wind, and in between, a lawn with trees shows.

"I want them to change as little as possible," she continues, "so that the character of Lethalis doesn't get lost, you know? It's a special building. With a lot of history." She looks at me meaningfully.

We turn another corner and I see the same white doors as before.

"If I may ask... how old are you exactly?" I ask cautiously. "You know so much about its history, but you seem to be only a couple of years older than me."

She smiles awkwardly. "I'm not much older, indeed. Let's leave it at that." She winks and turns another corner. "I'm curious to know what they plan to do with the carpet. I hear people find it dirty and tattered and that the lilies are too faded to keep it. They want to rip it out and put down floorboards. But that's a waste, isn't it?

I nod in agreement. "If you clean the carpet properly, I'm sure it will look more lively."

"Exactly. You understand me. We can clean it just fine, in every single room."

We come back to the stairs and go up to the second floor, making a lap there as well—everything looks exactly like it does on the first floor. We walk back towards the stairwell once more, and just when she puts her foot on the first step, she suddenly stops.

"I have to leave," she says. "Sorry, I would have liked to show you the entire place. But upstairs, it's..." she looks up into the stairwell, "well, it's a big mess up there sometimes. It's such a chore to keep things tidy. But then again, that's not surprising in a renovation, I guess." She sighs. "So we will, unfortunately, leave that mess for now." She takes her foot off the step.

"Can I help?" I ask abruptly.

She looks at me in surprise. "With what?"

"Whatever. Tidying up, cleaning..."

She opens her mouth for a moment, ponders and closes it again.

"I really hope I can remember something, by being here," I continue.

"Why do you want to remember?" She looks at me piercingly.

I bite the inside of my lip. "There are... things that need processing," I begin hesitantly.

She looks up the stairwell to the third floor. "If you think it might help you... But do you really want to do that now?"

"It's urgent," I insist. I remain silent for a moment. I can hardly tell her about my therapy, which is due to end in two months. She's never going to leave me alone here if I bring that up. "And I'd like to get to know Lethalis better," I add.

She draws her lower lip in and stares at me, pensively. "Where do you live now?"

"Near Vassen."

"That's not exactly within walking distance."

"I came by bus."

"Are you staying here?"

"I don't know i-..."

"The last bus has already left. You should stay here," she interjects.

"Well, I heard something about a bed and breakfast, Bullinger's if I recall correctly. It's near here, isn't it?"

She shakes her head. "A long walk and a waste of money. You said you want to remember your past, so... why not just stay here?"

"Could I?" I ask cautiously.

She nods. "Of course. Like I said, it's my home. I'm quite capable of sharing."

I smile, hesitant but relieved. "If you don't mind, then..."

"I don't mind." She looks past me, into the corridor. "Together, we can restore Lethalis to its former glory." She extends her hand to me and shows her toothpaste-commercial-worthy smile.

"I'll do my best!" I transfer the plastic bag to my left hand before shaking her hand with a broad smile. For a moment, it feels like all my worries have dissipated, and I can finally breathe.

"I have faith in you." She lets go of my hand and slowly starts walking down the stone steps. Just before she disappears from sight, she stops. She looks up at me. "I'm glad you're here, Amber." The corners of her mouth curl up and she raises her hand.

I wave back, smiling. As soon as she disappears from sight, I feel a wave of exhilaration wash over me. I am finally here, I think to myself. I'm in Lethalis—a place that has something to do with my past and why I am the way I am. And Toke even allowed me to stay here!

I walk down the second-floor corridor and slowly lower myself to the carpet in a kneeling position, putting my bags down against the wall. My fingers stroke through the carpet's short purplish tufts. The colour is not as vivid as in my memory. It's tattered and grey with a purple glow rather than intense lilac. The lighter-coloured lilies are hard to distinguish from the rest of the carpet—I can only see them because I know they are there.

As I sit, petting the carpet, my thoughts wander back to Danny. He would be proud of me for seeking this out, I know he would. But he probably hates *how* I'm doing this. My heart contracts with a stabbing pain, as if someone is trying to cut through it with a blunt bread knife. I put a hand on my heart and breathe in and out deeply. He will understand. Eventually.

I stand up and quietly walk down the corridor. My fingers glide over the wall. I walk into room 201 where I feel at the walls, the bathroom door, the rough stone tiles, the glue residue where the mirror once hung and, a moment later, the smooth plastic surface of the window frame.

I deliberately take in the smells: a fresh earthy air and a musty lime scent. The hotel wouldn't have smelt like this, back then. Back then... when was it?

Probing and sniffing, I want to scan every part of Lethalis, hoping for a vague memory that finds the strength to slip through the tiny cracks of my bricked-up memory. But the renovation doesn't make it easy. How much has been changed by the construction work? And what has remained the same all this time?

I walk to the end of the corridor and stand by the windows. The sky turns bright orange above the treetops as the sun sinks steadily behind the trees. I lean on the window frame and look between the plastic sheets at the birds flying overhead.

The shuddering warmth coils around me like a blanket.

My belly slowly expands as I inhale deeply. I blow out all the air at once through my mouth and turn around. The wall in front of me is bathed in sunlight. My shadow contrasts sharply against the orange canvas. Only my breathing and a few singing birds fill the silence in the corridors, until my stomach growls.

I walk back to where I put my bags and sit back down on the floor. My back rests up against the wall, my toes touching the wall opposite me. I snatch an oatmeal biscuit from the bag and open my third bottle of water. The cereal crunches between my teeth as I greedily chew on a piece of biscuit. Between bites, I rest the back of my head against the wall. The chalky smell of the plaster creeps into my nasal cavities.

Finally, I think to myself. Finally, I am truly alone. I try to let it get through to myself, but I'm having a hard time doing so. I image it would be nice to live by myself, with just myself to worry about or consider. No bedtimes. No parents watching everything I do. No disapproving looks or oppressive silences. No bloody shards on the floor.

I see Danny's cheek before me, first glistening with blood, then neatly dabbed dry. And no more Danny either, I realise. My stomach turns. Don't think about that, I appease. Don't think about that. Focus on the here and now. You're in Lethalis—the place that feels so familiar, yet so alienated.

Quietly, I steadily nibble the oatmeal bar and take a few sips of water, before I scramble to my feet and walk down the corridor, completely lost in thought.

That little blonde girl I saw during my last therapy session... that must have been *me*, right here on this very carpet, traced with blooming lilies. But why is this carpet the only thing I remember?

And what do the steak-cheeked man and the lady in red have to do with this?

I wander aimlessly through the corridors of the first and second floors. I had hoped that my memories would come back to me as soon as I entered here, as if some kind of barrier would dissolve and all the images from back then would flood back into my brain. But if I learnt one thing from Jack, it is to be patient. "You shouldn't rush into anything," he repeated with some regularity. Especially since I was so impatient during our sessions. I hoped it would go faster. I hoped I'd feel better again and would be able to move on. On with my life—with or without the man with the hat. Although, preferably *without*. I just want to be a normal twenty-something.

Meanwhile, the sun creeps further and further away, until only dim light slips in through the windows.

I walk up the third floor. My nostrils flare. A faint smell of smoke tickles my olfactory receptors. I look at the corridor ahead and see tiny flakes of ash swirling through the air, dimly lit by the twilight. I stand and watch the ash flakes settle on the carpet. Ash... Is there fire?

I walk around the floor, but don't stumble upon anything suspicious. I take another look on the second floor, but the air is completely clean. There's also nothing off on the first and the ground floor, neither inside the lobby nor in the dining hall. I rush back to the third floor and find only fresh air. Was it my imagination? Was this another one of those delusions Jack warned me about? I bite my lip furiously as I walk down the corridors. My legs come to a halt. This makes no sense, I think to myself. I keep spinning around inside my head and outside of it.

I walk back to my bags on the second floor and settle myself in room 299—the room that is as close to the stairwell as possible, without being directly in sight of the stairs, like room 201 and 202 are. It's warm inside the room, but I'm sure it makes for a quieter and more comfortable sleep than in the corridor, especially if I use my shoulder bag as a pillow.

I lie down on the floor and slide my bag beneath my head. I pull the heaped up fabric of my jumper from under my waist for a more comfortable pose. I remove my mobile phone, which is pushing against my hip, out of my pocket and toss it into a corner of the room. My gaze is fixed on the ceiling, from which the orange light is slowly receding. I turn my head towards the window and stare outside.

My eyelids feel heavy and I blink languidly. For a moment, it is completely dark when I blink. I blink again, this time more slowly. It stays dark for longer and longer, until everything turns to darkness.

7 TOURISTS

A slight twinge of pain surges through my ear canal, jerking me upright. My hands clutch my head as I moan in discomfort. "Ouch…"

I blink and lean my head back gently. I don't know for how long I've slept, but it's still dark outside. The light from the moon glistens in through the plastic sheeting in front of the windows. I follow the light with my eyes. It creeps across the white floor, along the white walls and across the ceiling.

My gaze lingers on a dark spot in the middle of the snow-white ceiling. I scramble to my feet and stare at the stain intently. My head throbs as I raise my arm, trying to reach for the stain with my fingertips. For just a moment, I feel a searing heat. My fingers flinch and withdraw.

Half asleep, I stumble out of the room, into the stairwell and up the top floor. The area is dark and completely silent. I walk down the right corridor, turn the corner and stand in front of room 399. The one room that's deemed off-limits by Toke.

My fingers reach for the door handle, but I stiffen. The chilly steel reaches out like a hand to mine and clamps around it. My hand cramps and my legs feel heavy. I stare at the room number on the door and pull back my hand with effort. My legs sway as I stumble back down the corridor, my right shoulder brushing up against the wall. I grab my head with both hands and groan at the continuous pounding.

Back in my self-claimed room, I pull the door shut behind me and carefully lie back on the floor. I stare at the stain at the ceiling. My eyelids grow heavy.

Dazed, I open my eyes and struggle to get up. My back muscles whine as I carefully stretch and yawn at length. My throat feels so dry that swallowing hurts. I open the last bottle of water and drink greedily.

Before leaving the room, I glance at the ceiling. The dark stain is still there. So, it wasn't a dream.

I step into the corridor, close the door behind me, and walk towards the stairwell. The warm light of the rising sun falls in through the windows further down the corridor and through the cracks of the open hotel doors. I see thousands of dust particles swirling through the air. I look at them with intrigue. It is both beautiful and filthy. The sight is mesmerising, but it constricts my breathing. I normally inhale this, but at least I don't see it then.

All this dust... It might be a first step to help restore Lethalis to its former glory. Dusting and vacuuming is something I can do, provided there's a vacuum cleaner around here somewhere. Toke left in such a hurry yesterday that I hadn't been able to ask her about anything else. I'll have to explore the hotel by myself.

I walk up the white stone stairs to the third floor and peek out over the steps. No swirling flakes of ash, no smell of smoke. I heave a sigh. And no mess, either, for that matter. Toke had mentioned clutter here, which we should leave for now, but the hallway is completely neat and tidy—just like it was last night, when I thought I was still dreaming.

My shoes touch the lilac carpet as I walk down the empty corridor. I check the rooms one by one. In one of the rooms, I find three buck-ets, two of which are still in one piece. In another room, I find a pile of cloths that look old and worn and must be meant for rough cleaning. In yet another room, I find a large strange-looking hoover—it's much taller than I am used to. I study it from all angles and decide to give it a try. I pull out the cord and find the nearest socket. The hoover starts humming loudly. It's ugly and makes a lot of noise, but at least it has great suction. I let the hoover glide effortlessly across the room and see the carpet underneath revive.

I probably would have ripped this carpet out if this were my renovation project. With what goes on in hotel rooms on a regular basis... that must be awfully tricky to clean. And it's a fire hazard as well. I picture the dark stain on the ceiling of room 299—is that what a burn mark looks like, through the ceiling? It felt hot, anyway. Unless I did dream that particular part. Or worse... hallucinated it. I bite my lip in frustration.

Don't trust anything I see or hear, I repeat Jack's words in my head. And yet, it felt so real and close as I laid on the leather sofa in his office. I felt that breath in my neck. I heard my name, over and over again. I could taste the sweat on my lips and I saw his face right above me. I shudder and shake my head. It's all just a delusion.

Suddenly, something dawns on me, and my heart sinks. Did I even kiss Danny? My pupils flick back and forth as I try to recall the events of that day. What if that didn't really happen? Then I have been worrying about nothing... And here I am now; complete radio silence. Danny must be worried sick! But... it felt way too real, all of it. I really don't know *what* to believe anymore.

I shake my head. There goes my endless train of thought, swirling through my head like a summer storm. It doesn't do me any good to brood. And while I'm here, at the place that has something to do with my past, I'd better investigate properly. I have to get my memories back somehow, so that the man with the hat no longer pesters me and so that the lady in red no longer disturbs my nightly peace. So I can go back to being a regular woman, finish my studies and get a job. I want to remember my real parents, without hurting Danny, and maybe even reconcile with them. I also want to understand what this lilac lily carpet has to do with my past. All under the guise of cleaning the hotel.

I vacuum one room after another. Twice, I have to change the plug into another socket, but I'm surprised at how enormously long the cord is. I vacuum the edges along the wall at rooms 396 and 398, turn around, and vacuum the floor in front of rooms 397 and 399. I look up.

Toke said I wasn't allowed in room 399. Something about an accident... I think of the dark stain, which may be a burn mark, on the ceiling of room 299. Last night, I couldn't open the door, but maybe, just maybe... I put down the vacuum cleaner and grab the door handle. I push the latch down and try to open the door, but the door doesn't yield. I push again, but it's in vain. I rattle it and look at the keyhole and the gap between the door and the doorframe. It is definitely locked. I let go of the door handle, slightly disappointed. I recall Toke saying all the doors were open, because of the whole missing keys ordeal back in the day.

I lift the hoover down the stairs, to the second floor, and start on the carpet in the corridor. I vacuum my own room and clean the other rooms one by one.

My stomach starts to rumble. Time must have flown by. It feels strange to play things by ear, without a timepiece to rely on. I have become a little too used to the clock I could always whip out of my pocket. Now, it's just guesswork and I have to rely on my biological clock. In any case, it is late enough for me to be very, very hungry—my hunger signal only kicks in at the very last moment, I've noticed. I finish vacuuming the last room and turn off the hoover, before stroking my rumbling stomach.

Let's grab a bite.

Back in my room, my hands rummage through the contents of the plastic bag. Mmm, noodles. I suppose I need a kettle for that. I raise my eyebrow. Although... in those Korean drama series, I see them chewing on uncooked noodles often enough. Under the authority of my growling stomach, I tear the package, firmly grab the block of noodles, and put my choppers on one corner to bite off a piece. I chew on it slowly. It's not to my taste, but I don't feel like starting a scavenger hunt for a kettle right now. As long as it stills the hunger, for now, it's good enough.

With narrowed eyes, I chump steadily on the noodles while sitting cross-legged on the floor. I should definitely look for a kettle later though. I sigh, feeling grizzled, and swallow the last bite. I wash it down, finishing my water bottle, and munch on an oatmeal bar to end the meal on a good note. I refill the water bottle at the bathroom tap and empty the entire bottle in one gulp.

I wipe my mouth with my wrist. Danny taught me that it is not healthy to refill a water bottle if it isn't reusable, but I don't care much right now. I refill the bottle once more, screw the cap back on, dump it in the plastic bag and walk towards the stairwell.

Suddenly, I hear footsteps thumping above my head. I stand still and look up. The footsteps move towards the stairwell. Is it Toke? I curiously look between the stairs and see a pair of feet encased in big dark boots. I take a step backwards. The boots are followed by two more pairs.

I take a few more steps backwards and then slip into a room to my left. The footsteps sound heavy on the stairs and then muffle.

"Where did that banshee go?" shouts a husky male voice. It sounds closer than I expected. My heart makes a jump. Silently I walk across the room to the bathroom door.

"I don't know," one of the voices shouts back, reverberating through the stairwell.

"I didn't see 'r," roars another voice.

I silently open the bathroom door and enter. My heart pounds in my throat. I pull the door shut until only a crack is visible. I dare not pull it completely shut because the noise might trigger them. A drop of sweat rolls down my nose and sticks to the tip.

The first pair of footsteps approaches the door of the very room I'm hiding in. The other two sound dully on the steps, going from softer to louder.

"Strange," I hear the man near me mutter. I hear his footsteps disappear further down the corridor.

"Who cares? It's our last day here, dude," roars one of the men from the stairwell. "Can we go home yet?"

The footsteps sound again and pass the room, as I press myself against the cool stone wall behind me with pounding heart.

"Well, looky, looky," growls the husky voice. The heavy footsteps move down the corridor into the stairwell. Not much later, they sound above my head.

I listen intently to the rumbling and their talking, but I can't understand what they're saying. I wipe the sweat from my forehead. Who on earth are they and what are they doing here? And who is this *banshee* they are looking for? I put a hand on my heart. Is it me? I shudder. Where is Toke?

I reach for my mobile phone in my pocket and realise I left it in my room. My throat squeezes together. I am not in danger, I try to soothe myself. I just need to avoid them. That shouldn't be difficult with so many rooms to hide in. As long as I'm quiet. Dead quiet.

Their footsteps stomp on the stone steps again and their voices echo through the stairwell. The sound grows softer and softer until it completely fades away.

Are they leaving? I carefully leave the bathroom and go back into the corridor. I sneak into the room in front of me and cautiously walk to the window. Between the flapping sheets of plastic, I see three figures walking along the path, away from Lethalis. Two of them walk towards a big white van and the other one walks towards a shiny black car. I watch as the black car leaves the grounds. The white van follows a moment later. Both vehicles disappear from sight. I breathe a sigh of relief. At least they're gone now.

I walk back into the corridor and start pacing. What were they looking for? And why did they leave so suddenly? Surely, construction is at a standstill... I shake my head. Stop. Worrying about it is pointless. For now, just go back to dusting, as a form of distraction. By now, I've gained a black belt in seeking distraction when brooding thoughts arise, thanks to Jack.

I walk up the stairs and look for the room with the worn cloths. I grab a light grey and dark blue cloth. I start dusting the window frame with the grey cloth, and continue on the bathroom sink. Every surface I can find, I make as dust-free as possible. There are dirty spots here and there; some sticky, others dingy. I use the other cloth, which I make damp first, to scrub them away. Occasionally, I cast a glance out of the window to keep an eye on the hotel driveway, hoping Toke will return soon so I can ask her about the unplanned visitors.

I finish the third floor and swap both cloths for cleaner ones. I then start on the second floor and, slowly but steadily, work my way towards room 299—the room I claimed as my own. When I finally arrive at my room, the dark stain on the ceiling immediately catches my eyes. I stare at it. My toes creak as I reach for the stain. The cloth can just about reach it, with much effort from my calves. I scrub as best I can with the wet cloth. Drops of water fall in my face as I squeeze the cloth harder and harder. My arm starts shaking and hurting. I lower it and take a bewildered look at the still equally dark stain.

"Amber?"

I look over and see Toke's bright red locks bobbing up and down as she hops towards me. I smile broadly. "Toke!" I greet her enthusiastically.

"I see you chose room 299."

"Yes, I liked this place," I respond.

She smiles warmly. "Me too. I always did." She breathes a heavy sigh. "How are things going?"

I point to the stain above my head. "Except for this one, it's going pretty well."

She looks at the black spot with a blank stare.

"It's just... there were others, just a while ago," I say in a serious tone.

"Others? Who?" She looks at me inquiringly.

"There were three men, wearing boots," I answer. "One drove a black car and the other two drove a white van."

Toke clicks her tongue. "I'm afraid you've met the tourists."

I look at her non-comprehendingly. "Tourists? Are they already staying here?"

She shakes her head. "No, but they come and go. That's why I call them tourists. They don't belong here, Amber. Outsiders have no business here. Lethalis is meant only for those who know the rich history of this special hotel." She looks at me with a fierce look in her eyes. "Or at least want to know more about it. But these... tourists... they leave a pigsty behind every time they come. You don't even want to know how many times I've tried to chase them away, but I still haven't succeeded. They keep coming back and they bang on the walls like a bunch of lunatics."

"Jeez. What about the police...?"

She shrugs her shoulders. "Do you really think they will come to help me? They don't see Lethalis for what it is. They only see an empty shit-hole with nothing worth stealing. You can't expect any help here." She looks at me thoughtfully. "But don't worry, they won't hurt anyone. Think of them as spiders. They will be more afraid of you than you are of them."

My head tilts to the side, as I try to make sense of her words. "I don't think that's the case," I start with a suppressed smile, gesturing at my petite stature.

"You can scare them away, Amber."

"How?"

She remains silent for a moment and smiles mischievously. "Well, I wasn't going to put it that way, but you could use a shower." She winks at me and lets out a girly laugh. "Anyway, I won't keep you any longer. I have to get back."

"When will I see you again?" The words are out of my mouth before I can even think about it. I open my mouth, searching for other words.

She looks at me gloomily. "Soon enough," she replies. "Lethalis is my home, remember." She winks again. "Toodles!" She waves briefly and turns around. Her dress swirls gracefully around her legs, making the embroidered daisies hop on the fabric. She disappears from sight.

I put the cloths in the sink and wipe the sweat from my forehead with the sleeve of my jumper. My whole body feels sticky. A shower certainly wouldn't be a bad idea. I kick off my shoes towards the corner of the bathroom, take off my jumper, and automatically turn my head to my armpit. My face contorts.

I look at the hotel room door and close it, before walking into the bathroom. I pull the door shut tight, wavering for a moment. The doors can't be locked. Toke may have gone home, but what if there is someone else? What if those tourists, as Toke called them, return? My incisor tears a piece off the inside of my lower lip—I taste the sweetness flowing from it. My hand rests on my arm, frozen in the motion of pulling up the bottom edge of my shirt.

"Toke!?" I call out, loud enough to alert a possible presence on the second floor. I remain standing for a while, waiting.

Silence.

I take off my shirt with my gaze fixed on the bathroom door, followed by my trousers and socks, and hang the garments over the sink to air-dry them. With my pants and bra still on, I step into the shower. I turn the shower knobs and feel ice-cold water pouring over me. I gasp for breath, quickly ducking away from the cold spray. I turn the hot knob further to the left and wait. My hand touches the water every few seconds to check if the temperature has changed, but the water is still freezing.

Is something broken?

My one hand throws small splashes of water from the jet onto my body, while my other hand quickly rubs my skin. I rinse off my arms, wash thoroughly under my armpits and throw water on my face. I turn around and let the water flow down my back with my molars clenched together. I scrub my pubic area and run a little more water over my legs before I turn off the taps. A shiver runs down my body. The heat outside makes this cold shower extra intense. Well, at least cold exposure is good for you, I think to myself, remembering the many cold showers at home.

I shake my limbs as dry as possible and carefully step out of the shower. I grab my trousers and try to put them back on, which is a tremendous task, seeing how clammy my skin is. Fake leather trousers aren't very convenient, after all, but they're my favourite. They look pretty and bold and are otherwise quite comfortable, disregarding the heat. And these particular trousers even have pockets that can hold a wallet, which you don't often see these days. Women's clothing is rarely functional, unfortunately.

I put my shirt, socks and shoes back on and stuff my jumper into the curve of the sink. I turn on the tap and submerge the jumper. My fingers knead the fabric and I focus my attention on the area under the armholes, where the smell of my sweat has settled. A moment later, I turn off the tap and wring out the jumper as best I can over the sink, hanging it to dry over the door of the bathroom after.

I walk out of the bathroom and look around me in the hotel room. My hair is sticking to my face and neck, dampening the back of my shirt. It would be nice to let my hair dry a bit before I continue cleaning again. I look at the sheets of plastic in front of the windows that break the sunlight. I pick up my wet hair and hold it up, pressing it against the back of my head. I walk out of the room, down the corridor, down the stairs to the lobby, towards the two glass French doors that give access to the garden. I gently push them opened and am greeted by warm sunlight. I squint my eyes and let my hair fall with a sigh.

My shoe soles muffle the feeling between my feet and the large white pebbles on the path in front of me. The path bends gracefully to the left, disappearing between shoulder-high hedges and finally coming back from the right with a big arc. To my right are several benches, with ornate white steel frames. To my left, I see beautiful rose bushes. The white roses are unfolded and spread a slightly sweet scent through the nearby air. An orange butterfly descends on one of the roses.

A group of clouds in the shape of a misshapen dog creeps in front of the sun.

I follow my feet, guiding me along the path, between the hedges. A small wooden roof, rising above the edge of the hedges, catches my eye as I arrive at a fork in the path. I follow the path to the right and keep on walking. The little wooden roof comes closer. Another fork, another turn, until I finally reach an opening in the hedge. Behind the opening is a cosy clearing with those same white pebbles, and in the middle is a large well with a wooden roof.

The brickwork of the stone well is overgrown with moss, giving a mystical feel to the whole courtyard. I walk up to it and look down over the edge. It is pitch black inside the well.

"Hooo," I say cantingly.

"Hooo," echoes the well. The resonance is full and clear.

"Hooo."

The well sings with me.

I smile.

At that moment, the sun breaks through the clouds. A beam of light streaks across the courtyard and reflects on the water in the well. I look at the rope stretching taut between the windlass and the water. Full of curiosity, my hands clasp around the wooden swivel stool at the side of the well. I push against it, but the swivel stool doesn't give way. I tighten my arm muscles and push harder. It moves slightly, but the bucket does not rise. I try to pull it, but that doesn't help either. I look into the well again. Is the bucket stuck? My fingers clench around the stone rim as I bend over. I wonder how deep such a pit is. I pull my head back and turn around, before leaning against one of the wooden posts supporting the roof of the well. I cross my hands behind me and raise my chin in the air. The warmth of the sun sweetly caresses the tip of my nose, my cheeks and my forehead. My ears perk up and catch the cheerful twittering of nearby birds. A gentle breeze rolls over my body. Warmth embraces my body and settles on my head. I heave a deep sigh.

This moment, right here, is everything.

The peace.

The warmth.

The silence.

For a while, I remain still, enjoying the moment. Just for a few minutes, probably, although it feels like half an hour. I sigh deeply. The fresh air feels pleasant in my lungs. I look around, wondering what this place would look like if the hotel would be fully booked. Would it still be this peaceful and quiet then? Or would you hear squealing children everywhere, roaring laughter and penetrating voices relaying every detail of a life?

I turn back to the well and look at where the rope touches the water. Maybe I can lower another bucket down to loosen the other bucket or I just to hoist some water from the well. I'm actually curious now; I have no idea how clean the water is in such a well and whether it feels hot or cold—the sun shines directly on it, but there is also a canopy above it that casts a shadow. This is the first well I have ever seen in my life. In real life, that is. I'm all too familiar with the horror movie, in which a creepy girl comes crawling out of such a well; Danny and I had a great time watching that after I turned sixteen, and it since became our regular treat at Halloween. Until last year. Because of my nightmares and delusions, Danny won't let me watch any more horror films anymore, despite the fact that I loved watching them with him. He's afraid the images will trigger me.

Lost in thought, I walk out of the courtyard. The pebbles crunch under my feet as I walk between the shoulder-high hedges. I follow the same path back as I had taken, and end up back at the rose bushes and white benches. I walk into the hotel and cross the stairwell to the third floor, where I had found the buckets. My fingers slide over the door of room 301.

HOOOONK!

My toes curl, stopping me in my tracks. A car horn... With bated breath, I walk to the door of room 302, push it open and step inside. The buckets are still exactly as I left them. I grab the bright red one —it is the heaviest of the three and also the most robust. With the bucket under my arm, I silently walk out of the room. My hand rests on the door handle. The door wasn't completely closed, but I don't remember how far it was open either. What if they notice? Will they start another witch-hunt for the *banshee*? I fervently hope they didn't mean me by that. I pull the door shut to half a crack and quietly walk down the stairs, moping over the fact that I am the one tiptoeing around here, while they are the ones who aren't welcome here.

I proceed through the lobby, towards the glass doors.

"Just hold on a little longer," sounds that husky voice from before.

I turn around at lightning speed. The one speaking is already at the grand doors of the entrance. I jump aside and disappear behind the counter, in close proximity to the man with the hat, who nonchalantly rests his hands on the counter.

The bright red bucket clatters to the floor. With a look of horror, I stare at it, hoping their chatter has drowned out the sound. But even so, I have a big problem. The bucket didn't fall behind the counter, safely tucked away from view. It lies completely in the open, for all to see, and it is too far out of my reach.

The front doors open creakily.

"But I don't want to anymore," sounds a barbed voice.

"Well, sucks to be you then. You've got no choice," the husky voice responds.

"I'm going upstairs," a third voice sounds.

I recognise the other voices as well. They are the same men from this morning. The tourists are back.

"Wait up..." says the rasping voice. "What's that?"

I can't see them, but I know what they're looking at. It's hard to miss.

Footsteps echo through the lobby. They get louder and the pauses after each step longer. The man slows his stride.

With beating heart, I press my back against the counter with force, pulling my legs up to my chest. I push myself further back and a sharp tip stabs into my shoulder blade, but I don't flinch. I try to wriggle my feet further back, hoping to make myself as little as possible, but I fear the noses of my shoes still stick out too far. I slowly turn my head.

A hand reaches for the bucket.

I see his watch, his light blue blouse, his dark brown hair, the tip of his nose.

His hand grips the bucket by the rim.

With bated breath, I stare at the man holding the bucket. Don't look. Don't look. Please, don't look.

He picks up the bucket from the ground. His nose disappears from my view. His dark brown strands of hair pull back. The colour of his blouse slips from my view, followed by his watch. His hand, clutching the bright red bucket, also disappears.

"Wasn't this upstairs?"

Moving clothes murmur, but there is no reply.

"One of you, huh?"

One of the men starts to cough. "Man, why're you so uptight, all the time? Putting everything back in place... As long as you find it, it's fine right? Seriously, how does your wife put up with you?"

"That's thanks to my late-night visits," taunts the other.

"A joke is nice and all, but don't get too cocky," says the rasping voice in a bidding tone.

Silence.

"Or I'll never let you return home."

After another short silence, all three men burst into laughter.

"But seriously, if someone's in here, we have to find them. Keep your eyes peeled."

Their footsteps echo through the stairwell.

The hairs on my neck rise up. They've noticed my presence. They're going to look for me and do something to me. I wait anxiously until their footsteps sound distant enough. I crawl out from behind the counter and look around the empty lobby. With buckling knees, I make my way to the French doors. I have to get out of here. I need to call Danny. I reach into my pockets and wince. I frantically pull my trouser pockets inside out. My phone is *still* laying in the corner of my hotel room. That's just perfect. I turn around and stare at my pale reflection in the glass doors.

First things first. I have to get out of sight. I walk along the path as hurriedly and quietly as I can. The white pebbles crunch under my weight and I cringe with every step. Why didn't they leave these hedges higher? I bend my knees and hobble along, hunching over, hoping the hedges will hide me from view. I cast a glance upwards and see the second and third floors towering over me. The windows of the various rooms all seem like eyes suddenly—if anyone looks out of a window now, they're bound to see me, with or without those plastic sheets. I lower down and crawl over the rough stones, bracing myself with my elbows, following the same path as before until I reach the stone well. I cautiously crawl along the edge of the clearing and lay down on my back, looking up towards the sky. I can't see the hotel, so they shouldn't be able to see me either. I should be safe here. For now.

I heave a deep sigh. A drop of sweat rolls down my forehead. But what if they find my stuff? My heart skips a beat. They may even snatch my phone...

My head is pounding with thoughts, spinning through my head like a tornado, as the sun burns in the sky. I roll onto my side, towards the hedge, to shield my face from the scorching sun rays.

Here, I lie—my ears perked for the slightest sign of life, agitated by every bird that perches in my near vicinity, bathed in sweat and with a mouth as dry as the Sahara desert.

Seconds become minutes. Minutes become quarters.

Sweat wells up from my pores and makes the scars on my arms itch even more than usual. I scratch my arms frantically with my nails, so violently that red welts emerge on them.

The only image I can still see before me is Danny's face with his crooked smile and his grey eyes with a warm glare. In my mind, I let him talk to me. He says my name, has his arms around me and holds me tightly. He tells me everything will be fine and he'll keep me safe. I put my hands under my head in a comforting gesture.

"I miss you..." I whisper. A tear rolls diagonally across my lips, spreading a salty taste.

Quarters become hours.

My head splits from the heat. I roll myself onto my other side and look at the well. All I want is a little water and some cooling. There's a small edge of shade around the well, but it is in the middle of the clearing and they would certainly be able to spot me there.

But, maybe they aren't looking for me anymore, reasons the one voice inside me.

As soon as you crawl to that well, they will grab you, reasons the other voice.

How much longer, I deliriously wonder, watching an orange butterfly flutter over my head.

"WOOHOOOOOOOO!" someone shouts loudly.

My body shakes. Who!? Where!? My eyes scan the surroundings. They're on my trail, I think, panicked. I lean on my elbows and try to lift my head.

"Finally," concurs one of the other voices.

The world dances around me, with a milky membrane over it. My stomach contracts. No, don't throw up. Not now, please! Swaying on my legs, I scrabble upright. My fingers squeeze the branches of the hedge as I peer over the edge. Where are they? I stumble across the gravel, away from the well, back towards the glass doors. Maybe I can call for help. All I have to do is go through the lobby and down the path. Behind it lies the gate and there will be people, somewhere close by. The village... the one that I had crossed when walking here... The old hag and her damn yapping dog. Mukkie.

My hand awkwardly slaps the door handle of the right-hand door. I pull the door with great effort. The coolness of the lobby comes to me as a cooling blanket. My stride quickens. The front door is just up ahead. My fingers reach for the door handle and I push my whole weight against the door to get outside. The door gives way and flings open with a bang.

But, there's someone on the threshold.

I gasp.

"Amber? Are you all right?"

I fall forward into Toke's arms.

"What's going on?" she asks, her eyes wide.

"Tou- tourists," I utter dazed.

"I'll deal with that in a minute, first we have to patch you up."

I feel myself becoming light as a feather. The door closes. I see the stairwell coming into view. We pass the first floor. The walls on the second floor glide by. The walls seem more grey than white. I squint my eyes. I see room number 299 and I see a bed. I feel the support of a mattress beneath me. I gently roll onto my side and look at her. "Toke, I..."

"Get some rest. I'll get you some water."

I feel the heat simmering on my skin. My heart seems twice its size. The mattress feels as hard as stone under my arms. I close my eyes for a moment and feel ice-cold water on my hands, forehead and sternum. I breathe a sigh of relief and blink my spiritless eyes. I see Toke's cheerful red locks dancing up and down. Her emerald green dress sways back and forth as she walks out of the room. And then she's gone.

My eyes feel heavy. I close them, vainly planning to open them again, not knowing that I will never see Toke again.

8 THE WELL

It takes a while before I can open my eyes again. I don't know how much time has passed. I slowly rise to my feet. "Thanks-" I start, abruptly falling silent.

Toke is gone.

I swing my legs over the edge of the mattress and stand up. My knees give out and hit the ground. I reach for the plastic bag of food and pull it towards me. I take out an oatmeal bar and greedily wolf it down. My gaze falls on the bedside table next to the bed. There are two filled bottles of water on it. I grab the nearest bottle and take a few big gulps. I grab two painkillers and swallow them with water.

Fidgeting, I pull out the dishevelled medicine box from my pocket, and take out the top strip of happy pills. I don't even know what time it is and how many doses I have skipped. I pop a pill from the strip and let it roll across my palm. I look at the yellow pill. My stomach contracts. My hand balls into a fist. I put the pill on the bedside table and walk to the doorway. I look back at the bed and the bedside table. There is even a desk with a chair in the room, by the left wall, and a lofty oak wardrobe. How did Toke get this furniture here so quickly, without me noticing and without a functioning elevator? And when did she do all this? Was it while the tourists were still inside?

"Toke?" I call out in a small voice. I walk down the corridor. My fingers stroke over the wall and alternately over the smooth doors of the hotel rooms. I walk into the stairwell and look up. The tourists were up there, on the third floor. Could they still be present?

I put my foot on the first step. It creaks slightly. Frowning, I walk upstairs as silently as possible. I peer over the edge of the stairs and observe the corridors of the third floor.

It seems deserted.

"Toke?" my voice breaks the silence.

No answer.

I walk down the stairs to the ground floor. "Toke?" echoes my voice through the lobby. I push open the dining room doors and walk in. My mouth falls open and I look around in amazement. There are many round and small square tables as well as a number of oblong tables, all with matching chairs. On each table is a fancy but old-fashioned tablecloth, covering most of the cherry wood top. Large gold-coloured chandeliers hang from the ceiling. I marvel at the splendour. The room seems extra large, oddly enough, now that all these dining tables are neatly arranged from front to back.

I look at the wall on the left, which had been freshly plastered and looked snow-white. Now, the wall is slightly stained and there is a door in it, instead of a gaping hole. I walk to the cherry wood door in the wall and gently push it open. There's a large kitchen, decked out with chrome tops, huge refrigerators, sturdy ovens and cherry wood cabinets. In the back wall is a steel door. I walk up to it and put my hand against the cool surface. A freezer.

It must have been quite an undertaking to haul this all inside, I think to myself. How long was I outside, laying between the hedges in the searing heat? Surely, not *that* long. My head spins as I run my fingers over all the surfaces in the kitchen, walking around slowly. There's all sorts of things here, but no Toke. She must have gone home again, I conclude. I leave the kitchen and walk back to the lobby.

My gaze lingers on the front door. Maybe the tourists are a sign that I should go home again. I walk up to the front door and push the handles down. There is no movement in the doors. My hands rattle the door handles. "Seriously?" I mutter, walking to the window next to the front door and peering out. The black car and the white van, which belong to the tourists, are nowhere to be seen. At least Toke has managed to chase them off, thankfully. As long as they don't come back again... My hands rub my upper arms. Maybe that's why Toke locked the door, so they can't come back. That's actually nice, I realise. Now they can't surprise me anymore and I'll be safe here once more.

My head feels heavy and I look around me in a dreamlike state. I stand next to the counter and look at where the red bucket had been. That moment was too nerve-racking. I crouch down. Those tourists are dangerous. Is that why this empty building is so appealing to them? What kind of sinister things are going on here?

I bend down and run my fingers across the cool stone floor. My gaze slides to the spot where I had been huddled, terrified of being spotted by the tourist with the blue blouse. I also see what must have poked my shoulder blade: a dusty old box of which the flaps aren't closed properly. I snort and walk back to the stairs, to the second floor and sit down on the edge of the bed. I drink some water from a bottle and look at the cheery yellow pill on the bedside table. I reach for the pill and keep it between my fingers.

If I just take my medication, things will get better, reasons one voice.

But you don't want that pill, reasons the other. You won't get better.

You take those pills for a reason. There's something wrong with you. Just listen to Jack.

Jack is lying to you. This is a placebo, to test how tame a lamb you are. Are you a lamb, Amber? Is that what you are? Then that's what you'll remain with these pills.

Danny also says you should take your pills. At least listen to him. He has your best interests at heart. You can trust Danny.

Danny is done with you. You've betrayed his trust time and again. Taking your pills or not is not going to change that.

At least you can show him that you want to change. He can learn to trust you again, but you have to prove it to him. Take your pills as they expect you to. Do what is required of you.

I bring the pill to my lips. My throat squeezes shut. I place the pill on my tongue. My whole mouth feels dry. I bring the bottle of water to my lips. My tongue curls up against my palate and pushes the pill against my front teeth. I spit the pill out on my hand and take a big gulp of water. I put the sticky pill back on the bedside table. I can't do it, for some reason. After all these months of persevering... I just can't stomach one fucking pill anymore. My whole body is fighting against it.

The dusk sets outside.

My stomach rumbles. I hunch over the plastic bag and grab the second pack of noodles. I will have to buy some more food soon, I realise. I eagerly open the pack and tear off a piece. As I chew, I look up at the ceiling with the dark stain. The ceiling shows greyish and dingy, even in the orange glow of the sun, which creeps further and further behind the horizon.

That night, I lie on my back on the mattress, which is barely more comfortable than the ground, with my knees pulled up. My shoes are placed neatly against the footboard. The chair, which appeared in my room with Toke's last visit, is slid under the handle of the door.

I stare at the moonlit ceiling. The dark spot is getting bigger, I realise. It started with the size of a breakfast plate, now it has grown into a pizza plate.

My eyes slowly fall shut.

"Amber," whispers the voice of the hotel.

I open my eyes.

The man with the hat is standing in the corner of the room. His steak cheek is turned towards me. He is not staring at me, as usual, but is looking at the door.

I sit up straight and follow his gaze.

"Amber," the voice whispers again.

The door handle begins to move.

I shift, my gaze fixed on the door.

The door handle rattles. The back of the chair shakes back and forth. The latch is pushed down and rattles once more.

I hold my breath.

The latch shoots up abruptly.

I look at the man with the hat. He's still facing the door, but has stealthily moved a metre closer to me. I pull my knees up to my chest, clasping them with my arms. The moonlight illuminates his back and part of his steak cheek. I stare at it. The longer I look at it, the less it bothers me. "How did you get that?" I ask in a whisper.

The man with the hat turns towards me. He brings his hand up and strokes his fingers down the mangled cheek.

My nostrils flare. I look back at the door and see a thick grey cloud rolling in below. Smoke rises and billows across the ceiling. My gaze is drawn back to the man with the hat. He is now standing against the footboard staring at me. I swallow.

He looks up. His eye lights up. Orange flickers dance in his pupil. He slowly lowers his chin and looks at me sternly. He opens his mouth and emits a chilling scream, making my eardrums flap and my heart skip. For a moment, half his face is ablaze, contorting into a painful grimace. His eye bulges out of its socket.

I press my back against the wall behind me, burying my nails in the rock-hard mattress.

The fire dies.

His face shrieks in silence. He steps backwards, away from the moonlight, until his back is against the wall. Concealed by shadows.

With pounding heart, I stare silently into the darkness, waiting for the next hideous display. The darkness remains what it is: infinitely dark. Nevertheless, I don't get a wink of sleep for the rest of the night.

. . .

The next day, I stand by the well, looking at the bucket hanging above it, which is no longer stuck in the bottom. Toke must have taken care of that. I gratefully lower the bucket into the well and hoist it up. It moves more smoothly than I would've guessed. I look into the bucket and see that the water is crystal clear. I feel the temperature with my fingers. It is cold, maybe as cold as the shower I took, but it feels pleasant. I grab the bucket, tilt it over my head, and stiffen under the icy water. Hm, not so pleasant after all. My tongue licks my lips. It doesn't taste weird, so that's something. It might even be drinkable. The bucket swishes, swirling the last remnant of water around. I put the edge of the bucket to my lips and tilt my head back. My throat cools as I drink eagerly.

I smell my armpits for a moment and fill the bucket with water again. I lift the bucket and pour most of the water over my crown. I tuck my hands under the fabric of my shirt and frantically rub my armpits —it's rather tricky, reducing this sweaty stench with no soap. I slosh the last of the water up at my armpits in turns. The water drips down my sleeves and soaks them to my wrists.

I would have preferred to take off my clothes and wash them separately, but I'm not sure if the tourists will really stay gone today—if they wanted to, they could go around the back of the building, after all. Also, Toke could suddenly turn up, and I don't need her to see me in my undergarments.

With a soaked shirt, I lean against the stone well, looking out over the hedges in Lethalis' garden. Beyond the hedges is a large lawn and a forest. Birds fly over the treetops, occasionally twittering loudly.

I look around and imagine lovey-dovey couples walking hand-in-hand between the hedges. I see two little blonde girls running around the well, circling me. One is wearing a dress with daisies on it, the other one wears a dress embellished with orange butterflies. I see a man wearing a chequered blouse sitting on one of the benches near the glass doors. The lower parts of his face is freshly shaved and he squints at the burning sun. Behind the glass doors stands a slender figure dressed in a bright red dress.

I imagine a terrace on the lawn, as an extension of the dining room. A waitress brings a cooled drink to a woman reading a newspaper at a white wooden table. Small drops trickle down the sides of the glass, glittering in the sunlight.

Now I see dozens of tables, all with a little white parasol to shield guests from the sunlight and heat. Some tables are vacant. At the other tables sit couples, families and loners. For some peculiar reason, all the children are girls with a similar shade of blonde hair and all the women are slim with copper-coloured locks and high cheekbones.

Footsteps crunch on the gravel.

I nearly twist my neck, jumping up in shock.

A young man with a narrow jaw, bright brown eyes, and hair shaved on the sides walks into the clearing. He leans casually on a rake. "Hiya."

I stare at him. "W-who are you?"

He smiles. "You look like a drowned kitten so."

My fingers pinch the edge of the well behind me. "Who are you?" I repeat.

He looks at me for a long time and sighs in the sultry heat. "I am *hurt*. You came all this way, but you don't even know who I am?"

I raise my eyebrows and slowly shake my head. Why doesn't he just answer?

"My pride's busted on me." He grins. "But I won't take it personal, will I?" He looks at me from head to toe. "Call me Henry then."

"What are you doing here, Henry?"

"Why?" He lowers his chin on top of his hands. The rake rocks back and forth a little.

I stare at him silently.

"Not much of a social lass, are you?" He chuckles and raises his head, slightly tilting the rake forward. "Well, what would I be doing here?" He playfully tosses the rake back and forth between his hands. "What would I be doing here... with a rake..." he continues in a sarcastic tone.

"I didn't mean that," I respond in an agitated tone. "Since when have you been here?"

"Here?" He points to the ground in front of him. "Ehh, a few seconds."

"You know what I mean." I cast him an unamused glare.

He grins. "Been here the whole time." He looks at me without blinking. "Can't say that about yourself. I should be the one asking. Is it not yourself?"

"I didn't know there'd be more people. Toke hadn't said that."

"There could be."

"What?"

He gives a nod. "This look suits you, lassie."

I wipe the moisture from my face, and look at him questioningly.

His intense chestnut eyes stare back. "What do you think of my garden now?"

I look around me and nod approvingly. "It's neat."

"I agree. It requires a lot of work. You should have seen it before I started working here. No overview, just walls. As if you were trapped in the crop. That's why I keep the bushes short and the openings wide. You can always find your way back so." His eyes skim over my face intently. He holds his one hand in front of him and stares at his stretched palm. "Otherwise it's like a maze in here. You'd walk in and..." he clenches his one hand vigorously, "...never come out again."

My eyes watch him closely.

He shifts his weight from one leg to the other. "You think you'll get yourself out, 'cause after all, you've seen the entry. But you've already turned so many corners you have no idea where you are relative to the hole in the wall. You wander on and on. You start running, and *whack*, another dead end. You turn around, go another path and hopelessly probe along the walls that are all the same. No one side seems to be the right one." He heaves a sigh.

I swallow down the lump in my throat.

"No matter how hard you look, you just don't find the exit." He lowers his eyes. "Everything starts to look alike and it's as if an entry never existed. Like you never even stepped foot inside. This is your life now. Right here in the middle, in the heart, where you're blind-est. Among the whispering walls, living out your days. Until, without realising, you walk past the exit." He looks up slowly with glittering eyes.

I stare at him silently.

"Do you know that feeling?" He takes a step to the side and tilts the rake forward.

I gulp, feeling frozen throughout my body.

"Do you recognise that?"

"I, ehh-"

He smiles crookedly. "Eh, maybe I'm the only one so." He scrapes the rake through the gravel. "I had hoped you would understand me, like Toke. But maybe she's the same then."

"It sounds... tough," I finally manage.

He looks at me. A smile still shows on his face, but his eyes are devoid of joy. "You're different, Amber."

My breathing falters. I stare at him blankly. "What did you call me?"

His gaze rests on my face for a long time. "Amber," he says in his husky voice. He lets go of the rake, and it clatters to the ground.

I take a step backwards. "How do you know my name?"

He steps over the rake and approaches me. I feel the well pressing against my legs as I vainly try to move further back. He stops right in front of me, bends down slightly and brings his face close to mine. His sweet breath gently touches my face.

I give him a hard shove, but he barely falters. "I never told you my name," I insist.

"Did you not tell me? Then how do I know your name?" He playfully bites his lip and looks at me with amusement.

My heart races in my throat. I give him another hard shove, slip past him and quickly flee the courtyard, deftly dodging the fallen rake. Pebbles leap aside in surprise as the hedges fly past me.

But suddenly, it dawns on me. My stride slows and my feet come to a halt. I turn my head and look over the hedges at the guy who calls himself Henry, heaving an exasperated sigh. "It was Toke, wasn't it?"

His face disappears behind the hedges as he doubles over with laughter.

"Bastard," I hiss, although I can't suppress my own laughter. Be it relieve or genuine joy.

"You should have seen yourself!" He gets up panting, holding the rake in his hand.

"How long have you been here?"

"Are we going to have our conversation five feet away now?"

I cross my arms, waiting for his answer.

"Not very pleasant, don't you think?" He saunters to the edge of the clearing, against the hedge in front of him—there is now about two and a half metres between us. "Or are you sacred I might bite you?" he asks playfully.

"Can you just answer my question?" I ask in a commanding tone.

He purses his lips. "What do you want to know?"

I think for a moment before answering. "I have lost part of my memory. I do know that I was here, in Lethalis, when I was a little girl."

"I still see a little girl," he responds sweetly.

I squint at him. "Do you know anything about the history of

Lethalis? From before the renovation? Something about an incident, maybe?"

He frowns for a moment. "Well, I should hope I don't look *that* old. But okay." He nods slowly. "I do know a few things."

"What do you know?"

"What is your question exactly?"

We stare at each other for a while.

Why doesn't he just answer directly, I think to myself, visibly irritated. "Has anything ever happened here? An accident? Something involving fire?"

He lifts his chin and at that moment an orange butterfly perches on his arm. He stares at it for a while. His gaze wanders to the horizon. "Maybe you shouldn't be here," he says in a mechanical voice. "I'd better get back to work. This garden doesn't keep itself." He saunters across the gravel towards the gap in the hedge.

"Is there anyone who can tell me more?"

He glances at me and shrugs. "I don't know. Why are you asking me?"

"Because I don't know who else to ask. Toke appears and disappears whenever she feels like it."

"Well, that's the way things work here. Isn't it the same with yourself? Appearing out of the blue."

I look at him with a slight frown on my forehead. "Is there, like, a town hall here or whatever? Some place where I can get more information or use a computer?"

He laughs out loud. "Who knows..." He saunters between the hedges, passing behind me.

I turn to him. "Just tell me! Where is it?"

He stops his stride. "Somewhere far from here," he replies gruffly.

"Thanks. That's... very helpful," I respond sarcastically. I look at my wet clothes. I can't go anywhere like this. "I'll check the village later today."

"Good luck with that," he respond, chuckling. He starts walking again and escapes from between the hedges.

"Why would you say that!?" I ask loudly.

He walks towards the side of the hotel, with the rake clutched in his hands, and glances back. "It's Saturday. Nothing is ever open here on a Saturday!" He disappears from sight.

I sigh. "Saturday?" In my mind, I see Danny sitting on the sofa, his forehead resting on one hand, his other hand dangling between his legs. He looks defeated. Desperate. My stomach churns and I anxiously try to banish the image from my mind. He must be pissed... No, he must be *furious* with me. I'll never be able to set foot inside that house again.

My hand slaps my cheek. *Not now.* Now, I have other things on my mind, other priorities. I want to know what happened here. Understand why the image of the corridor with purple carpet and lilies haunts me. Why the man with the hat is always in my wake. Who the fiery woman in the bright red dress is. I want to know why I have such violent anxiety attacks and have such huge gaps in my memory. I want to know... I want to know who my real parents are and what happened to them. Whether they are still alive. Where they are now. Why they got rid of me. And, as much as I miss Danny, the last thing I want right now is to go home.

I wring out the tip of my shirt. If I can't go exploring until Monday, I can at least make myself useful in the meantime by cleaning up, as I had pretty much promised Toke. Especially now that she's set up a room for me to make my stay as comfortable as possible. True, that mattress is like a block of concrete, but you should never look a gift horse in the mouth.

I leave the clearing and follow the path back inside, through the glass doors that are fortunately still unlocked. I walk through the lobby to the stairwell.

My thoughts wander to Henry, with his brown eyes and narrow jaw. Why didn't Toke tell me there was someone else around, apart from the tourists? If the locks on the doors don't work, he could get into my room at any time. It might have been him, rattling my door last night...

One of the steps creaks loudly under my weight and I look down in surprise. I shift my weight from one foot to the other and once again hear the step creak beneath me. I drop to my knees and run my fingers along the stone surface. Strange. It might be a construction error, I guess.

I quickly walk on to my room and take off my sodden shoes and clothes. I grab my jumper from the bathroom sink and pat myself dry with my eyes fixated on the door. Henry had better stay outside, with his silly rake and his stupid grin. And those chestnut brown eyes... How old is he anyway? I shake my head and sigh, then hang my clothes over the doors to dry.

I sit down on the bed with my legs pulled up, quietly, with nothing on but my lingerie. All the while, an attractive young man with a narrow jaw is working in the garden, who could stroll right in. I look at the door. It's open, because my clothes need enough space to air-dry—an occasional drop of water falls to the floor. I sigh and drop onto my back. Taking extra clothes with me would not have been an unnecessary luxury. But even so, this trip was anything but planned.

I lie staring at the ceiling. Before long, my thoughts wander back to Danny. Is he waiting for me to come home? Does he miss me? Or is he secretly glad I'm gone? And our kiss... our bittersweet kiss. Did that really happen and, if so, has he already told Kyra? I wouldn't be surprised if she forbids him from searching for me. Maybe she hopes I never come back. Maybe they both hope for that.

I stand up abruptly. The hell with these brooding thoughts! I'll just get to work in my lingerie, I decide. And who knows, if there's another one of those tourists, maybe Henry could protect me. I stroke my hands through my hair, gently touching my cheeks— they're rather hot to the touch. I glimpse outside. The sun is shining brightly in the sky and there is not a breath of wind.

My bare soles stroke the carpet as I leave my room and walk down the corridor. My heart pounds in my throat. This is strangely exciting and somewhat liberating as well. I walk up to the third floor to get the dusters, but the cloths I'd used have been moved. I turn a corner and then another. One room after another drifts by, until I see the red bucket in one of the rooms. I walk into room 398 and look into the bucket. There they are. Three dusters, dusty and crumpled. I pick them up and shake them, coughing silently.

I leave the room and find myself face to face with the room number in front of me. I think of the dark stain on the ceiling of my room, which only seems to be growing bigger and bigger. The cause of that is right here behind this very door, the only one in this entire hotel that has a damn lock on it.

Room 399.

9 ROOM 399

The carpet tickles my feet as I step towards the door. I place my hand on the latch and push it down. To my surprise, the door gives way with a slight creak. It's unlocked. I push the door completely open and look into the room. In the middle of the room, there's a large scorched stain on the carpet. That's the culprit, right there: the other side of the stain I see from my bed. But what is it and how did it get there? I kneel down beside it, my fingertips stroking the rough surface. I turn my hand and study my fingertips—they've turned dark grey. The only room that really needs cleaning is the very one Toke wanted to keep me away from, I realise. But, this will take more than just a little water. My eyes dart back and forth. Surely there will be cleaning supplies somewhere?

I get up and walk through the stairwell. All the rooms are empty except for the furniture in 299 and the buckets of cloths on the third floor. Where is that stupidly large hoover at? I walk down the stairs, into the lobby, looking around frantically. I walk towards the counter and look at the cardboard box, which had poked into my back earlier. I grab it off the shelf with both hands and pull it towards me. The box is as heavy as I'd expected. There must be something useful in there. Cleaning product, for instance.

The box lands on the stone floor with a thud. Dust particles jump up from the surface and invade my nose and mouth—my throat squeezes and I cough loudly. I glance at the French doors. If Henry were to hear me, he'd be bound to come looking and would find me sitting here on the floor, bent over a dusty cardboard box, clad in nothing but my undies.

I inhale, tighten my muscles and lift the box. With the box resting on both my forearms, I hurry back to the third floor. I walk into room 399 and carefully set the box down on the floor, near the scorch mark. I rub one of the dusters over the dusty top of the box, hold my breath, and wave the particles away from my face as I run my finger-tips over the now dust-free surface. The cardboard looks weathered and grubby, as if it's stood untouched for years. Lost and forgotten. In total oblivion.

Eagerly, I yank on the flaps of the box to reveal the contents and look inside. My face twitches. These aren't cleaning supplies. These are leaflets. Old leaflets, moreover. I grab the top one and examine it. *Lethalis* is printed on the front, in elegant silver letters. I unfold the leaflet. There are several pictures in it. One of a neatly decorated hotel room. One of the lobby, with a person behind the counter. I squint my eyes. That man behind the counter... He is wearing a modest dark grey shirt. His skin is dark brown. He has short hair, with light grey discolouration in the sideburns and at the roots of his hair. In front of him, on the counter, is a dark grey fedora. It is the man with the hat! The man with the hat is in this leaflet—without his current disfigurements. He's *real*!

I gasp and quickly look around me. "Where are you?" I shout. "Come out!" I scramble to my feet and walk into the corridor.

No one in sight.

"Come here, dammit. You know I'm looking for you. Show yourself when I ask you to!" I walk agitatedly down the corridor, sweeping every room. "Seriously, you always follow me wherever I go and now you're going to play hide-and-seek?" I remain still for a while, hoping the man with the hat will reveal himself. All this time, I've wanted him to disappear, but I didn't get what I wanted. Right up until the worst possible moment.

With my gaze fixed on the folder, I walk back into room 399. I lower myself to the floor, scanning the rest of the pictures. There's a couple of close-ups of the dining room and one of a fireplace, in the spot Toke had pointed out during her tour of the lobby.

There's a large picture of a corridor with the lilac lily carpet and white doors on either side. On one of the doors, I can make out room number 399. In the corridor, two people—a middle-aged man and a woman—stand in a dignified pose. Who are *they*? Could they be the former owners of Lethalis? I run my fingers over their faces. My finger gently strokes the woman's reddish hair. The coppery locks flow to just over her shoulders. She is wearing a beautiful dress, which starts to shine and turns bright red at the rubbing of my finger.

The folder slips from my weakened grasp and drops to the floor. The woman from my nightmares... The lady in red. It's her.

I squint my eyes as I look at her face. I rub my eyes and blink wildly a few times, but I can't manage to focus my vision. In the centre of it is a blurry white star. I heave a heavy, burdened sigh. It's that time again. Ocular migraine...

For the next half hour, I'll hardly be able to see a thing. Reading will be impossible and focusing on anything even less so. The star will gradually expand into a wreath, which will allow me to read and see details, but as soon as that wreath dissolves, the all-consuming headache begins, paralysing my limbs and making the light feel like sandpaper on my eyes. The smallest sound will thump on my eardrums like a folk fanfare and makes me gag, bathed in cold sweat.

Fortunately, I always have my medication with me. Not just the pills Jack prescribes, the so-called happy pills, but also pills to treat migraines. In silence, I thank myself for being so prepared in general. I walk out of the room and close the door behind me, before stumbling down the corridor. My arms lean heavily on the banister as I carefully move down the steps. I stop at the second floor. With eyes half-closed, I move down the corridor until I reach my room.

I reach for my bag on the bed and snatch my medication. I turn the box in front of my eyes, just outside of the white star. It is a green box with a thick red bar. I take out a strip and pop the first pill that touches my fingers. I swallow the pill with some water and sigh deeply. Although the pill doesn't stop the entire migraine, the headache is about 90% less severe when it starts. That's something, at least. I take two painkillers and move my clothes from the room door to the bathroom door. By touch, I slide the chair under the handle of the door, and put the window ajar for some fresh air. A pleasant summer breeze brushes over my face. It has cooled down a little outside, fortunately. I collapse on the bed, rest my head on the pillow and close my eyes.

It's only when the painkillers start to kick in that I notice how much pain I feel in my body. My shoulders are tense, my back is stiff and my neck feels like I've been sleeping on solid concrete. Slowly but surely, the pain fades away and is replaced by a feeling of sheer bliss.

The sunlight has dimmed the moment I open my eyes again. Groaning softly, I hoist myself to a sitting position, with my hands pressed against my head. The back of my head is throbbing, but luckily the worst of it has been stopped. I grab the last full bottle of water from my bedside table and empty it in one gulp. My tongue licks my lips. I slowly get up and walk into the bathroom. I fill the bottle to the brim and put it back in its place. I check my clothes, but they are still wet—too wet to go out and find a supermarket in the village to buy more food and drink. It'll have to wait. I move the chair and hang my clothes scattered among the doors, now that the room door is freed up.

I recall the leaflets that now lie in room 399. Who is the lady in the red dress, standing so majestically in her fancy dress in the corridor in the photo, yet is swallowed by blazing flames in my nightmares? I dreamt about her even before I came to Lethalis and before I had seen that leaflet. She looks exactly the same in my nightmares, wearing that exact same dress. That means I must have seen her at a time when she looked like she does in the picture—maybe even on the same day as that picture was taken. My head is pounding and I try again to silence my thoughts so as not to make my headache worse.

The carpet feels soft under my feet as I walk towards room 101. The carpet is intense purple and the pale, almost white, lily patterns are easy to see now. I look at it with a smile on my face and then step into the room.

When I look up, I am in for another surprise. I stare at the furniture in the room. I look at the desk, the chair behind it, the bed and the bedside table next to it, and the wardrobe. All five pieces of furniture are dark oaken. It's exactly the same as my self-proclaimed room. I know Toke wants to preserve as much of the hotel's original character as possible, but I don't know whether people still want this kind of furniture. I imagine the old hag has her house full of this kind of robust, old-fashioned furniture. Mukkie probably has some sort of ugly wicker basket, one you find at the flea market or a thrift shop.

Leisurely, I dust one room after another. Every window frame, desk and bedside table. I'll pat up the cushions later, I think to myself, when the headache has completely subsided. I casually wonder how Toke managed all this so quickly, again without me noticing. My head is pounding too much to concern myself with the logistics of it all. It is extraordinary enough that Lethalis is slowly but surely starting to look like its former self again, as it shows on the leaflets. *Restoring to its former glory.*

When I reach room 311, I stand still. I look at the carpet under my feet. Now that it's bright, it looks quite nice, and I can understand why Toke prefers to keep it. Maybe the guests will also find it comfortable, seeing how soft it is, leaving hygiene aside. How well can you actually clean carpet without destroying it, I ask myself, thinking of the scorch mark in room 399.

My toes brush through the short hairs of the carpet as I slowly walk out of the room, when suddenly my nostrils flare open. I follow my prickled nose and look towards the end of the corridor.

Smoke.

I walk towards the plumes of smoke slipping out from under the door of room 399, as flakes of ash dance in the air around me. I grope for the latch with the dusters still in my hand. The latch feels cold, strangely. I try to push the door open, but the door doesn't budge an inch. With a perplexed look, I lower my arm. It's not locked again, is it? Or does this thing jam every so often and am I just too weak to push it open? I haven't exactly been taking in a lot of nutrients these last few days.

"Wow," a voice sounds.

I look over and stare directly into Henry's warm brown eyes.

His eyes briefly shoot away from mine, downwards.

I clench the duster against my chest.

He casually leans against the wall. "A normal person doesn't run *towards* fire, but *away* from it, don't they now?"

"The door is jammed," I respond bitterly. "We need to break it open so we can put out the fire."

He looks at the door for a moment and then at me, expectant.

"A little help, please?" I gesture towards the door with one hand, while the other still covers my bosom with the dusters. Sweat glistens on my skin.

His eyes shine as he slowly shakes his head.

"Why not? Do you want the whole fucking hotel to burn down?"

"It never does," speaks his raw voice, as soft as a whisper.

I look at him non-comprehendingly. "What do you mean?"

"There is fire here so often. It never spreads." His gaze rests on the plumes of smoke creeping under the door. "You can just let it rage, lassie. It can't hurt you now."

I stare at the smoke. My eyes squeeze into slits as the burning smell titillates my nose hairs. "But..."

Henry steps away from the wall and towards me. "I'm being serious, Amber. That fire is there for a reason. Better to just let it burn and ignore it, best you can. If you get too close, then..." He gulps. "You should stay away from it."

"But it can't hurt me, can it? You just said that."

"You don't understand, Amber."

"Then explain it to me," I respond. By now I'm completely sick of his vague answers.

"This fire burns for you, Amber."

My breath falters. "If that's your pick-up line... I don't like chewed-out-" My voice drops.

RUMBLE.

Henry turns and listens intently.

"Tourists?" I ask.

He raises his hand to silence me and waits. "I know who that is," he says after an uneasy silence.

"Toke?"

He looks at me piercingly. "Why did you come here, Amber?"

"To remind me of my past."

"Why do you want to?"

I slowly lower the duster. "Because I... see things."

"Such as?"

I look at him silently. Can I trust him? Or will he spill everything to Toke, so that she can kick me out because she's afraid of another accident?

He takes a step closer, biting his lip. His breath caresses my collarbones. "Some things are better not to remember..." his honeyed voice speaks.

I swallow and close my eyes. The dusters fall silently to the floor as his warm breath caresses my neck.

"Go home, Amber."

My neck chills. I open my eyes. He has turned his back to me—his broad shoulder caps and narrow waist make his back flare out into a

V-shape. "Why?" I ask with a slight hitch in my voice. My fingers waveringly reach for his muscular shoulder blades.

"...the gatekeeper," he mutters. With a brisk stride, he walks towards the stairwell and down the stairs, leaving me by myself with a racing heart. I place my hand to my chest. I can still feel the effect of his caressing breath. I gulp. My hands stroke my heart. My cheeks feel hot. My fingers wander crosswise to my shoulders and descend to my upper arms, my sides, my hips and then my thighs. My fingertips slide up over my thighs. My lip dents under my upper teeth as the fabric of my panties tickles my fingers. I take several deep breaths. "The fire burns for me?" I repeat softly. He probably didn't mean it *that* way... why else would he turn away from me if he did?

My arms drop limply by my body. I look at the faded but still present scars on my arms, which I am only too eager to hide under my long sleeves. He must have seen them, I realise. That explains why he reacted the way he did. I curse my mutilation in silence. Of course he wouldn't want this, what am I even thinking? I yearn for my clothes, however wet they still are, purely to be able to shield myself from view. Me and my disfigurement.

I grab the dusters from the floor and turn my attention as best I can to dusting the rooms. I steadily work through the first floor. After dusting the last room, I return to room 299 and pull out the second-to-last pack of noodles. I sit cross-legged on the bed with my gaze fixed on the doorway. My clothes are still hanging to dry over the door. I tear open the package of noodles and open the packet of spices. I sprinkle the spice flakes over the noodles and then squeeze the bag of oil. My hands feel slippery from the oil as I take small bites off the pad of noodles. With glassy eyes, I stare ahead, devouring half the meal.

A cloud creeps in front of the sun and steals some light from the room.

My eyelashes bat up and down. A tip of bright red shiny fabric sways in and out of my vision. I stiffen, in the middle of taking another bite. My mouth is half-open as the noodles float in front of my chin. My gaze is fixed on the doorway.

"Amber," sounds the all too familiar voice, which makes the hairs on the back of my neck stand up.

The lady in red steps past the centre of the doorway with small, stately strides. Her reddish hair waves along the profile of her face. Her feet are bare. Her bright red dress is closed tightly around her figure. Without turning her head, she glances at me before walking on and disappearing from my sight.

I put the noodles on the torn-open package on my bedside table and get up cautiously. Tiptoeing, I walk to the corridor. I catch a glimpse of her dress as she turns the corner. I silently walk down the hallway, and at the very end, I peek around the corner.

The woman is standing in the middle of the hallway, facing the window. Her one hand rests on the other, on the window frame, as she looks at the horizon in silence.

I feel my heart beating on my tongue as I cautiously step into the corridor.

The woman shifts her weight from one foot to the other.

"Hello," I say in a small voice.

The woman doesn't even look at me.

I slowly step a little closer. My forearm strokes along the window frame. I try to read the expression on her face, but it's hard to do so from the side. "Hello?" I repeat.

The woman slowly turns her head towards me. A tear rolls down her cheek.

I am now about ten steps away from her, but I can clearly see the tear hanging from her jaw and falling onto the red dress—the fabric turns a deep red under the moisture. "Are you OK?" I ask hesitantly.

The woman turns her gaze back to the window. She brings her hand to her face and wipes the wetness from her cheek. For a moment she stares at the sky in front of her.

Who is this woman? Why am I seeing her? I study her face. Why does she look so lonely? My shoulders sag slightly as I take a few more steps towards her. "Who are you? Why are you here?"

She turns her face towards me once more. She's really beautiful, I think to myself. In her late forties, with some telling lines on her face. She has high cheekbones and thin eyebrows, adorning the arches above her dark green eyes. She has narrow lips and a wide forehead.

The woman twitches the corners of her mouth and shows a small smile—one without joy. She turns and starts walking away.

"Wait," I exclaim. I search for words as she keeps on moving. I follow her stride, still keeping my distance. "Do you know me?" I ask loudly.

The woman turns the corner and disappears from my sight.

I quickly run to the end of the corridor and come to an abrupt halt.

The entire corridor is empty.

I put a hand to my forehead and feel my heart thumping in the back of my throat. On weakened legs, I walk back to my room and sit back down on the bed. Bewildered, I stare into the distance. Is she a hallucination or a ghost? Why am I seeing her? What does she want from me? And what does she have to do with Lethalis and my past?

Lost in thought, I munch on the leftover noodles, gently scratching at the itchy scars on my arms.

With a sigh, I lean back. Could she be trying to convey something to me? Could she even tell me anything at all? If I was here as a little girl, back in the day, would she have seen me? But if she was indeed the owner of Lethalis, I am quite sure she wouldn't remember any random guest. But there must have been special circumstances, for why else does she appear in my nightmares?

My thumbs twirl around each other in circles as I wonder what's with that red dress of hers.

I straighten my back. Thoughts creep through my head as I walk out of my room and wander through the corridors. The walls of the first and second floors glide by again and again. Strolling aimlessly, I see the light from outside slowly fading.

At every corner I turn, I expect to see the lady in red. I want to see her. I want to be ask her questions. Whether she can answer them is a different matter, but I at least want to try. Every corridor I search, again and again, is empty. Not a soul in sight. No lady in red, no Toke, no Henry and no scary men—or tourists, as Toke calls them. Not even a steak-cheeked man, who's keeping a surprisingly low profile. With every step I take, I feel more alone.

Each hallway seems to get more and more narrow, as if the walls are closing in on me, and they seem to stretch in front too, as if the horizon is drifting away from me. I turn the corner at room 199 and walk towards the stairwell. The soles of my feet burn. Gusts of pain surge through my insteps with every step I climb and each step creaks beneath me.

I walk up the stairs to the second floor and look at the ground. There is a shoe lying there. A single shoe. White in colour, once, now grey-ish, with red and blue curved streaks down the side and tawdry white laces. I bend down and pick up the shoe. Does it belong to the tourists? But that would mean they have returned, and the front door is locked. The back door, however, is not, I realise. And at the back door... I sigh. It's probably just Henry playing a stupid joke on me. I throw the shoe to the floor and take the short route to room 299. I turn the corner and am about to walk into my room when my feet stop me. I look up from the carpet.

Something is moving in the doorway of room 267. It has disappeared from view before I can see it properly, but I am sure it is still there. Company.

I suppress the urge to shout something and walk silently across the lily carpet down the corridor. I pass the closed doors of rooms 261 to 265. I push my toes into the carpet and peer around the doorframe, trying to take a peek into room 267.

On the gaudy bed sits a little girl with long blonde hair. She emits a laugh when she sees the top half of my head in the doorway, jumps off the bed and runs in my direction. I take a step back and see the girl run out of the room, down the corridor, her blonde locks dancing up and down. She's wearing a blue dress with daisies on it and worn sandals of a pale green colour. She stops at the end of the corridor and looks back at me. Before she disappears around the corner, she giggles.

I follow her without a sound. As soon as I turn the corner, I see her standing halfway down the corridor, holding her finger up and tracing imaginary shapes on the wallpaper. I walk over to her and look at the shapes she's tracing. "What are you drawing?" I ask.

She looks up with glowing eyes and points to her invisible drawing. "Daisies," she says.

I crouch and raise my eyebrows for a moment. "They're beautiful," I say softly.

"Have you seen my markers?"

I slowly shake my head. "No, I haven't seen them."

"Hmm... that's what Lessie said too."

"Who's Lessie?"

The girl ignores my question and continues drawing.

I watch her intently. She seems as real as Danny is. In my mind, I see him shaving himself in front of the mirror in the morning light. She looks as real as Reina, who's only a few years older probably. In my mind, I see her sitting on the bed, fluttering her little hands, waiting for her bed time story to be told. She seems as real as Jack on his leather chair, with his fingertips pressed together and his penetrating gaze. And just as real as the man with the missing eye, the steak-cheek and the worn fedora. I look around, but the man with the hat is still nowhere to be seen. Why do I hardly see him anymore? Is it because I'm off my meds?

The girl hums softly as she draws something that looks like a butterfly near one of the flowers.

I look at my hands, turn them over, and look back at the girl. Could it be...? My right hand reaches out, my heart starts beating faster and my breath falters. My fingers close in on her hair.

"Amber," Lethalis' voice roars through the corridors.

The girl turns away from me and hops down the corridor, leaving me with goosebumps and upright hair on my arms. For a nanosecond, I felt something. For just a mere nanosecond I could feel the softness of her hair. She's tangible. I find support against the wall as my heart races like a track horse. How can she be tangible? The man with the hat isn't tangible—Jack went straight through him, as did that business man walking down the street. Is she really here, alive and present? Although... Have I evert tried touching the man with the hat myself? No, on the contrary. I tried to stay as far away as I could from him. Until I found those leaflets, that is. Now he's the one keeping his distance.

"Hi!" A jolly little voice sounds.

I look to my left and see the girl standing at the end of the hallway, half hidden behind the wall. She looks at me with a glint in her eyes and an unfettered, candid smile on her face. I respond to her with my usual tight-lipped smile.

She recedes her head behind the wall. A few seconds later, she jumps into the corridor with both feet, coming into full view. "Djaaaa!" She chirps, as if she's just performed some kind of magic trick.

I laugh awkwardly as my stomach rumbles harder and harder with excruciating hunger—a hunger like I've never felt before, even with my usual abstinence from food.

The girl repeats her trick and looks at me expectantly.

I step away from the wall and take a hesitant step towards her. She shrieks, jumps in the air and semi-steps back behind the wall with an amused expression and twinkling eyes.

I take a few more steps towards her and hear her giggle. She disappears from sight again as I walk down the corridor. I turn the corner and see her standing a short distance away, waving at me. She hops ahead of me as I walk behind her. She stays a few metres in front of me, glancing at me. She displays an uninhibited smile with white teeth, two of which are missing.

I feel a stab in my heart and look at her mouth. I recognise the position of her teeth. It isn't a clear memory, but a blurred smudge from a distant past—a grainy image creeping from the shadows. This little blonde girl hopping carelessly through the corridors of Lethalis... is she me? I collapse and lean on my knees. If that's me, how could it be that I felt something on my fingertips? And yet she *must* be a memory: a living memory, rather than a hallucination. The girl is as bright as the corridor with the lilac lily carpet. Just as present, solid and tangible. My head even feels clear. I haven't felt this lucid in ages.

I get up and look past the girl to the end of the corridor. Something protrudes above the top step of the stairs. A dark grey hat, followed by a snow-white eye and fused skin. The man with the hat grows taller and taller, until his dull patent leather shoes touch the carpet. For fuck's sake, I think to myself. You've finally showed yourself. It's about time.

The little girl turns to him, while he puts one foot in front of the other, stepping over the lilies. His hand moves upwards, into the air, towards his head. He clasps the brim of his hat between his fingertips and removes it with a graceful bow.

The girl is still watching him, with her back turned towards me—completely motionless.

I take a few hesitant steps towards her. She is still six metres away from me. And only three metres from the man with the hat. He looks at her with a stern gaze. And that's when I realise he hasn't even looked at me for the briefest of moments.

My calf muscles contract as my upper body bends forward. My feet shoot forward one by one, seemingly in slow motion. The walls slide by my side. The girl is almost within reach. I look down at her blonde crown and extend my arm, reaching for her shoulder. But my fingers miss her by inches.

She runs forward and leaps into the arms of the steak-cheeked man. His hat falls to the ground. His white teeth stand out sharply against his skin as he shows a broad smile. Soft slits form next to his one eye and above the scar, right next to where his other eye must have once been. The girl strokes his scarred cheek. Then she reaches for his greying curls, which are less than six millimetres long. He bounces her up and down on his arm.

My eyes follow the man and the girl walking towards the stairwell with big smiles. His curls disappear from view.

"Amber," whispers the voice from the hotel.

A sigh caresses my neck, perking up the hairs. I slowly turn my head and see the lady in red passing to my left. She halts in front of the dishevelled hat, looking down at it. The muscles in her upper back visibly contract as she bends forward and snatches the hat from the carpet. She straightens her back. Her nails dig dimples into the hat. Both hands ball into fists. She lowers her chin. Her reddish locks fall in front of her face. She slowly turns to me, the hat still clenched in her fists, and looks up. The dim light falling through the corridor reflects on her damp cheeks. Her flashing eyelashes push tears from her glassy eyes.

"Are you OK?" I hear my voice ask feebly. I want to swallow, but my throat is way too dry.

"*Hnnng*," moans the lady in red.

I take a hesitant step towards her.

One hand lets go of the hat and hits her left ear with an audible slap.

I stiffen and stare at her.

"*Hrrrg*," she snarls. She hits her temple. Again. And again. And again. Her other hand begins to join in. The hat crumples in her iron grip. The brim shoots up from the impact of her fist against her head.

My feet shuffle backwards. This is bad.

Her fists hang motionless in the air, one close to her temple and the other, holding the hat hostage, near the wall. Her head lifts so slowly it sends shivers down my spine. Her piercing eyes stare into mine.

My right foot slides back as inconspicuously as possible. I want to get out of here, away from her—every fibre in my body feels that urge but at the same time is frozen with fear.

The lady in red lowers her arms until they're limp by her body. Her chin drops to her chest. Rusty tufts of hair conceal most of her face and one of her eyes. The eye that is still visible is fixed on me like that of a hawk.

My throat squeezes. I slide my left foot back too.

She throws her head into her neck and roars like a maniac.

ROOOOAAARRR!

I almost fall backwards, tripping over my own feet, as I turn and run. Her footsteps thump on the ground, right behind me, as I round the corner, my shoulders scraping along the wall. Even barefoot, her sprint makes noise. I nearly bump into the window frame. My breath trashes in my throat. I fly around the next corner and run straight to my room. I dive through the doorway and slam the door behind me. The door almost pops at the seams when the woman slams her entire weight onto it.

I quickly jam the chair under the latch, using the last bit of energy in my limbs, and step backwards on swerving legs. My knees buckle and give way. My butt hits the edge of the bed. My hands reach for the edge for extra support. With eyes as big as breakfast plates and clammy palms, I try to catch my breath without losing sight of the door. I wait for a sign from the other side, like a loud thump as if a battering ram were being banged against the wall. I wait for the door handle to rattle up and down. I wait for the moment when the back of the chair breaks in half, giving free rein to the predator in the corridor.

Grooowwl.

The growling is quiet, but it drowns out all the other sounds inside and outside of the hotel. My knuckles turn white as I desperately search for a viable weapon out of the corner of my eye. I only see two stupid water bottels in my trembling field of vision, one of which is empty—that's not even going to make a dent in butter.

The growling slowly hushes. A heavy blanket falls over the hotel, now filled with silence.

I rub my sternum. The affectionate stroking cannot slow my heart rate of 210. My head spins and tilts backwards. My body has no way of resisting it and I let myself fall backwards, my right arm in an uncomfortable bend. The image before my eyes narrows and is covered with swirling white orbs.

My stomach contracts and I gag. The slightest content of my stomach sputters up my throat and heaves into in my mouth. I cough and wheeze and try to swallow down the burning sensation. With all my might, I turn onto my side and spit a few pieces of undigested noodles across the mattress, gasping for breath. I desperately want to grab the bottle of water from my bedside table and rinse the burning sensation, along with the rancid sour taste, but my limbs refuse. My chest expands as a hoarse rattle erupts from my throat. The dancing orbs slowly fade on my retina.

My hazy gaze is focused on the bottle standing some three arm lengths away from me—just two too many. If I could roll over once, I might be able to grab it, is a thought that slithers through my head like thick shit through a funnel. I take a few deep breaths and wiggle my tingling fingers back and forth. Come on, I cheer myself on. You can do this. You have to.

With a bout of willpower, I roll through my own vomit, onto my stomach and onto my other side. Pieces of undigested noodles stick to my cheeks and nose. I gasp and feel my stomach contract again. I cough and huff. Stinging pain stabs through the muscles between my ribs. I gasp for air and manage to roll onto my back. With my final ounce of energy, I bring my arm towards the nightstand. My fingers brush along the plastic. Almost. My head rolls to the side and I look at the bottle still standing there, mocking me, just outside of reach. Come on, I think. Come on... *please*.

Groaning, I make one last half-baked attempt to roll onto my side, then roll back onto my back.

I laugh out loud at the cooling sensation in my palm. The plastic crackles in my weakened grip. I flaccidly pull my arm towards me and feel the water bottle land on my stomach. Both my hands grope for the cap and frantically struggle to twist it open. Luckily, the bottle has been open before and I don't have to fight the little plastic teeth anymore. I probably never would've succeeded if that were the case. After a few seconds of struggling, I feel the cap give way, just a little bit.

I laboriously bring the bottle towards my face, without taking off the cap. Now I have to figure out how to drink the water without choking. Kyra taught me that you can't drink whilst lying down. She believed it was important for me to know that in regard to Reina's care, so she made me try it out for myself several times. Time after time, I choked. Eventually I figured out that it could work, provided I took tiny sips and lifted my head slightly. Kyra considered that cheating and she pushed my head back before smacking the bottom of the glass, causing the entire contents to pour down the back of my throat. I was still coughing two days later. But at this very moment, right now, it might just work. Now the only question is whether I have enough energy to keep my head raised. Or should I use my energy to roll onto my side? Do I roll towards the vomit or do I try to roll in the direction of the nightstand? If I choke, I might be finished. What a way to end a life. I can already see the newspaper headlines in the back of my mind. *Woman choked to death in hotel by her own vomit.*

My chest rises relentlessly towards the ceiling. I let out a deep sigh, cutting through the sides of my gullet, and close my eyes. It's all or nothing. I roll back onto my right side, facing the leftover vomit that has already semi-dried. I slowly manoeuvre the hand with the bottle towards my face. My wonky wrist narrowly misses the vomit. I fiddle with the cap once more, now that I have only a single hand at my disposal. My other arm is wedged halfway under me. After some ten seconds, I feel my insides go numb. I take another breath and close my eyes. *Please.*

Water flows over my index and middle fingers as soon as the cap falls from the bottle, at last. I quickly put the bottle to my mouth and place my lips around the opening, drinking with small but eager sips. The sour taste in my mouth fades. My throat cools. I gratefully close my eyes and drink until I can no longer manage to suck water from the bottle. I lie too flat to take in the final remnant, so I leave the bottle beside me, right in front of my mouth, and breathe slowly. Finally, some relief. My eyelids feel heavy and press my eyes shut.

I just hope the chair holds, is my last conscious thought before I am pulled into an intangible world—one where anything is possible and nothing can really touch me.

Deep shadows trail across the ceiling as the sun creeps further and further behind the horizon, shrouding the room in darkness. However, the real darkness is yet to come.

10 WATER DROPLETS

When I open my eyes again, it's dark, and I need to give my eyes a moment to get used to the darkness. The moonlight is diminished by the covers of clouds which float through the sky with dead ease, as well as by the plastic sheets in front of the windows.

The rancid taste of vomit lingers in the back of my throat, as I carefully hoist myself up to a sitting position. A droplet dribbles down my nose. I wipe my face and feel my clammy forehead. My palm touches a leftover noodle still sticking to my cheek. I grimace and turn to the bottle still lying on the mattress. I pour the remnant of water down my parched throat and swallow gratefully. I would have loved to use the water to wash my face and get rid of the pungent smell of vomit, but that's not the most important thing right now. I suddenly remember the wet wipes in my bag and the pack of gum that I bought. I roll off the bed with just my upper body, reach for my bag and grab the pack of wipes. I wipe a few tissues over my face, heaving an enlightened sigh, and throw them into the corner of the room. I then look for the gum and gratefully chew on it. Finally, some refreshment.

With a throbbing head, I wonder how long I have been in Lethalis now. Two days? Four days? A week? What day is it anyway? Henry said something about it being a Saturday and since then... how much time has passed exactly?

With a nagging growl, my stomach pleads for food. I don't even know how long I haven't eaten properly. Maybe it's indeed time to go home, like Henry said. Back to Danny—I'll weather that storm when it comes to it; this is no way to live. The hallucinations are becoming too real and they are getting too close. I think of home and see the beige wallpaper in front of me, in my room, coming loose from the walls in places. My desk, where I sometimes sit drawing well into the night, with my desk lamp aimed at the paper in front of me. There, on that paper, all my thoughts take shape—pure and sincere, without filter and without camouflage.

My computer screen is in front of me, showing my favourite website: VampireFreaks. I see the messages pour in and the new comments on my photos. Like that last picture, on my dark green duvet. Or the one in front of the mirror in the bathroom, with my scars in plain sight.

My mind wanders through my room, to the corridor that connects my bedroom and Danny's office. I can see his bookcase filled to the brim up on the rear wall—I miss browsing through his books and picking one that piques my interest, only to finish reading it within a few nights. I see his outdated laptop and usual coffee mug on the top of his dark desk. His desk reminds me of the one Jack's got. That one is even bigger and fancier.

Now, I see Jack's office before me with that leather sofa, making crackling noises. I can hear the crackling, as though it occurs close to my ear. I also hear breathing, first slow, then heavy and rushed, almost groaning, and I can taste the salty sweat on my lips. I recall Jack's face hovering over me, his eyes wide open. I hear my own voice pleading for help.

My stomach turns and I shake my head. I can't go back. I don't want to go back. Lethalis is where I'm supposed to be, I feel it in my toes, and it is trying to tell me something, I just know that. I get up from the bed and stagger ahead, grabbing my damp shirt from the door.

My crown is struck by something cold and wet. I startle and place my fingers on my head. A drop of water falls right on top my fingers. I step back and look at the ceiling. Even in the dim light of the moon, I can see it: the dark stain now covers half the ceiling. Droplets stick to the surface, falling down one by one. A water droplet falls on my nose and I pat my face with my shirt.

As the droplets fall on the shirt that's clenched in my hands, it finally makes sense. My body isn't wet from sweat, but from the water droplets falling from the ceiling for however long. Is there a leakage? I frown at the speed at which the drops succeed one another. The intervals seem to be getting shorter and shorter. I can't keep sleeping underneath this. Sulking, I hang my shirt back to dry.

I don't know where I find the energy, but I manage to pull the mattress off the bed and drag it across the room with great effort. The mattress wobbles in all directions. I pull the chair out from under the latch and push it aside. I open the door and move the mattress into the corridor, where it slumps to the wall with a dull thump.

I grab the two empty bottles, put them in my bag and swing the bag over my shoulder. The weight of the bag almost yanks me to the ground, tripping me over my feet. I catch myself against the wall and hunch over, panting heavily, propping myself up on the bedside table. My legs sway almost as much as the mattress. I carefully bend down to the plastic bag in front of my feet and lift it up. It holds three remaining oatmeal bars, one pack of noodles and a can of energy drink. I lick my lips, but realise I'd better save the drink for later. I grab a bar, stuff everything into my shoulder bag, and eat the biscuit in small bites as my mouth gets drier and drier and my crown gets wetter and wetter. After the last bite, the wrapper slips from my weak grip and swirls to the floor.

I stumble out of the room, grab the mattress and drag it down the corridor past the other rooms. I think for a moment and then drag it along towards the stairwell. I try to push the mattress up the stairs, but it folds in half and slides to the side. I step over it and try to hoist it up by one of the corners, carefully moving up a few steps. The corner slips from my fingers and the mattress slides down until it hits the ground of the second floor. This isn't going to work, I realise. I walk up the stairs with just my bag and arrive at the third-floor corridor. I look sideways towards room 399, which only comes in clear view when I round the corner. Inside lies the origin of the dark stain, and now this damn leakage too.

This room must be cursed, I conclude, thinking back to all the horror films I watched on the sofa with Danny. So often those stories involved a curse or an evil spirit. I often found it entertaining, but it also scared me. I'd snuggle extra close to Danny, as he rested his arm across the sofa railing, and he would gently grab my shoulder. The warmth of his body always made me feel safe. I could really use that right now. I want someone by my side, even if it's just Toke. Or Henry.

But I know I'm not alone here. I recall the lady in red and how she had sprinted after me. I shudder. Would she still be here? What if, just like the man with the hat, she never leaves me be anymore?

I look into room 399. The door is open and I see the box of leaflets in the middle of the room. Those leaflets should be able to tell me more —they show both him and her, after all. I set my bag down, rummage through the box and take out a stack of leaflets. I tilt them left and right in an attempt to read the text, but it's just too damn dark. This will have to wait until tomorrow.

The carpet underneath the box catches my eye. Despite the lack of light, the stain is easily visible. I touch the carpet and half-expect it to feel wet, but it feels as bone dry as my mouth.

I get back up and cross the corridor to room 398, where the now empty bucket from which I had taken the dusters stands. With the bucket, I walk back to the stairwell, to the second floor and into room 299. At least ten water droplets fall down every half-second. The carpet is damp in several places, but in particular right next to the bed. I place the bucket on top of the wet spot and hear the droplets clatter into it. I step back as I pat dry my neck.

The sound of the splashing droplets is remarkably soothing. I take a deep breath and heave a loud sigh. The sound of the sigh hushes under the creaking noise above my head. I look up and see cracks forming in the ceiling. My eyes open so wide they almost pop out of their sockets.

I jump backwards and bang my back against the doorframe, one foot out of the room and the other barely manages to dodge a chunk of ceiling, which crashes into the floor and hits the front of my shoe. A smaller chunk of concrete hits my shin and bounces to the side. My arms shield my face from the spraying water, which pummels at me like a rain of needles. My right foot refuses to move as I try to turn away from the strong jet of water. I turn my face behind my arms and gasp for breath, but the water squirts past my defences and invades my mouth and nostrils. Coughing and sputtering, I collapse through my knees. My arms mow and grasp at my foot, which is stuck between the debris and the wall. Tears sting my wet sprayed eyes. My lungs burn. My eardrums ring as I make a frantic attempt to kick the debris aside. I wriggle my foot back and forth until there's a small opening, but a stabbing pain shoots through my ankle.

I let myself fall to the side, away from the crushing blast of water. The muscles in between my ribs acidify as I cough fiercely. I gasp for breath, but don't get the chance due to my sputtering diaphragm. My lungs fight the fluid ferociously. My vision spins and narrows. Dark spots coat my visual field. Water droplets shoot through the air with every thrust from my chest. My head hits the sodden carpet and I lose consciousness.

Bright light bursts on my tear ducts. My body feels calm and still. In the middle of that ocean of serenity, I see her silhouette before me: the silhouette of my mother. She floats towards me through a space where gravity does not seem to exist. Her hands reach out in front of her and grab me by my shoulders. I still remember this embrace, my thoughts tell me. I find myself in the water as I thrash around me with my infant arms and watch the splashes fly through the air. I feel the pressure of my mother's hands on my shoulders.

I watch her face as she slowly comes into focus. Her broad forehead with slight furrows. Thin eyebrows and high cheekbones. Her dark green eyes, carrying unspoken thoughts. I gasp as her reddish locks ripple through the water, along the red fabric of her dress, which is tightened around her figure like a cocoon. Her narrow lips part before pressing firmly together to form deep wrinkles around her mouth, while her eyebrows dip to her nose, accumulating the skin between them. Her nails dig deep into the skin of my shoulders, holding me firmly in place.

I open my mouth and attempt to scream, but water forces its way into my mouth. I swallow the water and feel my ribcage shock as wildly as it did a moment ago. My tiny hands smack her arms and her head, making no impact whatsoever. A second wave of water sloshes in. My epiglottis sputters under the strain. I try to shove myself away from my mother, but I don't have the strength left to escape her clutches. The water sears into my nasal cavities.

Well before I waste my last bit of energy, I realise it's futile. I cannot break free. I cannot escape. I can only endure it. To let go and draw my last gurgling breath. This is where I cease to exist.

My body stops jerking. My limbs relax. The pressure on my shoulders disappears and I feel a warm sensation around my wrist. I feel thin lips pressing around my lips. An oppressive sensation follows, violently invading my throat. A heavy punch dents my diaphragm. My mother's copper locks tickle under my nose after each forced breath.

Water is violently squeezed out of my lungs and shoots up into the air like a little fountain. My own coughing and panting sound soft and inane next to my mother's panting and excited laughter.

"Well done, Amber," her voice sounds, both sweet as honey and sharp like a knife. She presses a firm kiss to my forehead. "You can't leave me."

I regain consciousness and hear the water still squirting from the ceiling. I open my eyes and slowly blink a few times. My throat is sore, my chest expands steadily. *Ah*, I think. *That's* what had happened in the past. I wasn't swimming, but I was in the shower with my mom. It was on or close to a birthday, but not mine. How do I even know that? Hmm, because it was hot that day. Yeah, I could see the sun shining, even from inside the bathroom. That couldn't have been on my birthday, because it's typically gloomy and grey then, with a chance of snow.

Water sloshes up against my body and streams down the corridor behind me. I follow the water with my eyes. My gaze lingers on the bathroom. That bathroom had looked the same then, in terms of layout. So it must have happened here, inside this hotel. In Lethalis.

My right hand slides halfway under my neck. I push myself up off the floor and slide my elbow under my body to support myself. With arms buckling, I bring myself to a sitting position. My head pounds violently. I move myself backwards into the corridor, sliding my butt over the soaking wet carpet. Defeated, I look at the water that has flooded the entire corridor. The water flows gently through the doorways and below the room doors, partially sinking into the lilac tufts of the carpet. I don't know how carpet handles this much water exactly, but it can't be good, I fear. I need to stop the water. There must be a main tap, somewhere, that can shut off this never-ending stream.

I seek support from the wall and scramble to my feet with throbbing temples. My one foot places itself clumsily in front of the other as I make my way to the stairwell. There lies my mattress, half on the stairs and half on the wet carpet. The water has already reached the stairs, playfully dripping down the steps.

Water taps are somewhere downstairs, in the crawl space or under the welcome mat, Danny once taught me when we had a leakage in the kitchen—one that quickly flooded the entire kitchen floor and seeped into the dining area. I stagger down the steps. Lethalis doesn't have a welcome mat, but it should have a crawl space or something. Or maybe... a basement?

I pass the first floor, where the water has done little harm yet. I stagger further down the stairs and end up on the stone floor of the lobby. Down here, at least, the water won't do much, other than give the tiles a good cleaning. I look around the lobby and see the entrance, the doors to the restaurant, the glass French doors leading to the garden, the wide white counter, and to my right the steel door of the elevator and a white wooden door. With soggy shoes, I stumble to the white door and push it open. I enter a corridor with another door in it and a wooden staircase leading down. I push open the other door and find a large empty room with small windows high up in the wall. Only a tiny bit of moonlight creeps in through them.

I turn towards the stairs and stumble down in a hurry. With every step I descend, it gets darker. At the bottom of the stairs, I stand in near-complete darkness. My hands fumble along the walls, looking for a light switch. I frantically search at the height where I expect it to be, but all I feel is cold stone and unevenness. My fingers tip upwards as I ardently wish for my eyes to get used to the dark well enough to spot the switch. Again, I feel nothing but wall and it is still pitch black.

I grope a little lower than I would expect it to be. My right pinky strokes along a bump. I hold my hand on the spot and feel a switch under my palm and push it frantically. Bright light begins to flicker and I squeeze my eyes shut. Even before my eyes can get used to the light, I keep tracing the wall. My fingers feel gritty bricks, cold pipes and strange objects. I blink wildly and look ahead. More bricks, wall boxes, two shallow cupboards on the wall and pipes running in all directions. My eye catches one of the pipes, which has a grey round thing on it and a gold-coloured tap. *There*! I stumble towards the tube, grab the tap and start turning. My knuckles turn white as I try to get it to move. The tap is stuck.

My other hand joins the fray. "Come on!" I groan desperately. My cramped fingers concede the battle. I stagger backwards and barely manage to keep my balance. I take a deep breath, pull my right leg off the ground, aim for the tap's left arm and kick it hard. I collapse through my knees, gasping for breath. I look at the position of the little arms. A wave of hope rushes through me. I straighten my back, raise my leg again and kick the tap once more with all my strength. *Yes*! It gives way! My hands finish the job and turn the golden arms until they won't go any further. I breathe a sigh of relief and shamble back to the stairs. But before I can go back up, I plump down on one of the bottom steps, tilt my head back, and let the stairs support my entire weight. My chest puffs up and down in a frantic manner. I stay in my uncomfortable pose to catch my breath and until the pain in my flank subsides.

At least the water problem is solved. Although, the flow of water has stopped, but I still have to get rid of the water itself, I realise. I bring my hands to my face and rub slowly from top to bottom. My feet feel heavy. The stairs are anything but comfortable, yet I don't want to get up. I'd rather not even move. I want to lie in a nice comfortable bed, one that is softer than the block of concrete I have been lying on for the past few nights, which is now lying half soaked on the stairs.

Reluctantly, I hoist myself up with my elbows. I break free from the stairs, slam the light switch with one hand and walk up while seeking support from the wall. Back in the lobby, out of the corner of my eye, I see the ground shimmer. Without glancing at it, I know the water has already reached the ground floor. I walk through the water, up the stairs and back to the dark second floor.

The carpet is as soggy as the socks in my shoes, yet I no longer see any reflection. Either the water has flowed down or it has been soaked up by the carpet, but most probably both. It's hard for me to solve this with a couple of buckets and a hoover, which I can't seem to find anywhere anyway. This probably just needs to air-dry. I make a tour of the floor and open each room door as wide as possible, so that the draughts have free rein. This brings a little light into the corridor as well, which is a bonus for me.

I trudge back to my mattress, which still lies halfway across the steps like a soggy brick, grab the edge of the mattress and try to push it up, but the mattress feels extra heavy and water seeps down my arms, causing me to lose my grip. I look around me in defeat. I don't know what I'm expecting to find. The answer, for one thing, but I see no solution to my situation; nothing that could make it easier for me to hoist the mattress upstairs. That's when I finally remember that Toke has already furnished nearly all of the rooms. Plenty of places to sleep, in other words. I leave the mattress as it is and walk dejectedly to the third floor, where my things are. I step into room 399, expecting to find an insane havoc, but the floor is completely intact —I can tell even with the dim moonlight. From the centre of the room, on top of that big dark stain, the box of leaflets smirks at me, like it's mocking me.

I carefully test the floor with my toes. I hear no noticeable creaking, but I don't fully trust it either. I quickly walk to my bag, grab it off the floor and start to walk out of the room. But before I leave the room, I cast another glance at the box. I grab it and drag it out into the corridor. I don't know what it is with these leaflets, but there is *something*. Maybe I can find the truth in there, if I look closely enough, as soon as there's sufficient daylight.

I enter the opposite room, which has no window, and push the box into a corner of the room. I lower myself onto my butt and place my bag beside me. The back of my head rests against the wall and my eyes immediately fall shut. Nodding, I try to find a more comfortable position, but I'm out before I know it. Sleep overtakes me like a muscle spasm.

My dream is hectic and muddled. All sorts of things are happening, but there is no coherent narrative. No beginning and no end. Sometimes I seem to wake up, but that too could be part of the dream. All that sticks with me is the smell of smoke and the light of flickering flames, stealing the darkness from behind my closed eyelids.

Thud. Thud.

I also detect the sounds echoing through the stairwell of Lethalis as part of my dream. Loud thudding, a bang and then softer thudding. Again and again.

Thud.

11 THE HISSING VOICE

The first thing that greets me that morning is the stabbing pain in my neck and back. I carefully get up while placing a hand on my neck and applying pressure. I've been lying against the wall in a strange curve, with my head tilted to the side and my spine in an unhealthy twist. I clench my teeth in pain.

I reach for my shoulder bag, rummage through it, and pull out the strip of painkillers and one of the water bottles. The plastic creaks under my grip as I realise it's empty. *Fuck*! Why didn't I refill them when I had the chance, I think in a panic. I could have just filled them under the tap. Now I'd have to put the water back on and there'd be another flood.

I swallow. My throat feels as dry as sandpaper. I contemplate going to the well. The water inside was clear and it didn't seem to taste strange. Maybe I should make do with that for now.

Or you could just go to the supermarket, urges the one voice inside me.

I look at my body, clad only in tawdry lingerie. My clothes are still hanging over the door of room 299.

Surely you can't go out looking like this, you look like shit, chimes the other voice. They will think you're a whore. Everyone will look at you and point at you, whisper behind your back and make ugly faces.

You'll be at the centre of the attention you so desperately want to avoid but also crave so much...

Or they'll think you need help and call the emergency services... Maybe you have been reported missing and the police are looking for you as we speak. Then they will come and get you right away and you will never discover the truth you so desperately seek.

If that were the case, Mukkie and the hag would have betrayed you by now, reasons the other voice. Nobody benefits from helping you. They don't give a damn about you, why should they?

I shake my head to silence the voices and that's when an idea pops in. I rummage through the bag once more and retrieve the energy drink. I open it and gratefully swallow the painkiller with it. I sit quietly as I keep taking small sips of the refreshing liquid. When the can is almost empty, I feel the painkiller starting to kick in. Another ten minutes or so later, the sharp edge has faded and the pain has gone blunt.

I decide to use the little bit of energy I gained from my broken sleep to walk to the well, carrying the four empty bottles with me in my bag. A cloud drifts before the sun as I walk between the hedges in the garden towards the clearing with the well.

At the well, I lower the bucket until it's in the water. I wait a moment to hoist it back up. I carefully place the four empty bottles in front of me on the gravel, with the cap off, and aim the bucket above one of the bottles. A splash of water knocks the bottle to the ground. I set the bucket down beside me, clamp the bottle between my legs and try again. The bottle dents between my thighs as I try to hold it in place, and I manage to fill it to the brim. A small excess drips down my bare legs. I screw on the cap and fill the other three bottles in the same way.

At least now I have something to drink. I greedily empty one bottle down my throat and fill it again, before putting the bucket to my lips and lifting it skywards. A stream of water pours down my throat. With quick, big gulps, I drink from the bucket until my stomach and oesophagus have had enough. I let the bucket dangle above the well and put the bottles back in my bag, with a sense of satisfaction. I already feel a lot better than 15 minutes ago.

I sit with my back against the well and watch the clouds pass by in the sky. I remember enjoying looking at the clouds when I was little. I could see all kinds of shapes in them, no matter how weird. Sometimes I could see human heads. Sometimes prancing horses or fire-breathing dragons. Sometimes I saw fanciful creatures with five arms, two horns and a huge belly. I would lie on my back in the grass as I watched them. I have no idea where it was, but I do know I was with *someone*. With whom? Danny? No, it was someone smaller, someone my height or maybe slightly taller. A child, in any case. It wasn't Reina, because she wasn't even born yet. Was it a friend? I frown. No, I was even younger... It was before I was adopted. Maybe someone from the foster home, I presume. Although I don't know how long I stayed in that foster home and with whom. I don't remember *anything* from that time. Maybe I was right here, between the hedges, provided there was grass instead of pebbles back then. Maybe I was on the grass behind the maze, which stretches for tens of metres—an empty plain so large that a small building could easily be placed there. A shed, for example.

The image of my mother looms before my mind's eye. I see my tiny arms whipping around in the splashing water. My breath falters. That look in my mother's eyes... I remember not understanding that look, not being able to grasp it. After all, I was just a child. It had been a look full of hate, full of disgust and envy. And it wasn't in a swimming pool or play pond either, as I always thought, but in a shower. In this hotel, of all places. I can finally understand why the newspaper article attracted me so.

I rest the back of my head against the cool stones. My own mother wanted to kill me, right here in Lethalis, I realise slowly but surely. I repeat the situation several more times in my head. The realisation is more or less there, but the emotion is absent. No anger. No sadness. Not even fear, like I felt when I ran from her in the corridor. I just don't feel anything at all.

My mind wanders to Jack and all his analysing questions, which he fires at me like a platoon at every situation or thought I describe. His piercing eyes make the questions all the more intrusive. I shudder. *Intrusive*, that's exactly what he is. He has to crawl into my head to understand me and be able to help me, but I don't want him there at all. I want him to stay outside.

I shake my head and immediately regret it. The sharp pain in my neck hones in on me like a missile. I wait a moment for the pain to subside and then carefully stand up. I hang my bag with the water bottles over my shoulder and walk back into the hotel.

Now that it is light and I am back in the land of the living, I can take a good look at the water damage. The water that had reached the lobby floor is nothing more than a sheen on the white stones. I did expect the stones to get cleaner, but I did not expect them to shine like this. I step onto the first step of the stairs and hear it creak. I frown, looking at my foot and the step below. I pull my foot back and crouch in front of the steps. My fingers glide over the white stone surface. It feels pleasant. I thought it would feel cold. I push down on the step with my hand, but it doesn't make enough impact to provoke creaks. Why does this keep creaking anyway?

I continue my way upstairs and glance at the first floor. The carpet has also enjoyed a decent cleaning: ornate lilies bloom on the bright purple carpet. Apparently the water has flowed further than it seemed yesterday after all, because as far as the carpet reaches, it has the same intensity of colour. On the second floor, the ground is just as purple and the walls are just as white. I walk to room 299 and take in the havoc. The floor is littered with debris, a kinked pipe protrudes from the ceiling that is partly gone. If the floor above it wasn't supported by wooden beams, it would've come down too, I realise. I look at the pipes. Maybe Henry can fix this, if he's handy like that. I'll go and find him in a bit.

I grab my clothes from the door and get dressed. Finally. I pull my long sleeves further to my wrists. It's warm, but pleasant. At last, I am concealed again.

I walk to the stairwell. The white steps make cheerful sounds below my feet as I walk up the stairs to the third floor. I stop and look across the carpet. The lilies proudly pop out of the purple and dance down the empty corridor between the clinically white walls. The carpet seems as clean as it is now on the first and second floors. Toke may not be happy about the burst pipe, but I am sure she will be happy about the sight of the lilac lily carpet. If she wants to restore Lethalis to its former glory, this should do the trick. The carpet really is special. Somehow I know that I used to think so too, back in the day. As the carpet tickles my toes, I *know* that I've experienced that for hours, day in, day out.

My rumbling stomach sends a small echo through the hallway. I walk to room 399 and look at the dark spot on the ground for a moment. I turn to room 398 and walk straight to the box of leaflets. No migraine, no tourists, no leakage. Now I can finally focus and examine those curious leaflets. I plop down on my butt—a pain surges through my lower back—and lean back against the wall as I grab a leaflet.

Thud. Thud.

My finger strokes the ornate silver letters spelling *Lethalis* on the front cover. I turn the page and look at the pictures. My eye immediately catches the steak-cheeked man standing behind the counter in the photo. My fingertip strokes the fedora lying on the counter in the photo. "What happened to you?" I ask aloud. I look around, but the man with the hat is nowhere to be found, yet again. "What was our relationship?"

I think of the little me, in the floral dress, jumping into his arms. All this time, I thought I was crazy, having hallucinations. But the man with the hat actually exists. Or existed, perhaps. It might be that I've been seeing a ghost all this time. What do they call it, a poltergeist? One that keeps bothering and scaring you. Or did he come to me for help? I wouldn't know how I'd be able to help him in his state. Or maybe he wants revenge on me—I have no idea what happened between us and how he came to his end after all. Maybe I played a part in that myself. If he is indeed dead, that is.

Thud.

I look at the two people in the corridor. The woman in the bright red dress with the copper-coloured locks and wide forehead stares into the camera with a sullen look. I recall feeling her hands on my shoulders in the shower. Mom. I swallow. Seeing how she's portrayed in this photo, proud and imposing, it would be no surprise to me if she indeed was the *owner* of Lethalis. That might mean we all used to live here.

I try to focus my attention on the man. If she is my mom, then would this guy with the checkered shirt be my father? My real, biological father? The man has blond hair, small eyebrows, close-set eyes whose colour I cannot make out, a fairly wide jaw and a short chin. He wears a white and blue checkered blouse that contrasts with the rest of the picture—my mother's dainty red dress and the chic interior—and bulges over his waistband.

A nagging feeling trashes my insides. My diaphragm feels like a block of concrete pressing against my heart and my heart feels like a music box—flip it open and a polished ballerina does her trick in the empty shell. My fingertip slides along the face of my possible father and for a moment Jack's face looms before my mind's eye.

Thud. Thud.

The veins on my forehead bulge as I try to push the image from my mind and think of the old days. If this man is indeed my father, he must exist somewhere in my memory. I must have seen his face in real life. So then why do I only see darkness in front of me, without sound or smell or taste? The darkness feels like a wall with a front and a back. I stand in front of it and right behind it lie my memories for the taking—so close, almost tangible, but completely untouch-able. The wall doesn't need to fall, but a keyhole to look through, that would be something.

Thud.

I frantically think of the scene in the shower and imagine my mother walking through the corridors with us. I try to visualise my father in one of the rooms. But the more I force it, the blurrier the image becomes. Until I can't even manage to see the man with the hat in front of me. How ironic... Where has he gone at all?

THUD.

With an exasperated frown, I scramble upright and hurl the leaflet at the floor. What is that damn thudding sound? I walk down the corridor towards the stairwell, fully ready to smack Henry over the head for his obnoxious shenanigans, but what I find is far more absurd than Henry banging his rake against the ceiling.

A small stout man tumbles down the steps. So slow, in fact, that he nearly comes to a halt. He has short blond hair and he's wearing a checkered blouse. His body vertically rolls over itself, down towards the flat area of the stairs. Head over feet, feet over spine.

Mesmerised, I stare at the freakish scene.

The man rolls across the flat part. His feet slam upwards, towards the ceiling. One shoe comes loose and flies through the air—it doesn't seem to abide by the same rules of gravity the man seems to be suffering from and bounces with a loud bang on the wall, only to fly down the stairs to the second floor. Even from up here, I can see that it's the same shoe I had grumpily thrown to the floor earlier, assuming Henry was trying to play a prank on me.

Thud. Thud.

With each thud, the body of the man in the checkered blouse rolls on. As soon as he reaches the wall, where his shoe had bounced off from, he dissolves into nothingness.

I stare at the empty staircase and silently curse my absurd delusions.

Suddenly, the man's face appears right in front of me, his nose tip brushing against mine. I let out a loud scream and step backwards. The man looks blankly ahead, as if he's looking right through me. It's the man from the leaflet, I realise. The man who stood next to my mother. He starts tumbling backwards again in slow motion. I want to grab his wrists to stop him from falling, but my hands move right through him. "Fuck!" I yell. These fucking delusions, they really seem to have their own rules. As I watch the man fall backwards and see his neck make a strange kink on the steps, I wonder why I had felt the tip of his nose but hadn't been able to grab him by the wrist to save him from his ghastly-looking fall, which is happening all over again before me.

I heave a sigh and turn away from him. It's nothing but a delusion. I cannot save him and he cannot harm me either. With goosebumps and shivers running down my body, I walk back to the room with the leaflets. I kneel down and look at the rest of the pictures, without really seeing anything special, and I fold the leaflet shut with disappointment.

Thud. Thud.

The back of the leaflet is now facing upwards on my outstretched palm. On the back are a number of portraits with names underneath. At the top left is the man who could be my father, with a frugal smile on his face. Below his portrait reads *Ethan Price, owner*. I squint my eyes. Next to him is a picture of my mother, the lady in red: *Lilian Murphy, hostess*. A cold shiver runs down my spine.

Below them are four smaller portraits. The man with the hat: *Lester Wright, doorman*. A bald man with a grey stubble beard and moustache, full eyebrows and a robust nose: *Irvin Dunne, cook*. A woman with big black glasses, a warm smile, puffed-up frizzy hair and big yellow earrings: *Sia Lachman, maid*. A younger man, about my age, with a narrow jaw, bright brown eyes and hair shaved on the sides: *Henry Shaw, gardener*.

My breath falters. Henry!? I stare at his picture, my head starts spinning.

Not only is the man with the hat a ghost, but Henry is too? The handsome guy leaning casually on his rake, with a rebellious tuft of hair dropping in front of his mellow brown eyes. I sigh, slightly disappointed. I think back to our first encounter. Is this what he meant by that odd maze story? If he's a ghost, then he can't help me with the spill or fix the havoc either. But how was I able to feel him? His breath. His warmth...

My thoughts get drowned out by my rumbling stomach and then I realise that the thudding sound has finally stopped. I reach for my bag, grab the final pack of noodles and start chomping off chunks in a daze. Chewing slowly, something begins to dawn on me. If Henry is a ghost, then what does that make Toke?

I stand up and start pacing, the leaflet clutched in one hand and the chunk of noodles in the other. My feet automatically take me back to the second floor, where I have spent most of my time so far. I carefully study the back of the leaflet but I don't see a portrait of Toke anywhere. I breathe a sigh of relief. Maybe she is like me and she's just able to see them. I chew thoughtfully on a big bite. However... she never mentioned Henry, he only mentioned her.

BANG!

For a moment, I believe the man has started falling down the stairs again, but the sound comes from the floor above me. My ears prick up. What is it this time? I take off my shoes and sneak down the corridor. My footsteps sound muffled on the vibrant carpet.

I approach the stairwell and hear a voice. It is a soft, high-pitched voice with a full sound. I listen intently. Could it be my mother? I put my foot on the bottom step of the stairs and carefully walk up a few steps.

The voice echoes through the corridors. I cannot understand what is being said. From here it sounds like gibberish. Incoherent sounds in an endless brew. I climb a few more steps and am now standing on the flat part connecting the two staircases. I approach the last part of the stairs and take a step up.

Kkkkrrrrrrrrk.

I stiffen under the loud creaking of the step. Silently cursing, I look at those darned steps that keep acting like wood but instead look like stone.

Hobba wam plom kobb bob.

I prick up my ears. As quietly as a mouse, I sneak further up the stairs. I place my feet as close to the banister as possible, wary of further creaks. On my socks, I step onto the third-floor rug and stay put.

Mup kes soph naz ga res hus.

The sound is coming from the right section of the floor, I realise. Where I had been sitting quietly, not too long ago. It's where the box with the leaflets is. I silently move down the corridor towards the corner, where rooms 399 and 398 are. The closer I get to the sound, the more the babbling becomes hissing. I stop next to the doorway of room 399.

Shush nah som gissh saaa.

I take a hesitant step forward. A small creak under my feet causes a deafening silence. With pounding heart, I peek around the corner of the doorway, into the room.

Amid the debris sits a crouched being.

My throat clenches shut and all the air squeezes from my lungs. My eyes twitch in their sockets as I stare at the guise.

It stares back at me.

12 MUKKIE

her smooth-ironed yellow floral dress and with a large mug of fresh coffee in front of her on the lacquered table top of dark oak. Plumes of steam form above the dark blue mug. At her feet lies a small dog with curly white fur in a braided basket, which Aagje had once scooped up for a bargain price at a local flea market. Mukkie has his eyes closed and his flank slowly rises and falls.

Aagje turns the page of the Sunday paper and pushes her horn-rimmed glasses further up her nose. She slowly moves her head from left to right. Her gaze falls on a short article halfway down the page. She places the newspaper on the tabletop and straightens it, almost knocking her coffee mug off the table. She frowns her eyebrows and purses her lips, making the furrows in her face show even deeper, as she intently reads the typewritten words.

MIDSBERG - 22-year-old Amber Collins from Vassen has been missing since Tuesday morning.

She was last seen in Vassen-North, where she was on a regular appointment. After this appointment, she was supposed to take the bus to Vassen Central, from bus stop 1315, to go home. She did not return home. None of the drivers on duty have identified her.

The article is accompanied by a small photograph of the young woman.

"Oh dear," Aagje says in her rasping voice.

Mukkie raises his head and looks at her with his black beady eyes.

"Look at that, Mukkie. Another young brat who ran away from home."

Mukkie lets out a shrill yap, before jumping up and wagging his tail. He runs around the table once and then disappears into the L-bend of the kitchen.

Aagje slides her chair back and gets up while huffing. "Yes, I know, I know." She follows the little dog into the back part of the kitchen. She is halfway to the back door when she suddenly stops. She looks down at Mukkie and frowns. "Hmm, that girl... didn't we run into her? That beautiful blonde, she was very petite as well and she had an urban accent." She scratches her chin. "Yes, maybe..."

He yaps.

"One moment, Mukkie. This is important." She turns and shuffles back, around the table, to the bright red phone hanging on the wall between the big oak kitchen cupboard and the door towards the hall. She presses her finger on the wide keys and a moment later takes the receiver off the hook.

Mukkie yelps again.

Aagje purses her lips as she wraps the phone cord around her index finger. "Yes, hello," she says after a moment. "I'm calling about the newspaper report of that missing girl from Vassen." She listens for a moment. "Yes, that's right. I saw her on Thursday, I believe."

Mukkie pokes his head around the L-corner and looks at his owner, who has turned all her attention to the phone call. He darts back to the back door and whimpers. He pushes his nose against the closed door. His tail gently sways back and forth as he impatiently circles the dark grey exit mat. He remains standing and curves his back, squinting his beady eyes.

"Okay, that's perfectly fine. Then I'll make sure the tea is ready. Yes, thank you kindly. See you soon," Aagje answers the person on the other end of the line. She puts the phone on the hook and smoothes her dress.

Mukkie comes running around the corner wagging his tail and jumps into his basket next to the leg of the kitchen table.

"Don't you need to go anymore?" She bends down, groaning and bracing, and strokes its head. Before she can get up, the doorbell rings. "Well, well. Are they here already?" She leans heavily on the armrests of the sturdy chair and rises. She opens the door next to the phone and waddles down the hall to the front door. A white curtain with sunflowers hangs in front of the front door window. The curtain lets just enough light through to see a silhouette standing outside.

She turns the key in the keyhole, loosens the door chain and pulls the door open. She squeezes her eyes slightly against the bright morning sun.

"Aag, how are you today?" sounds a heavy voice. A tall man in light grey overalls stands on the porch. His ragged face is framed by a stubble beard and shiny silver hair that falls to just above his eyebrows. He displays a warm smile under his light brown eyes.

"Is it you, Frederick? I thought you were the police."

"The police? What have you been up to this time?"

Aagje emits a girly laugh. "Oh dear, what a rascal you are. What can I do for you, Frederick?"

"Well, I just looked out of the window and saw the sun shining so beautifully that I was reminded of you and your sunflowers." He gestures to the sunflowers that are in the wide garden boxes in front of the porch. Their yellow leaves wave sweetly at the sun. "So I thought, let me pay a visit to that bright lady and ask if she would like a cup of coffee."

She rubs her hands. "Now that you mention it, I haven't had any coffee at all! I do crave some. Go on and have a seat and I'll make you a lovely cup." She gestures to the wooden garden bench on the porch, which is decorated with green and yellow cushions.

"Can I help you with anything?"

"Don't be silly, it'll only take a few moments. You go and enjoy the sunshine." She smiles longingly and strokes her gaudy silver necklace.

Frederick walks towards the bench and sits down in a comfortable position. He glassily stares ahead.

Aagje glances at his stately posture for a moment and walks back into the hall. She hobbles to the kitchen and looks at the dark blue mug on the tabletop. She looks out through the open doors. In the door-way, nothing but the porch, a few sunflowers and the street are in sight, with the house of the new neighbours across from them: a young couple looking for a quiet place to live before the twins arrive.

She snatches the mug from the tabletop and walks to the side of the kitchen, where there is a dark green plastic wastebasket. She tips the mug through the bin's lid and walks to the coffee machine next to the fridge. There is still a small layer of fresh coffee in it. She takes out the jug, rinses off the coffee and puts the empty jug back. From the cupboard, she grabs a tall tin with slight rust marks. Her carefully varnished nails flip the lid up. She grabs the old filter from the coffee maker, inserts a new one and scoops eight scoops of filter coffee into it from the tin. She throws the old filter full of coffee grounds into the bin before opening the crockery cupboard. With pursed lips, she looks inside. She takes out two ornate cups with saucers: beige in colour, with a gold decorative border and tiny pink flowers dancing along the sides. With a satisfied look in her eyes, she sets the cups next to the coffee maker. She fills the water tank and presses the power-button, which turns bright orange.

Mukkie raises his head as she waddles past.

Aagje walks up the porch and looks at Frederick. He sits on the bench with folded hands and closed eyes. The rays of the sun caress his slightly wrinkled face. Despite the substantial scar on his left cheek, he is a handsome figure. Maybe even thanks to that scar, Aagje believes. She looks at his hands, thick with calluses with some small pigment spots. He owes his strong build both to his genes and to his work. Even at the age of 73, he is still out in the wheat field, working every day. The man with the golden hands, that's what they call him here in the village. He is said to have worked as a caretaker in the past, doing all kinds of odd jobs from fixing pipes to laying bricks and unclogging toilets. She plays with her necklace as she stares at him. Her fingers slide to her cheekbones and caress her stretchy skin.

Frederick slowly opens his eyes and looks at her.

She coughs for a moment and smiles. "Milk and two lumps of sugar, right?"

He shows a delicate smile and sits forward, with his elbows resting on his knees. "Actually... I'm trying to cut down on sugar."

"Really?" she shows her best Bambi eyes. "But you look great the way you are!"

His warm, hearty smile rolls across the wooden floorboards. "It's on the doctor's prescription. I have to watch my sugar intake."

"Oh dear, what a pity that is. You love those cakes from Fliens Bakery so much!"

"Well, a small slice once in a while should be okay, Barto assured me. But I'd have to be mindful for the rest of the day."

"Gosh... what a shame."

"It is what it is. But you're sweet as can be, so I don't need sugar for now."

Aag's knees buckle from his boyish laughter. She giggles. "Oh, you sweet talker. I'm going to get your coffee." She turns and darts back into the kitchen. She waves one hand at her face while grabbing the coffee pot with her other hand. The coffee pot shakes in her trembling grip and she quickly grasps the handle with both hands. She carefully pours the cups and sets them on a tray. From the fridge, she grabs the milk and from the cupboard above her head, next to the tin, she grabs the pack of sugar cubes from a plastic bag. She adds a dash of milk to both cups and puts one lump of sugar in the left one. She opens the drawer in front of her and looks at the cutlery. On the far right are the small silver spoons. She puts a spoon in both cups, pushes the drawer closed and walks out with a slight hop in her step.

"There you go, treats with no sweets." She shows him a bold wink and sets the tray with the cups on the small table next to the bench. The cups bounce on their saucers as she tries to move the table across the wooden floorboards.

"Let me do that." Even before the words leave his mouth, he is already standing next to her and takes over the small table from her. He lifts it and gently sets it down in front of the bench so they can easily reach the cups.

"Thank you, kindly." Aagje holds her breath and lowers herself onto the bench.

He comes and sits next to her and stirs his cup. He lifts the spoon, gently taps it on the edge of the cup and lays it down on the saucer. He brings the cup to his mouth and takes a small sip of the hot coffee, while Aagje looks on in admiration. He licks his lips, looks into the cup and takes another small sip. He puts the cup back on his saucer. "That's a good cup, as usual. You always brew it just right."

They sit silently side by side on the bench, looking out over the sunflowers, the deserted road, and the house of the new neighbours. The curtains at the front of the house are opened one by one by a young woman with a noticeable swollen belly. Aagje watches her closely as the woman opens the windows slightly ajar.

"It's been a year already, hasn't it?" remarks Frederick.

Aagje turns her head to him. Their eyes meet.

"Omar." He gives a nod towards the house.

She nods slowly. "If he could see who has moved into his beautiful cottage... He would turn in his grave."

Frederick smiles weakly. "Well, I can understand them coming to seek peace and quiet. They came from Vassen, didn't they?"

She nods wildly. "But that's only what Rosaline told me. Do you know they haven't even introduced themselves yet? Spring has already come and gone. It's not as if they don't walk the streets." She gestures to the front door flinging open, to reinforce her point. "Maybe life's like that in the city, but over here you introduce yourself to the neighbourhood when you move here. You do your rounds, bring something like a pastry and properly introduce your family."

The neighbour from across the street waddles across the driveway to the letterbox. She yanks open the lid and takes out the newspaper. She looks at Frederick and Aagje who are watching her from the porch. She raises her hand in the air as a greeting.

Aagje crinkles her nose.

Frederick raises his hand in the air and nods briefly.

The woman turns around and walks back to the front door.

"It will take some getting used to, with all the different norms and values," Frederick's warm voice sounds, "but they'll figure it out. Once you know about each other, you can depend on one another."

"That's exactly the way it works. A good neighbour is better than a distant friend."

The front door closes behind the woman, who has now disappeared from sight.

"I heard her partner is a painter. Maybe she could give your porch a fresh coat sometime."

Aagje crinkles her nose again. "You always do a wonderful job."

He chuckles. "I'm getting a day older too, Aagje. The ailments of old age are slowly taking over me."

Their gazes meet again. "Yes, our youth is well behind us now, isn't it?"

They stare ahead in silence.

Two pigeons startle at Mrs Bullinger's fat black cat making a half-baked attempt to grab one of them. They flutter their wings wildly as they soar into the air. With a thud, they land on the porch roof.

Frederick coughs for a moment. "They're predicting thunderstorms for this afternoon. You wouldn't say that huh, looking at the sky now."

"Hmm, they tend to get those predictions wrong. But they have to write *something* in the paper..."

He nods in agreement.

"Oh!" she interjects. "That's right!"

He looks at her questioningly.

"Did you see that report about that girl who went missing?"

His fingers slide along his stubble as he nods thoughtfully.

"I saw her!" she continues gleefully.

He raises his eyebrows.

"Last Tuesday. I was walking Mukkie when I bumped into her. She was wearing one of those tight black leather trousers, far too hot for this kind of weather, if you ask me. And a big light blue jumper with long sleeves. It was like she'd walked out of a freezer."

"Have you notified the authorities yet?"

"Sure, they'll be along shortly. But the strangest thing was, right... she was looking for Lethalis."

His face tightens. "Lethalis?" He stares into the distance.

She nods fiercely. "Such a young girl wouldn't have heard of a place like that, would you think? And it's not even open yet. But she insisted she had to go there. I still advised her to go to Bullinger's B&B, but she didn't want to. Very peculiar. I wonder if she has found it and what she was looking for there..."

"Lethalis," he whispers.

"Didn't that friend of yours work there, Lester?"

He turns his head slowly in her direction. "W-what did you say?" he stammered.

"Maybe you could call him, I'm sure he'll be able to tell the police something worthwhile."

Frederick looks at the half-empty coffee cup in front of him. He reaches for it with his fingers and closes his right hand around it. He brings the cup towards his lips, but lowers it again. He turns to Aagje and opens his mouth.

"Mrs Williams?" sounds a high-pitched voice.

Both Aagje and Frederick look at the two people approaching the porch. A middle-aged cop with her copper hair twisted up in a bun and a young cop with short black hair.

The cup falls from Frederick's grasp and clatters on the wooden boards.

"Oh dear," moans Aagje. "Yes, that's me," she responds briefly to the officers, before turning her attention back to Frederick. "Are you all right? Is your arthritis acting up again?"

He rubs his fingers. "I'm afraid so, yes." He picks up the cup and places it back on the saucer. "I won't keep you any longer, Aag." He gets up and walks across the porch.

The officers are now standing in front of the porch steps. They step to the side and greet Frederick as he passes them. He nods at them and crosses the street with large strides, past the opposite neighbours' fence, around the corner and out of sight.

The officer walks up the porch. "You had called us about the missing woman from Vassen?"

13 THE GATEKEEPER

An icy iron grip clamps firmly around my diaphragm. I am face to face with the guise I had seen once before, on the sixth day of my sleepless week. Only this time it does not disappear when I look at it. It appears crystal clear, like the freshly painted window frames in the room. My nostrils flare and catch a wet lime smell.

The guise seems to be getting taller, I realise. I take a step backwards as it rises chillingly slowly from the crouching position in which I found it. Small black flakes swirl from its arms, which are coloured black and dark red, with creases and tears. The two eyes, lying deep in their sockets, are fixed on me.

A loud bang outside lifts my feet off the ground in terror. A flash of lightning pierces through the sky, illuminating the air behind the flapping plastic sheets that hide the outside world from view.

The involuntary leap helps me regain the strength in my legs. I stagger backwards into the corridor and sprint towards the stairs. Before I know it, I slam to the floor with a hard thump. I look up shocked, expecting to see that horrific ghoul right in front of me. I look up into Henry's warm brown eyes. He offers me his hand.

"What's wrong with you?" he asks bewildered.

I gasp and gesture towards the corner of the corridor. I don't need to explain anything because the guise appears right at that moment.

Henry pulls me to my feet and we rush down the stairs together, past the second floor. Our feet thump on the wooden steps. We run down another floor and another and another. My head spins. Our feet come to a halt.

"What the f-" I exclaim, looking down through the stairwell. The stairs, suddenly made of oak, get smaller and smaller and the stairwell gets darker and darker until only darkness can be seen. I look up and see exactly the same thing there. It's a never-ending cilinder of stairs.

"Shit," Henry curses. "Shit, shit, fuck!"

"What's happening? How do we get out?" squeaks my voice.

He looks around us, tightens his grip around my wrist and drags me towards the nearest floor. We run past rooms 301, 311, 323... He busts open the door of room 325 and pulls me inside. He closes the door gently and puts his finger to his lips. He walks past me to the window and looks out. A second flash of light lights up the sky.

"What was that? Or who was that?" I whisper as I walk over to him.

"The gatekeeper," he responds gruffly.

"The gatekeeper?"

He bites his lip. "You need to get out of here, Amber. It's no longer safe here. You have to get out while it's not too late."

I look at him inquiringly. "Can you tell me what's going on? Who is the *gatekeeper*? A gatekeeper of what? What the hell is happening?"

He shakes his head abruptly.

Mass os haa kesh che saaah.

I look at the door and see a shadow creeping under it. I look at Henry, who desperately looks down from the window.

"It's too high," he hisses. He grabs me firmly by my shoulders and squeezes for a moment. "You've got to get out of here, Amber."

"Please tell me who this gatekeeper is!"

He bites his lip. "She's the beginning of the end," he says softly. "She's the one who opens the gate."

"The gate to what?"

"To yo-"

The door blasts open with such force that it bursts from its hinges. I press myself against the wall screaming.

Henry runs towards the guise and crashes into it with all his weight. They plummet to the floor. "NOW!" he shouts in desperation.

My feet kick off from the floor. I sprint out of the room, past them, into the corridor. The windows fly by on my left. I race around the corner, approaching room 399 and blink avidly through the flakes of ash spewing out of the room. My feet stop abruptly and I stand still in the doorway. There is now a desk with a chair, just like in room 299, and an oak wardrobe. There is also a bed with a bedside table next to it. At least, what's left of it all. The carpet is now completely greying with dark discolouration and scorched tufts and completely decayed patches. The blackened wooden parts of the bed have half collapsed and the bedspread has completely perished to white and grey flakes.

My feet drag my body into the room. My eyes glide over every inch of every object. I remember this... I remember this big black stain, the swirling flakes of ash and the pungent smell of burnt flesh. I look down at my mutilated arms.

A third flash lights up the room and reignites the flames. I stand nailed to the floor, watching the flames grow and swirl around me. Not just the flames grow, but everything around me increases in size. The window gets bigger and slides further away from me. The burning bed growls taller. The ceiling rises higher above me.

I look at my arms again and swallow. The skin is flawless. I fidget my little fingers back and forth. Yes, that's right. This is what my arms used to look like, way before. Before all this happened. I look up and see my mother's face, outlined by copper-coloured locks. Her breasts jiggle in her shiny red dress as she violently shakes me. She has that same strange expression on her face: full of anger, full of sadness, full of fear.

"Tell me!" she screams.

My eardrums burst.

"I need to hear you say it!"

I feel her hands squeeze tightly around my wrists. Her nails split the skin underneath and dig deeper and deeper into my flesh. I see it and I feel the pressure, but the pain stays away. "Daddy!" my childish voice moan.

She rattles me severely. "That man is evil," she hisses. "He took her from me and now he wants to take you away."

"Daddy!"

"But no one will take you from me. I will purify you. Yes, I can purify you. Your soul must be cleansed! I can bring you back. I can do that. This time I will succeed."

Blood streams down my tiny wrists and drips onto the carpet. The heat from the flames sears my skin. And with that heat comes the pain: the rending all-consuming pain from which there is no escape. The pain I remember like yesterday, but had managed to repress for so long.

My high-pitched voice screams. And screams. And screams.

A dull thump behind me is followed by the sensation of an arm clenching around my waist. I see a large black fist smashing my mother's face. Her head tilts backwards on impact and her hair goes up in the flames behind her.

I am lifted off the ground and carried out of the room. My little back hits the wall of the corridor. Through my tears, I see the face of the man with the hat, Lester, in front of me with flawless skin and some small pigment spots around his nose and eyes.

His head suddenly tilts and he falls onto his side.

I see the splintered wooden chair in my mother's hands, towering over us in the doorway. My high-pitched voice wails.

Lester scrambles to his feet and pushes my mother back into the room, chair and all.

By now, the flames have overtaken half the room.

I hear footsteps rumbling across the floor.

My mother's face contorts in the midst of the flames as her nails dig into Lester's shoulders.

I am lifted into the air once more and hear a loud scream as soon as I disappear around the corner. I look up into Henry's brown eyes. He pushes room 301 open, rushes into the bathroom and sets me down in the bathtub. He turns on the tap. His fingers feel the jet of water before he lets the water wash over my little arms.

"Stay put like this, I'll get back to you soon, promise," his voice sounds agitated. "Stay put!"

"Henry," I hear my adult voice say softly, as the image of the bathroom fades around me.

I blink. I am suddenly sitting with my back against the wall in room 399. I dazedly look around the blackened room. Everything is back to its normal size, I am no longer a child. I am out of my memories, back in the present moment. At least, that's what I suspect.

"Amber," sounds a voice.

I lift my head. Standing in the doorway is a small middle-aged man with dark blonde hair, small eyebrows and close-set blue eyes. He has a robust jaw and a short chin. Over his jeans, he wears a checkered blouse. I immediately recognise him from the picture on the leaflets: Ethan, the owner of the hotel. The man who kept rolling down the stairs in slow motion, his shoe flying through the air. The man who could well be my father. He looks at me and slowly turns his head towards the corner of the corridor.

"Amber," the voice sounds again.

The man disappears from sight. I slowly get up and follow him. Our feet guide us to the stairwell. I stand at the top step and look down between the familiar oak steps. I count six flights of stairs and then the white stone floor that transitions into the lobby. Between the bars of one of the stairs I see a copper-coloured crown. I squint my eyes in pain.

I should never have been curious about my mother. I should never have come to Lethalis. Now it has all come to life and it won't leave me alone. It tugs at me and suffocates me and sticks to me like industrial glue.

The copper hairs come closer and closer, climbing one step after another.

My name echoes through the stairwell.

My fingers feel limp, my knees weak. She is coming for me, I realise. This time without Lester or Henry to protect me. What Ethan's part in all of this is, I have no idea. The latter still stands motionless in front of me, like a shadow. Maybe he is protecting me, I think groggily.

"Amber!" The woman with copper-coloured hair remains standing on the flat section between the stairs. She looks up at me.

A memory comes back to me. My mother was standing right here on the stairs before Ethan started rolling down them. I've seen his limbs make kinks they shouldn't. I've seen his blood splash against the wall. And now she's going to do the same to me! I shudder.

She slowly comes up the stairs, repeating my name, in a calm voice.

I'm sick of hearing my name like this. I've heard it too many times here. The hotel keeps calling me. Maybe it'd be better if I were pushed down, now that I'm no longer safe here either. Perhaps it'd better to close my eyes forever. I just hope it's all over with a single fall. Just like with Ethan, that time.

Her arms stretch out in front of her and reach for me, but Ethan stands between them. His hands slowly come up and his arm muscles tighten. With all his strength, he pushes her down the steps. Her eyes snap open as she flies backwards through the air.

I gasp for breath.

The back of her head slams against the wall of the stairwell. Along with the blow, dozens of blood splatters sprawl across the wall.

Ethan slowly walks down the stairs in front of me. I follow him closely, as if we are one.

The red of the blood mixes with the copper shade of her hair.

He crouches beside her and looks up at me. He runs both his hands through her hair. His hands soak in the blood. He looks at his palms and presses them against his face. He rubs his hands up and down and then lowers them.

Between the bloodied skin, a row of white teeth protrudes, grinning wide.

14 DANNY

Danny taps his fingers on the steering wheel. He pays half of his attention to the traffic lights in front of him, which still show red. The rest of his attention is directed towards his mobile phone. The blue device sits loosely in a holder next to his steering wheel. He waits in anticipation of the familiar sound of a chime and the icon of an envelope on the screen.

He taps the screen and opens his messages. He looks at the texts he has sent himself:

Mom says you're not home yet. Where are you?

Pick up.

Amber, please, call me back.

I'm worried. Are you OK?

I'm not angry, so please come home.

If this is about yesterday... it's alright. You didn't do anything wrong. You have nothing to worry about. Please just call me back. I love you.

He is startled by a loud honk coming from behind him. His eyes dart to the green lights in front of him. He pushes the accelerator forcefully, ignoring the indignant stares of the pedestrians besieging the pavement to his right.

"Call me," he says aloud as he drives past the bus shelter near Jack's practice. He turns the steering wheel to the right, drives into the street where the practice is and fiercely slams on his brakes in front of the stately old building. "Call me now," he pleads softly. He snatches his phone from its holder, gets out and shoves the door shut.

"Sir, you can't park here," sounds a voice from a little further away.

He casts the person an angry stare. "Call the cops, see if I care." With brisk steps, he moves towards the entrance to the practice. He walks past the squeaking receptionist, up the stairs. Without so much as knock, he steps into Jack's office.

Jack looks up from his screen with wide eyes. He sits behind his dark wooden desk, one hand on his computer mouse and the other out of sight. "D-Danny," he stammers. He frantically clicks the left mouse button a few times. "What are you doing here?"

"Where's Amber?"

A brief silence falls, in which the receptionist's slow footsteps can be heard on the stairs.

"Where is she, Jack!?"

"Sir, you can't just come in here without an appointment!" The woman from the reception finally catches up to him. She gestures at Jack. "I'm sorry, Jack, I was trying to stop him."

Jack exhorts her to silence, without breaking eye contact with Danny. "Go downstairs, Pam, it's fine."

Danny hears her footsteps shuffling across the wooden floor, back down the stairs. "Where is she?" he repeats.

"I have no idea, Danny. She left here at a little past eleven, as usual on a Tuesday. Why, did something happen?"

"She didn't come home and neither of us can get hold of her." He paces back and forth around the office. His heavy footsteps make the wooden floor creak.

Jack removes his other hand from under the desk and intertwines his fingers. "That's odd." He frowns.

"Did something happen? What... what was she like during the session? What-" Danny swallows. "What did you talk about?"

Jack raises his eyebrows for a moment. His upper teeth bite gently on his lower lip. "There's something I wanted to discuss with you, but I was going to..." he glances at his watch, "...call you about that in ten minutes."

"What is it?"

Jack releases his fingers and taps the surface of his desk with his fingertips. "Amber is not adhering to the prescription of her medication."

Danny places his hands on the desk and leans forward. "What do you mean?"

"She's taking more pills than she's supposed to," Jack replies.

"More? How much more? And why!?"

"I wondered that too..." He straightens his back. "She wasn't particularly talkative today and it seemed like something serious had happened." He is silent for a moment. "Do you have any idea about that?"

Danny stands upright and takes a step backwards. His gaze drifts to the window behind Jack. "She had a rough night," he responds gruffly.

"Hmmm." Jack clears his throat. "The side effects of the medication are quite diverse and not harmless. I explained to her that it can cause hallucinations." He tilts his head. "I advised her to stay indoors because of the risks. Maybe... she saw something?" His eyes squeeze to slits.

Danny looks at him for a moment. "She's always had hallucinations, that's what she comes here for, mind you. If it was the man with the hat, she wouldn't have run away from that. She knows how to deal with that by now. I know her. And she always calls me back or at least she texts me. Always! Something must have happened."

"Is it really that unusual that she's not home by now?" asks Jack with a certain tone in his voice.

Danny nods thoughtfully and starts pacing again. "Shit, shit, shit," he says softly.

"I think it's best to go home now," Jack sighs. "Go home and wait for her. If she's not back by tonight..." He gestures with his hands for a moment. "Wait it out quietly and don't worry too much. Maybe she's with a friend and her mobile is out of battery."

"She doesn't have friends," Danny responds bitterly.

"Go home, Danny," Jack says in an imperative tone. "I'll keep my eyes and ears open."

Danny rubs his lips with his fingers. He nods briefly, turns around and leaves the room with Jack's eyes burning at his back. He dashes down the stairs, passes the sputtering receptionist whom he again ignores, and walks back outside. He gets into his car, drives down the pavement and follows the road towards home. His gaze wanders from one side of the street to the other. Searching for her long dark blonde hair, swaying in the wind. Searching for her favourite black leather trousers, which as usual are far too hot for this kind of weather. Searching for one of the oversized jumpers that dominate her wardrobe. What colour would she be wearing today? Black? Dark green? Light blue?

His thoughts stray to last night, when his hands rested on her shoulders. Her cheeks were bright red and almost seemed to glow in the dim light of her bedside lamp. He can still taste her on his lips.

He pushes the gas pedal down further. "Where the hell are you, Amber?"

Danny grabs the three empty coffee cups from the dining table and walks to the kitchen. With his head down, he waits for the coffee maker to do its job. He places the three cups, filled to the brim, back on the table. One for Kyra, one for himself and one for the detective sitting at the dining table with them. It is a man in his sixties with sallow brown hair full of grey streaks and an impressive greying beard. He has introduced himself as Morgan.

Morgan glides his pen across the paper in front of him, from bottom to top. "What does Amber look like? Starting with her hair and eyes."

Danny swallows. "She has long blonde hair."

"Light or dark?"

"Dark. Light brown, nearly."

"How long?"

Danny looks at Kyra, who shrugs her shoulders for a moment. "In terms of inches, I don't know, but it reaches down to her waist."

"That's good," Morgan responds. "And her eye colour?"

"Green. Dark green, with a few amber streaks and flecks."

Morgan looks at Danny for a moment and then calmly writes down the details. "Posture and height?"

"Skinny," responds Kyra.

"She's quite slim and about five feet and eight and a half inch," Danny adds.

Morgan nods. "Any notable characteristics? Tattoos, birthmarks...?"

Kyra and Danny look at each other briefly. "She has scars on her arms," Danny starts. "From about here to here." He gestures to his own arm, from his wrist to halfway up his upper arm. "She had those before we adopted her."

"By self-injury?"

Danny shakes his head. "From what we understand, it's from third-degree burns."

Morgan diligently writes down the details.

"She also has birthmarks," Danny responds. "One on her left shoulder blade, at the bottom, one on her cheek, just below her eye, and another above her collarbone, over here." He points out the spots on his own body.

Kyra grabs her coffee cup from the table and takes a sip of the hot coffee. She glances at Danny from the corner of her eye.

"The more details, the better for us," Morgan responds. "We don't put everything in the missing persons report, but it's important for our own records. Look-a-likes get identified at times and details like these are crucial in that way. Is there anything else you can think of?

Kyra silently looks over the rim of her coffee cup at the agent and shakes her head.

Danny twists his wedding ring around his finger a few times and shakes his head as well.

"Good. Now that we have noted all the details, it is important that we can make an outline of the situation so that we can prioritise this appropriately and conduct a more focused search," he speaks in a low voice that in itself commands authority. "Has she been missing before?"

"No," Danny replies.

"Never been away for long periods without communicating anything? Or failed to turn up for appointments?"

"Yes," Kyra says immediately. "She didn't go to school on Monday."

"That's the day before she went missing, correct?"

She nods. "And she didn't notify us at all."

"She sent me a message," Danny corrects her.

"And was that the only time she stayed away?"

"She's usually at home," Danny replies. "For the past ten months at least. Before that, she lived in a dorm room for her studies."

"Were you in touch with her regularly then?"

Danny nods as Kyra takes another sip.

"Did anything like this ever happen back then?"

Both shake their heads.

"What was she wearing on Tuesday?" he asks as he holds his pen at the ready.

"I was off to work before she woke up, so I didn't see her at all," Danny says. He looks at Kyra.

"I was busy with Reina, so I didn't see her either."

"Is there anyone who would know?"

"Jack," Danny responds immediately. "He should know."

Morgan looks at him questioningly.

"Her psychiatrist," he explains.

"He's the one she had an appointment with?"

Danny nods.

"Good, then I'll inquire about that with him, if you give me his details. We also need a list of the things she had with her. Is that something you can answer on your own or do I need to ask Jack as well?"

"She always has her mp3-player and phone with her," Danny begins. "A pink flip phone. Her mp3 is black, as are her earbuds." His eyebrows dip towards the corners of his eyes. "Her wallet, too. And her shoulder bag, she always has that with her when she goes to therapy, and it's not in her room either. She also carries her medication; the pills Jack prescribes, painkillers and something to treat migraines."

Morgan writes along diligently. "Do you have the exact names of the medication?"

"We have some boxes lying around." Danny nods to Kyra, who gets up and walks out of the room. "She had her bus strip card with her too," Danny continues. He heaves a sigh.

"Jewellery?"

Danny shakes his head. "She doesn't like them."

Kyra re-enters the room and places the medicine boxes on the table.

"OK, this is very helpful," Morgan admits. "We're going to find out where she was last seen, when and by whom. I will ask Jack about that as well and we will request CCTV footage from the street, if possible. My understanding was that you had already called the bus company and that no one has seen her on her usual route, is that right?"

Danny nods repeatedly. "She has been taking the same bus at the same time three times a week for months. The bus driver recognises her every time she gets on. She was seen on the way out, though, before she arrived at Jack's."

"And you had also called hospitals in the area and she hasn't been found there as yet either, correct?"

"Yes," Danny replies with a worried look.

"Are there any other places, where she frequented, where she might have gone?"

Danny shakes his head. "We called Mrs Katen, our contact at her school, but she couldn't tell us anything either. She's mostly at home, really..."

"And what does she do when she's at home?"

"She mostly sits at her desk, doing homework and drawing."

"Can I see her room?"

"Of course." Danny shoves his cold coffee aside and gets up. He and Morgan leave the living room and walk down the hall to the door leading to the annex. He opens the door and leads Morgan down the corridor, passing his own office door.

Morgan casts a glance at the door and follows Danny, through the back door and into Amber's room. He looks around and looks at the most noticeable things first. The unmade bed. The cluttered desk with a computer screen, keyboard and mouse and a small calendar. He looks at the calendar and flips through several pages. It has only the appointments for therapy and school on it. His attention is drawn to the pinboard on the wall to the right of the desk, which is cluttered with drawings. He studies them. "How would you describe her state of mind, the last time you saw her?" he asks slowly.

Danny thinks for a moment. "Quite alright. A bit stressed maybe and-" He stops talking abruptly.

Morgan turns and looks at him sternly. "And?"

"...maybe a bit confused," he replies hesitantly.

"Confused? How so?"

Danny is silent and bites his lip.

"As difficult as it may be, it is important that you are honest and don't hold out on anything. That could get in the way of the investigation. Finding her is the top priority right now."

"She..." he sighs, "tried to kiss me."

Morgan raises his eyebrows for a moment. "Kiss?"

Danny nods slowly. "I pushed her away. I think... she's a bit confused and maybe expressed her feelings differently." He sighs deeply.

"When did this happen?"

"Monday night."

Morgan nods slowly and turns his attention back to the pinboard. With his thumb and index finger he pulls aside each drawing one by one to look at the ones hidden behind them. He stares silently at the back few ones. "Is she depressed?"

Danny comes up beside him and also looks at the drawings, which had been hidden in plain sight all this time. His breath falters. "N-not that I know of."

Morgan casts a glance at him and then turns to the desk. "Can this be turned on?" He points to the computer under the desk.

Danny kneels and presses the power button. He turns on the monitor, which lights up brightly a moment later. He bends over the keyboard and enters the password, while Morgan watches him. He steps away from the keyboard and gestures at the screen.

Morgan sits down on the desk chair and drags the mouse and keyboard towards him. He opens the internet browser and is greeted by a cheerfully designed Hyves page. He scrolls down. His eyes glide over the screen. Then he opens the messages and reads the few that are there. "Hm. Are there any other social media websites she uses?"

"She has a... hmmm, MySpace, I think it's called," Danny responds. He places his hand on the back of his neck as he watches Morgan accessing the bookmarks and opening Amber's MySpace page. The page is mainly black in colour with pink accents, like skulls.

Morgan looks back for a moment. His eyes meet Danny's. Together they comb through Amber's friends list, which is considerably larger than the one on her Hyves page. They look at her playlist and photos, which includes some of her drawings and pictures of herself. Morgan raises his eyebrows. "Were you aware of these pictures?" He looks at Danny and watches his reaction closely.

Danny shakes his head. "No, I... I've never seen these before."

Morgan accesses the bookmarks once more and scours the saved websites. Music. Drawing styles. Games. Studies. His eye catches a tucked-away folder. He clicks on it and sees a single bookmark. "VampireFreaks?" he responds aloud. He clicks on it and the website opens.

Danny leans forward, closer to the screen. His finger points to a number at the top of the page. "What's that?"

"Looks like... a rating," Morgan responds.

"Of what?"

"Of Amber."

Danny frowns deeply.

"You didn't know she was on this website?"

Danny slowly shakes his head and kneels down beside the desk chair, his gaze still fixed on the screen. His one hand covers his mouth as Morgan opens the photo section. The gold ring on his finger feels cold on his lips. His hand slides upwards, over his eyes and against his forehead. He averts his gaze, gets up and walks away from the desk.

"You weren't aware of these pictures either, I suppose?" asks Morgan in a soft tone.

Danny lowers himself onto the edge of the bed and rests his elbows on his knees. He drops his head. "Why..." He closes his mouth, opens it and closes it again. He rubs his face for a moment and then grasps his wedding ring with two fingers. He twists the ring back and forth and slides it up and down.

"Unfortunately, we see this quite often," Morgan responds. "Even with much younger women than Amber. Thirteen-, fourteen-year-olds, even. And they all manage to keep it a secret from..." His voice fades away. "Hmm, Danny?"

Danny raises his head.

"There are some worrying writings on here," Morgan begins. "I'll have to discuss some things, but I believe her disappearance is urgent."

Danny comes up beside him and reads the most recent writing on Amber's page. A hoarse sound slips out of his mouth.

Morgan looks at him gravely. "I believe she is a danger to herself."

15 HOT LEATHER

Morgan steps on the gas. Next to him sits a person of about fifty years old with shoulder-length brown hair. On their nose is a pair of striking red glasses with oval lenses.

A cheerful ringtone sounds from the phone sitting in a holder on the dashboard.

"Can you answer that?" Morgan asks with a quick nod.

"This is Robin," says the person, who has wriggled the phone out of its holder and presses it against their ear, before adding "it's Danny," in a quieter tone.

The tyres come to a squeaking halt at the traffic light at the busiest intersection in Vassen-South. Morgan's eyes track the vehicles cruising in front of his car.

"He's asking about the missing persons report."

"Tell him we are on our way to Jack and = we will then post the report on our website. It sometimes takes a while for the media to pick this up, but we will also submit it to the newspaper. Hopefully before it goes to print. It will be on the doorstep tomorrow morning."

Robin repeats Morgan's words on the phone and listens intently to the voice on the other end of the line. "Ahem... why we're only now going to see Jack?"

"Gimme." He gestures with his hand and takes over the phone. "It's Morgan."

"That's not hands-free," she whispers to him.

He ignores the remark and deftly turns a corner with one hand on the wheel. "I understand that Danny, but you have got to understand that we need to follow procedures." He shakes his head for a moment. "I promise you we're doing everything we can to find Amber as soon as possible. Trust me, Danny." He listens and nods briefly. "I'll call you as soon as we know more. Make sure you and your wife get some rest." He steers around another corner. "That will be fine. I'll talk to you soon, Danny. Yes. Yes. No, no problem. Okay. I'll call you, Danny. See you soon." He puts the phone back in its holder and pushes down on the throttle. He fiercely overtakes another car and swerves around another corner.

"Mind the coffee, will you?" she grumbles.

He remains silent.

"I get that this one is urgent, but why the extra rush? That's not like you."

"That psychiatrist..." he begins.

"What about him?"

He frowns deeply. "You brought her medication, didn't you?"

She snatches a bag from the back seat, opens it and takes out the medicine box. "Bromazepam... are you familiar with that?"

He shakes his head. "Only from what I've read on the leaflet."

She carefully opens the box and pulls out two empty strips. Her fingers grope for the leaflet, which is stuffed down the bottom of the box. Her finger glides over the text on the paper as her eyes move along. "If you stop taking this medicine..."

The traffic light turns green and he accelerates the car quickly.

"Always consult your doctor... hm, hm. If physical dependence has developed, sudden termination of treatment will be accompanied by withdrawal symptoms... How long has Amber been taking this medication?"

"Since Jack prescribed it, about ten months back," he responds, not slowing down for the approaching threshold. The coffee sloshes over the rim of the cups sitting in their holders.

She looks at the cups with a slanted eye, before studying the leaflet again. "Loss of sense of reality, whereby previously familiar surroundings seem unreal... alienation from oneself, increased auditory acuity, perceptions of things that are not there."

He casts a glance aside. "Not very promising, is it?" He retrieves a cigarette case from his breast pocket and flicks a cigarette into his mouth. He lights it with one hand and takes a deep drag.

She straightens the paper with a sigh, then rolls down the car window at her side. "No, definitely not. But these things happen very rarely, probably. They have to write it in here to cover their own asses, in case of an incident, just so that they won't get sued. And we can't be sure if Amber has stopped taking her medication, either. She might still be taking her pills on time and in the right dosage. She had been given a new box..."she opens a notepad and flips through the full pages scribbled on it, "on Wednesday the 16th of July, last week."

"She may have enough pills for another week, but she wasn't taking them properly. Danny said so too," he responds. "We have no idea what state she is in now. And the withdrawal symptoms aren't even the most worrying to me."

She looks at the leaflet again. "Possible side effects...repeated use over several weeks may lessen the effect...daytime sleepiness, confusion...oppositional reactions such as delusions, nightmares, fits of rage...physical and psychological dependence..." She bites her lip. "...headaches, dizziness... memory loss during the period after ingestion...?" She falls silent.

He steers the car around another corner and slows down. He rolls down his own window, takes another deep breath and blows the cigarette smoke out the window.

"She's in treatment for amnesia, right?" she asks.

He nods. "Among other things. She's being treated for fears and delusions, but where they stem from, that's exactly what this drug suppresses. So why is..." he grunts, "Jack Reed prescribing *this* particular drug?"

She folds the leaflet with a deep frown on her forehead. "What are you trying to say?" She puts it back in the box and stuffs the medication back in the bag.

"Remember that case Harris had handled in "92? That mother, with bipolar disorder and delusions, who was deliberately given the wrong medication by her psychiatrist?" he asks with a telling look.

She nods slowly. "She had died, right? But that was unconnected to that medication, they declared. She had been burnt alive..."

"It was, but... do you remember the psychiatrist's name?"

"Reed, wasn't it?"

He casts a meaningful glance at her, with one hand on the wheel. He puffs on his cigarette.

She stares at him silently and starts shaking her head. "You can't be serious...*Jack*? Jack Reed?"

He nods slowly. "It's him. He changed his name fourteen years ago, his surname, that is."

"Dammit!" She angrily slams a fist against the dashboard. Coffee sloshes over the edge of the cups and smears the dashboard. "What have you said to Danny?"

"Nothing at all yet."

"Hnnng... if he finds out about this..."

"Precisely. All we can do now is catch the bastard," he says with a fiery look in his eyes. He releases the throttle.

"And make sure he never opens another practice again," she adds. "What he did to those women... Are you absolutely certain?"

"There's only one way to find out." He extinguishes the fag in the cigarette holder, which now has a small layer of coffee in it.

The car comes to a stop in front of a path leading to a medium-sized gloomy-looking building. They both get out. He hoists up his trousers, looking at the second-floor window. From down here, he only sees a ceiling with wooden beams.

A cool summer breeze rolls over them as they walk to the front door. He pushes against the door and they step into a dusty hallway. The floor is lined with various shades of brown mosaic. The sole illumination stems from the sunlight pouring in through the two front windows.

"Good day, how may I help you?" sounds a rasping voice to their left.

Morgan casts a glance at the counter next to the window. Behind it is an old female with curly white hair and small glasses. He promptly looks in front of him at the oak staircase leading upstairs and struts towards it. The steps creak under his weight.

"Excuse me, hold on! You can't just go up there if you don't have an appointment!" the woman's chirpy voice rasps.

Robin waveringly looks at her and then at her partner's back. She hurries after him up the stairs.

Morgan enters the first floor and walks towards the very first door. He pushes down the latch and watches the door open. He stares into a room that is mostly empty, aside from some stacked boxes.

Robin opens the next door, where there are mostly lots of storage boxes. She walks in and runs her hand over the box, while Morgan already walks to the stairs towards the top floor. She opens the box at the top and glances at the contents. "Morgan," she hisses. She pushes her glasses, which are sliding down, further up her nose.

Morgan stands still. His foot hovers above the bottom steps. He withdraws his foot and walks towards Robin, who is holding a DVD in the air. He reads the title as the steps of the bottom staircase creak under the weight of the little old lady, struggling up the stairs. He puts his hand into the box and grabs a stack of DVDs. They all have the same title: Amber.

Robin covers her mouth.

"Confiscate everything." Morgan turns abruptly. He rushes up the stairs to the second floor, with the stack of DVDs still clutched in his hand.

The old lady has almost reached the first floor when Robin is already behind Morgan, aggressively pushing open the only door on the second floor.

The DVDs clatter to the ground. For a moment they both stand rooted to it. Then Morgan starts shouting. Jack jumps up from the brown leather sofa and is immediately pushed to the ground by Morgan, who gets on top of him and pounds on him.

Robin quickly takes off her jacket, knocking over the camera pointed at the sofa in the process. The camera slams shut against the floor. She throws her jacket over the disrobed woman lying on the leather sofa with her eyes closed.

Morgan rubs his discoloured knuckles.

Robin sets a cup of hot coffee in front of him on his desk. "We watched some of the DVDs..." she begins in a soft voice, "and it's all what you think."

He nods briefly.

"Should we inform her parents?"

He slowly rises to his feet. "Not yet. Let's find her first. The rest will have to wait. Unless you want murder on your conscience, because Danny is not one to remain calm." He casts her a glance.

She slowly shakes her head. "They are searching near her GPS location. It was last picked up in Kobbel. An employee at the local supermarket presumably saw her. They are checking the cameras now."

"And the dogs?"

She shakes her head. "Nothing yet."

"At least that's positive... sort of."

She hesitantly stays by his side.

"What is it?"

"Jack's lawyer is here."

He heaves a deep sigh. "I have other priorities right now."

She gazes at him inquiringly. "Are you sure? If-"

"Yes," he replies briskly. "This woman's safety comes before this..." He clenches his fists and takes a deep breath. "Amber comes first. That's final."

"Okay, I'll pass it on to Jerry, so that he can pursue it further."

He nods. "I'm going to have another smoke and then we'll drive down to that supermarket."

She nods and walks away.

He strokes over his mouth. He snatches his jacket from the back of his office chair, puts his hand into his right pocket and takes out a pack of cigarettes. He wedges a cigarette between his lips as he walks down the corridor. He takes out his lighter and pushes open the door to the car park at the back of the building. His stomach expands as he takes a deep breath of fresh air, before lighting the cigarette and blowing out a meagre cloud of smoke.

The tip of the cigarette smoulders under each puff he takes. His gaze is fixated on the sky. Every now and then he flicks some ash, which blows along in the feeble wind and spreads across the car park until it cannot be seen with the naked eye. He strokes his left hand through his thinning hair, deep in thought. He startles when the shortened cigarette butt sears his finger. "Damn." He dumps the stub and cools his finger with his tongue.

The door behind him opens and Robin walks into the car park. "Jerry's taking the case. But you have to be there tomorrow, at ten o'clock."

"We'll see about that when tomorrow comes. Let's go." He crosses the car park to the white Volkswagen, printed with blue and red stripes. "This is going to be a long evening," he says before opening the door and getting behind the wheel.

"I have nothing better to do on my Friday nights anyway," she replies nonchalantly as she gets in on the passenger side.

"What's the address?" he asks.

She silently types in the supermarket's address on the sat-nav and buckles her seatbelt.

"Here's to hope, I guess," he says. His foot steps firmly on the throttle.

It is dusk when Morgan and Robin arrive at the supermarket in Kobbel. They get out and Morgan raises his hand to the young female officer waiting for them in front of the sliding glass doors.

"We have her on camera," the officer says as she walks towards them. "Both inside the supermarket and outside by the bus shelter." She points to the bus shelter on the side of the road. "But it's only partly in view. You can see Amber's shoes as she walks back and forth, they disappear and reappear, but we have absolutely no idea which bus she took. That's completely out of view."

"Do you know what time she came out?"

"She came out at three past four, according to the screen. But that doesn't seem to be entirely accurate."

Morgan walks towards the bus shelter with Robin and the police-woman in his wake. His finger slides along the schedule hanging on the inside. "Bus 54 goes at eight past four... Bus 55 goes at twelve past four. Both in the opposite direction to each other." He looks around. "Call the company and ask if the drivers on duty have seen her."

The policewoman nods and grabs her mobile from her pocket. She separates herself from them.

Morgan strokes through his hair. "For a moment I hoped it was going to be easy."

Robin purses her lips. "It never is."

He takes out his packet of cigarettes and opens it. He looks down at it with a disappointed frown. "Last one," he growls. He shoves the cigarette between his lips and lights it. He takes a deep breath and quietly exhales his breath. A playful cloud of smoke dissolves into the sultry air.

"I'm going to talk to the shopkeeper," Robin says briskly as she starts walking away.

He chuckles. "You'll get used to it one day."

She glances back. "To that smell? Never."

He takes another deep drag and blows the smoke towards the ground. His head turns to the schedule. He stares intently at it as he smokes his cigarette. He takes his last puff and licks his lips as he drops the fag on the floor. His shoe steps on it and moves back and forth. "Where are you?" he whispers with squinting eyes. Then he marches towards the supermarket. The glass doors slide aside and he steps inside. Robin is standing at the checkout counter talking to a lanky young man. Morgan walks towards them and puts his empty cigarette case on the counter. "Is it him?" he asks with a sidelong glance at Robin.

She shakes her head. "His colleague Rosie was working at the time. He's tried to call her a few times, but she doesn't answer."

"She's always like that," the boy begins. "Even when she does have a shift."

"What's your name?"

"Farid."

"Morgan," he responds, holding out his hand.

The boy grabs his hand and shakes it.

"You weren't on duty on Tuesday, I take it?"

Farid shakes his head. "Never on Tuesdays, that's my study day. Apart from holidays, that is..."

"What do you study?"

"Biomedical sciences," he responds with a glint in his eyes. "I want to be a forensic scientist."

Morgan smiles. "How many years do you have left?"

"I start my final year in September."

"Then I hope to run into you again during my career. Preferably before I retire."

Farid smiles broadly. "I hope so too!"

Morgan slides the empty cigarette case forward. "Do you have one for me?"

Farid looks at the box and grabs the same brand and size box from the shelf behind him.

"Make it a bigger one," Morgan says. He puts a tenner on the counter. "I expect I'm going to need it."

"In this way, yes," Robin snarls.

Farid puts the box on the counter, grabs the tenner and taps the till. He shoves the note in and takes out some change, which he then hands to Morgan.

Morgan puts it in his pocket without looking at it and opens the box. He takes out a cigarette and tucks it behind his ear. "Can we see the footage from Tuesday?"

Farid nods. "You can walk around the counter over there." He gestures to the path to the right of the counter.

Morgan and Robin follow his lead and come to stand next to him with their gaze fixed on the monitor showing the camera images. They look up when the sliding doors open and the policewoman steps in.

"So?" urges Morgan.

The woman shakes her head. "None of the drivers on duty on that day remember her. I sent them the link to the search report on the website, hoping they would recognise her, but unfortunately it wasn't that easy."

Morgan sighs. "It never is." He turns to Robin. "Notify Danny and his search team, so they can scour this neighbourhood. And ask Ben to bring three dogs. Hopefully they'll pick something up."

Robin nods and walks out with her phone to her ear.

The woman remains standing by the sliding doors and watches Morgan bend over the screen, which is in front of Farid, intently studying the camera footage.

"Can you replay it?" he growls.

Farid nods and rewinds the image.

Morgan watches the footage again. And again. And again.

The woman, meanwhile, walks further into the supermarket with her phone pressed to her ear.

Robin re-enters the shop. "They are coming." She walks to the counter. "All of them," she adds.

Morgan casts a glance outside. "We have maybe two hours of daylight left, so let's hope they get here soon."

Robin leans over the counter and looks at the screen, which has paused at a moment when Amber's shoes can be seen in the bus shelter. She points to the image. "You can't tell if a bus is coming, can you?"

Farid and Morgan shake their heads.

"Then who says she went by bus?"

Morgan raises his eyebrows. "Can you call your colleague again?" he asks Farid. "Rosie, was her name?"

He nods and quickly grabs his phone from his pocket. He dials the top number on his list of recent calls and waits patiently. A moment later, he lowers his arm again and shakes his head defeated.

Morgan and Robin snort at the same time.

"Ah!" the policewoman exclaims. "There was another driver on Tuesday!"

Morgan looks up and frowns. "What do you mean another one?"

"Apparently the driver, who normally drives that route, wasn't present. But he didn't want to get in trouble with his boss, so he lied at first. He just called me back."

"Why was he absent?" asks Morgan.

She bites her lip. "He had a relapse."

Morgan nods slowly. "And the stand-in driver? Do we have his details?"

Her phone hums a happy tune. She looks at the screen and raises it in the air with a proud expression on her face.

"What do you mean, it's not in there?" responds Morgan irritably. He looks briefly at Robin, who is standing next to him, and rolls his eyes. "It's urgent for a reason." His fingers clench around his phone so tightly that they are turning pale. "No, that's why it should have been in the paper today." He listens and shakes his head several times. "Get it done." He lowers his hand, ends the call and puts the phone back in his pocket. "Unbelievable..." He settles his heels against his desk, rolling backwards with desk chair and all.

"At least we know which bus she took," Robin responds, bringing the desk chair to a stop.

"Do we also know where she got off?"

She shakes her head. "But at least not before Redwing Road. He looked back then, apparently, and had seen her sitting there. But otherwise he hardly remembers that ride. At the terminus, in any case, she was no longer there."

"Where is it?"

"At the Lindeleuve."

He frowns. "Why did Amber go that way, of all places?"

She stares ahead. "Maybe she didn't really have a plan," she begins. "Maybe she just got in and didn't care where she ended up. You can't rule that out after seeing that last tape."

He growls. "Let's hope someone saw something."

She nods in agreement, before looking up and then giving another meaningful nod. "Jerry."

He looks over and sighs. "Get ready to head out that way in a bit." He gets up from his chair and walks towards the man who comes running in a three-piece suit. "Oh, and call Danny! But not about the paper!"

Later that afternoon, Morgan and Robin stand with their hands in their pockets on the Redwing Road in Rodsberg, a village about ten kilometres from Midsberg.

Further along, Danny and an older man walk side-by-side. They go by the doors one by one. On the other side of the street a man and a woman do the same.

Morgan studies them. "Did you also notice that the mother is never present?"

"Kyra?"

He nods slowly as he lights another fag.

"She must be busy with the daughter."

"But still." He blows his smoke aside, away from Robin. "I haven't heard a word from her, not even through Danny. And he calls almost every hour when he's not with us."

They look at the three cops walking by with sniffer dogs.

"Come," he says to Robin as they follow them. "It's still a long way to Lindeleuve."

A few hours later, the sun disappears behind the horizon. Several people from Danny's search team have already gone home. They have completely scoured the Redwing Road and the surrounding area. Then the Vale Street and the Wallowing Shore, and a radius of a few kilometres around it. Without a single trace. Without a single clue. Darkness descends gloomily over the streets.

The birds whistle loudly as Robin and Morgan, with thick bags under their eyes and a cup of coffee in their hands, get into the car in the car park behind the office.

Robin silently enters the address of Birch Avenue, which is in Padsberg, just two kilometres from Chestnut Avenue in Midsberg.

Morgan quietly turns on the radio as they drive up the near-empty motorway at a leisurely pace.

"If only it was this quiet on a Monday," Morgan says languidly.

Robin slowly pats the red frame of her glasses, lost in thought.

They have been on the road for a little over an hour when Robin's phone rings. "Robin Smith," she says with the phone to her ear. She listens intently.

Morgan casts a questioning glance at her.

"Okay, we're on our way," she replies after a while. She disconnects the call.

He casts another glance at her and sees the corners of her mouth curl up. "Yes!?"

"Most likely," she responds glowering. "We have a tip-off."

"Where?"

"A hotel in Midsberg. Kenna and Jake are at the scene and have found her belongings. A pink flip phone and a shoulder bag matching the description."

"What about Amber?"

"They're still looking for her."

They are both silent with straight faces.

"Send a team after them," he says demurely.

"What about Danny?"

He shakes his head cautiously. "We don't know what state we're going to find her in."

16 THE STAIRWELL

Loud footsteps echo through the stairwell. There is shouting.

I see a young man with short black hair standing on the stairs, just a few paces away from me. He holds up a gun with his arms outstretched, which is staring at me with its single black eye.

I look straight ahead, crouching down. My eyes shift from left to right, but Ethan is nowhere to be seen, because Ethan has never been here. I look down at the strange woman lying on the floor in front of me, the back of her bleeding head against the wall. My cheeks feel hot. I stroke the outside of my wrist along my face and see that my hands are stained red. *My* hands.

The young man shouts again.

I cannot hear what he is saying - it is as if he is three metres underwater, as muffled as his voice sounds. I slowly stand up and I can tell he doesn't like that very much, but my body does what it does.

The man's arms tremble.

I take a step forward.

The loud bang that follows surpasses any other sound I have ever heard in my life. The echo in the stairwell makes the sound all the more insistent. My hands push hard. Not against my ears, but against my stomach. I stagger backwards and blink. Stumbling over my own feet, I fall to the ground, right next to the woman.

He kneels down beside her, placing one hand on her wrist and pointing the other in my direction, with that gazing gun clutched between his fingers. A mobile is wedged between his ear and shoulder. His mouth moves wildly and more of those unintelligible words resound.

I tilt my head.

The young man's mobile clatters to the ground as his whole face twists to a shocked grimace. The hairs on his arms rise up straight. His wide-open eyes twitch in their sockets.

I stare at him with a wide, joyless grin. My snow-white bared teeth starkly contrast with the blood of the unconscious woman on my face.

It is not long before a whole platoon of people swarm through the stairwell, like a plague of flies. Shoes and boots rumble over the stone steps without so much as a creak. People in uniforms scour all corridors and rooms of the building. The box of leaflets is carried outside. There is talk of water damage and a collapsed ceiling, and of an old burn mark in room 399. Now the woman with copper-coloured hair is also being lifted out on a stretcher. They call her Kenna. Flashes of lightning shoot through the air and illuminate her face.

I watch everything from behind the window in the stuffy car, while an older man with grey-brown hair and a full greyish beard asks me questions, in the presence of a woman wearing striking red glasses with oval lenses, who sits silently in the passenger seat.

"Do you hear me, Amber?" the male voice asks.

I look back at him. "What are they going to do with the furniture?"

Both persons in front of me frown.

"They're a bit old-fashioned, but they belong to Lethalis," I explain calmly. "Just ask Toke."

"Who is Toke?" asks the woman with glasses.

"She lives here." I smile. "Lethalis is our home."

The two people slowly turn their heads towards each other and stare at one another.

My gaze is drawn to the small panel hanging from the front window. "Why is that woman covered in blood?"

The persons also look at the image and then back at me.

"We were hoping you could tell us, Amber," the bearded man says. "Why is... she... covered in blood? Why did she attack one of our officers?"

"She didn't," I answer briskly. "That was Ethan."

"Ethan? Who is that?" The man casts a glance at the building. "Does he live here too?"

I nod slowly. "But you should stay away from him, you know. That man is evil."

The uniforms swarm like ants and buzz like bees. In and out of the stairwell. They arc around me as I stand at the foot of the stairs, looking up, with my hands gagged behind my back and my waist tightly wrapped in bandages.

"Can you tell me what happened here, Amber?" the bearded man asks.

"Stop that," I respond brightly.

A silence falls. The buzzing and swarming stops.

"Stop what?"

"Saying my name," I respond, still looking up. I put my foot on the first step and remain standing. "It doesn't creak anymore," I say to the woman with glasses.

"What doesn't?" She looks at me non-comprehendingly as she holds a notepad at the ready.

"The stairs. It doesn't creak anymore."

The woman writes something down.

I walk up the stairs and remain standing on the second floor. "What do you think of the carpet?" I ask the bearded man.

"What am I supposed to think?" he responds, speaking the words slowly.

I giggle. "It's beautiful, isn't it? And it belongs to Lethalis. They mustn't rip it out. If you do, then..." I shake my head. "Toke also thinks they should leave it as it is. They should keep it like this, don't you think?" I look at the man again. "Did you know it's fire-retardant? Fire-retardant carpet... It's even more special than I first thought. This is why I came back to this place."

"Because of the carpet?"

I nod. "The lilac lily carpet."

The woman grabs her phone from her pocket and holds it to her ear as she turns away from us towards the stairwell. She talks softly into the phone and hangs up not much later.

"It's completely washed clean by the water," I say.

"It looks nice," the man responds in a heavy tone.

The woman gives him a small poke between his ribs and whispers something in his ear. She covers her mouth with her hand, but I don't need to read her lips. I can hear very well what she is whispering.

The two construction workers and the superintendent, who had made the final touches here before construction paused because of the holiday period, have come forward. They will report to the police station tomorrow. But that is not what's important. What is important is the person currently on his way to Lethalis.

Danny slowly comes walking up the stairs.

I study his straightened face, without an angry frown, just tears glistening in his grey eyes. I breathe a sigh of relief and attempt to approach him, but am stopped by the bearded man, who gently grabs my arm.

"Amber..." Danny utters.

I close my eyes for a moment at the sound of my name, reassured by Danny's smooth voice.

His eyes slide from left to right and top to bottom. He bites his lip hard. "Honey... what... what did you do?"

I incline my head and out of the corner of my eye I see the woman with the glasses shaking her head. "What do you mean?" I ask.

Danny's Adam's apple moves up and down as he swallows. "What happened?"

"There was leakage," I begin, "but I managed to stop that, because of what you taught me." I look at him expectantly, but the desired pat on the head fails to materialise. I take a step forward and am stopped again. "Room 399," I say loudly. "They took the box, but I found them, Danny. I finally found them."

Danny raises his frowning eyebrows. "Who did you find?"

"Mom and Dad."

It remains silent.

"They were here too," I continue. "Maybe you can still see them, but then we have to go up. And Henry, Henry's here too. But he might be in the garden now..." I bite my lip softly and try to successfully read Danny's face, but I can't make sense of it.

"Who..." Danny swallows again. He casts a glance at the man and woman on my either side. "Who's Henry?"

"The gardener. He works here, like Lester." I look at him expectantly.

"Who is he?"

"Him you know."

Danny looks at me silently with a questioning look in his eyes.

"The man with the hat," I say cheerfully. I smile broadly. The woman's dried blood breaks from my skin and the flakes swirl down.

Danny widens his eyes and takes a step backwards. "Amber, I-love..." he stammers. "I... I don't want to hear about it. I don't want to hear about any of your delusions right now." He pronounces that particular word in a harsh tone, as if it were something dirty and scandalous.

The woman with the glasses starts to sputter.

"Look at what you did to that poor woman!" Danny gestures furiously at the wall of the stairwell.

I stare silently at the blood sticking to the wall. "I didn't do that," my monotone voice says. I stare at him sternly without blinking and open my mouth one last time. "That was Ethan."

Danny's mouth falls open slightly. Deep furrows form on his forehead.

The bearded man steps forward and grabs him by the arm. "There are things you don't know about that you should know about," he hisses. "They are..." he is silent for a moment and looks at him seriously, "...extenuating circumstances."

"What do I need to know?"

"It's about Jack." The man sighs deeply. "You'd best sit down for this. And..." he turns to me, "take her to the car."

The woman with the glasses gently grabs my elbow and guides me down the stairwell. I take small, slow steps, descending deeper and deeper down the stone steps, and look up at Danny. Words creep into my ear canal. When I prick up my ears, I can even overhear half-sentences.

THUD!

Danny's fist bangs heavily into the freshly plastered wall beside him, spraying it with splashes of blood, bright red and glistening.

17 IN BETWEEN WHITE WALLS

There is a soft tapping against the window.

I slowly open my eyes. I shield my eyes from the bright morning light. My gaze moves to the window. From behind the window, I'm being stared at by two small black beady eyes. Between the beady eyes, an orange beak taps against the window once more.

With a soft groan, I get up.

The blackbird flies up from the window frame.

I walk towards the window. My fingers slide along the thick black bars that front the window, forming a huge tic-tac-toe field. My gaze drifts over the car park outside, covered with freshly fallen snow. My nails scratch at the scars from the old third-degree burns on my arms, which now itch even in the cold. The few ointments they are allowed to prescribe here do a lousy job.

My legs lead me to the bed again. I sit down and pull my knees up to my chin.

I haven't counted the days, but I know roughly how many months have passed since I went to Lethalis and apparently left a police-woman named Kenna with serious brain damage by pushing her down the stairs. I listened to the stories from my new therapist, a woman who calls herself Lain, and overheard the words of the various policemen who came to visit. Some seemed angry, others seemed defeated. The young man with his short black hair seemed especially... afraid. But there was also an older man with grey-brown hair and a big beard, who remained curiously calm and asked thoughtful questions with a deep voice. I had seen him before, in the car outside and in the stairwell, in the company of a woman wearing red glasses. They had talked to Danny and what they said, I didn't like much.

Those first few weeks here had been noisy, but now it is mostly... quiet.

I bite my thumbnail and get up from the bed again. I pace between the white walls of the tiny room, which is about half the size of the hotel rooms in Lethalis. I wonder if the construction has resumed yet, now that it is the middle of winter and the blood on the wall has probably long since been cleaned up. I wonder if there are still signs of the water damage and if they have been able to repair the ceiling of room 299 after the leakage. I would love to see it in its restored glory, without the shadows of the past. But that won't happen. For now, after all, I am trapped here, between walls as white as those in Lethalis.

My fate is now, by court order, in the hands of Lain and in the hands of the actual owner of Lethalis, Barbara Bunning, who saw the name of her future gem dragged through the mud for months on end on television and in the newspapers. Her decision will determine how long I have to stay here. If only Toke had been the real owner, I sigh. She would have forgiven me. If only she had been real at all...

There is a knock on the door.

I look at the face in front of the little window in the door. It is one of the caretakers. That's what they call themselves here. A caretaker.

A rattling sound is heard and the door swings open.

"Amber, it's time for your appointment," says the man whose name-plate reads Manny.

I walk out of the room and go ahead of the man, down the corridor. We turn a corner, go through a door, down a flight of stairs, through another door and down another corridor. Halfway down the corridor, I stop with my ears pricked. I look into the television room. On the small square screen I see a fat man in workwear - he is one of the construction workers who made some final touches at Lethalis during my stay.

"I had thought it was strange," I hear him say. "Things would just be in other places than we put them, like a bucket and our hoover—we call 'r a banshee, cause that thing screeches, so loud. We looked for it for hours and finally found it, but it was in a whole other room than we left it. But you can't expect some lunatic to be in there, you know. You're just doing your job and you're focused on nothing but that. Yet there's some crazy girl slithering about, like a cockroach hiding in the cracks. It might as well have been one of us, you know. It's a good thing we didn't bump into her, really, because we might not have been able to recount it. I still have sleepless nights sometimes, because of that."

I roll my eyes. Some people try to cash in on just about anything, to the most pathetic extent, even this many months after the fact.

I follow with the caretaker and stop in front of one of the doors just a moment later. I look at the sign next to the door. *Visiting Room* it reads.

Visitors, I think to myself. The only visitors I've had in here are the policemen and the therapist, who will greet me again in a moment with her wide snow-white smile and her braided blonde hair. No Danny. No Kyra. No Reina.

"Go on in," says the voice next to me.

I look at the ground. Would Danny have tried to visit me? Maybe the police won't let him have contact with me and that's why he stayed away, otherwise I don't understand why he hasn't come to see me yet. I bite my lip. It has been months, I think gloomily. I miss him and I miss that sense of security he provides me. I so want to be held by him right now. But he doesn't even show his face. Has he abandoned me over the whole thing? Surely he can understand that I wasn't... me, not the true me, at least?

"Amber."

My nose curls up. With bared teeth, I look at the caretaker. He steps back and is already reaching for his pocket with one hand. My smile weakens and I roll my eyes. I know the blows of the whip, I think grimly, as I place my own hand on the door handle in front of me. I push down the latch and step inside. Snow-white teeth greet me from one of the chairs.

The man follows me into the room and stands in the corner, against White Teeth's advice. She has explicitly asked for a female caretaker, repeatedly, but she got shot down every time. A woman would be no match for me, they pointed out to her. I am too strong. White Teeth then asked for two caretakers or, if necessary, three, but that too was out of the question. There are already so few caretakers; they cannot babysit me during every session.

The white teeth ignore the man in the corner and urge me to do the same.

I look silently at the window. It's not as if I have no experience with that.

"How are you feeling today, Amber?" she asks.

I look at her eyes. She has brown eyes, darker than Henry's. Her hair is lighter than mine and always carefully tied together in a neat braid. I look at her dark eyebrows and the few millimetres of dark outgrowth on her crown.

"What do you want to talk about today?"

My head turns to the window. My gaze fixates on the bare beech tree in front of it. On one of its branches sits a brambling.

"We talked about Jack last time. At least... I did," she clarifies. "How do you feel about that now?" She shifts on her chair. "It's quite devastating to go through something like that and it should never have happened." She studies my expressionless face intently. "I can imagine that you might be feeling angry... sad... unsafe. You have every right to feel that way."

Jeez, really?

"It's okay that those feelings are there... that's proper, actually, it's natural. It's important that those feelings find a way out. In a healthy way, that is." She clears her throat for a moment. "Your trust has been deeply damaged, even in something as mundane as a cup of tea, which should have just been a cup of tea."

I cast a glassy stare outside. The brambling hops from one branch to another.

She makes eye contact with the caretaker standing in the corner of the room and takes a deep breath. "Can you remember anything at all about what happened? For example, of that last time, that you had woken up during..." She is silent for a moment. "Did you ever feel him on you? Or noticed that your clothes were different when you came to? Did you ever notice anything about the drink he gave you?"

My eyes follow the snowflakes swirling past the window.

"Morgan, the detective who stopped by to ask you some more questions a few weeks ago, is working on a case. They want Jack to pay for what he did," she begins. "And your story can help them do that, but you'll need to answer."

Another silence follows in which she watches my eyes closely.

"I understand that video tapes were found in his practice and at his home..." she folds her hands together, still waiting for the slightest shift in my attitude or behaviour, "...and that you are also on several tapes. Your parents have since been informed of this. Your mother, Kyra, and your father, Danny..."

My jaw clenches.

"Or would you prefer me to call them your adoptive mother and adoptive father?"

I swallow and keep my gaze fixed tightly on the window.

Her sigh fills the room. "Let's talk about something else, then. The reason you came to see Jack: the man with the hat."

I stare into the distance. I hear her rambling on about Lester as the wind whistles outside. She asks what he means to me now and if he is still with me. The sound of her voice slowly blends into the ambient noise as the snowflakes steadily cover the window.

I lie with my back on the soft mattress, staring at the white ceiling above me. I have already studied every discolouration and crack and compared it to the ceilings I have seen in Lethalis and the ceiling at home in my room. My thumbs twist around each other. I wonder if my room is still my room. Maybe Kyra has already had it emptied and there is a new coat of paint on the ceiling. Maybe Danny helped throw out the furniture.

I turn onto my side and sigh deeply.

The room around me is empty. It has been empty for ages. Since my last day in Lethalis, I have been alone, apart from all the people around me. No lady in red. No Henry. No man with the hat. I could have used your company right now, I realise amid the bittersweet silence. I smile crookedly, paralysed by the irony.

The next morning, there is a knock at the door. I lift my head slightly off the feather pillow and frown at the face of the usual caretaker peering through the window.

The key rattles in the lock and the door swings open. "Amber, you have a visitor."

I scurry to my feet.

He smiles. "I've never seen you this excited. Get changed quickly, I'll see you in a minute." He puts down a pile of clothes, closes the door and locks it. The back of his head covers the window.

I hastily take off the dotted white pyjamas and hoist myself into the dark blue sweatpants and light grey shirt that now lie on the floor by the door. My knuckles tap against the window.

The caretaker turns around and unlocks the door once more.

I step away from the door as he pushes it open and holds it for me. I walk out into the corridor and walk ahead of him in a brisk pace.

Down the corridor, around the corner. Through the door, down the stairs. Through the other door and down the last corridor, past the television room. With pounding heart, I stand in front of the white door with the sign next to it that reads *Visiting Room*. I exchange a silent glance with the caretaker before pushing the door open forcefully. I step into the room and remain motionless.

On the couch, where I normally sit during conversations with the white teeth, sits an older man of tall and stately stature. He has broad shoulders, sinewy arms and bony fingers intertwined in front of his chin. His chin is covered in short greyish stubble, as are his cheeks and sideburns. His shiny silver hair reaches to just above his eyebrows, and beneath it a pair of piercing light brown eyes adorns his face. The man's left cheek is marked by a sizeable scar that has largely faded. In front of him, on the small coffee table, is a weathered grey fedora.

I stagger to the chair, which I normally sit opposite, and plop down. My fingers clasp around my swaddling knees.

We look at each other. Looks without words, but full of meaning.

"Good morning, Amber," the man greets me in a deep voice.

"Good morning, Lester," I respond with dry mouth. I swallow. They are the first words I have spoken in months, my first words since I left Lethalis.

Lester smiles warmly. "No one has called me that since your mother." He pulls his fingers apart and places his hands flat on his thighs, just above his knees. "These days I introduce myself as Frederick. But... you can call me Lester."

"You're real," I react abruptly.

His eyebrows raise slightly and he emits a boyish laugh. "As far as I know, yes."

I shake my head. "No, I mean... You're real. You really exist. You're alive." I look at him thoughtfully. "But you look different. Your cheek..." I stop talking.

He smiles. "It took some surgery and years of recovery time, but it's better this way, isn't it?"

"I thought you lost your eye."

He raises his eyebrows, his mouth slightly ajar. Then he puts his finger on the surface of his eye. "A glass eye," he explains. "I didn't expect you to have remembered any of that."

"I saw it, that you were pushed in the fi-" I gesture with my hand over the left part of my own face.

He nods slowly. "That must be an unpleasant memory for you."

I shake my head again. "I only remember it... since just before I came here. Before that, I didn't have any memory of before, except of my mother and me in the water and the vision of the carpet with the lilies."

"Ah, the lilac lily carpet," he responds.

"And a hallucination of you," I add cautiously.

He raises his eyebrows. "Of me?"

I nod. I open and close my mouth again. How do I explain this? I swallow. "I didn't know you were real. I only remembered that on the last day in Lethalis. It showed me."

He looks inquiringly at my face. "It?"

"The hotel. It showed me all sorts of things. What happened on that day with my mother. How my mother was. How..." I am silent for a moment, "...how she could look."

"I don't know exactly what you saw, but Lilian, your mother, was much more than just her last months."

"What do you mean?"

He exchanges a glance with the caretaker and then looks at me thoughtfully. "If you want, I can tell you a few things to fill in some blanks, but do you feel stable enough?"

A muscle in my neck contracts nastily under my wild nod.

"Okay... let's see. Let me start at the beginning." He lowers his head slightly and breathes a sigh. "I remember the day I first saw her." He looks up at the ceiling. The right corner of his mouth curls up. "A beautiful sight, with big open eyes and a closed soul." His gaze focuses on me again. "Even the air around her felt mysterious. Almost every man who met her fell under her spell. Ethan, the owner of Lethalis at the time... your father."

He swallows and frowns. "The wildest stories circulated as soon as the male guests had a drink in them and made themselves comfortable in the lobby." He casts a glance out of the window. "Every night they sat there, with a glass of whisky in one hand and a fat cigar in the other. Outdoing each other with bizarre stories and grand victories. One guest after another, coming and going. And in a quarter of those stories Lilian played the lead role." He looks at me piercingly. "She was a regular guest at the hotel, for months. Nobody knew where she got the money for such a long stay, but rumour had it that her father was immensely rich. The owner of a coal mine. A real estate tycoon. A successful golfer. The head of a bank. Even a mafia boss, it was said. There was even a pot full of gambling sums, which in the end was never paid out. Partly because Lilian stored it, probably..." He chuckles. "In reality, she had never paid a bill. Not for the room she stayed in permanently, and not for the food or drinks she ordered. She had a debt of thousands; a fair amount in those days." He is silent for a moment.

"How come you knew?"

"She told me." He has a dreamy look in his eyes. "I don't know exactly why, but Lilian was one of the few who said more than two words to me."

I look at him non-comprehendingly.

He looks at his hands, dark brown in colour with tiny pigment spots. "Different times," he sighs. "At least..." He looks briefly at the care-taker in the corner of the room. "Something has changed, anyway. But back then I was lucky to have a job in the first place. One that earned enough to keep the lights on at home and where I was even at the forefront of interacting with guests."

I look deep into his eyes and notice the small shades of orange in the light brown. "Why wasn't she kicked out, if she had racked up such a debt and wasn't paying?"

"Hmmm. Initially, I believe, because Ethan had fallen for her, hard." He pauses for a moment. "He soon made her move in with him, in room 399," he then adds. "But that wasn't the only reason. Your mother, with her looks, was an excellent hostess. And Lethalis..." he casts a suspicious glance at the caretaker, "...had an underground side income in the 1980s."

"The Golden Ten games," I respond.

"Do you remember that?"

I shake my head. "There was something about it in the paper." I pull my lower lip into my mouth and waver. "Because of that leaflet, that piece of paper, I went to Lethalis. Just because I saw a picture and it attracted me so much that... well," I explain.

"Yes... Lethalis has a curious... attraction," he admits slowly. "It has always had that and I don't think it was only because of the Golden Ten. Ethan made tons of money there. Especially when he had appointed Lilian as hostess. She pulled in one man after another and with that one wallet after another inside-out."

I frown slightly.

"Yet nearly every man left grinning. And so Lethalis gained quite a reputation for its size and location, in addition to the dance parties in the earlier years. That reputation did not go unnoticed." He smiles delicately. "The authorities were not happy with us. They were on our doorstep every other month with all sorts of claims and ruined many a dance party for nonsensical reasons. They put more and more pressure on Ethan. Fines for the smallest things. Chasing guests away. They even destroyed hotel rooms and the restaurant several times. Ethan was finally so fed up that he quit."

My throat feels groggy.

"You can perhaps imagine how surprised he was when quite a bit of money still kept coming in. He thought he had squeezed the supply and was preparing for the worst, after all the trouble and damage the authorities had caused." He looks at me meaningfully.

"My mother?"

He nods. "Lilian brought the gambling game underground. That's how it managed to continue for a few more years. But it didn't really stay underground, because people talk. That's just what they do. The authorities soon got wind of it and resumed their harassment. They did everything they could to shut down Lethalis."

"To close it down?"

He nods. "They didn't settle for less. So when the game was banned in 1991, they were only too happy. They finally had the official means to shut down Lethalis. That was quite a blow to your parents. Ethan went down with it and Lilian... she refused to accept it. She had quite a lot of willpower, that lady." He shakes his head slowly. "But at the time they had you and your sister to look after, so they had to come up with something."

My stomach turns. "W-wait a minute... did you say... my sister?" I stammer.

He looks up at me, his mouth hangs open a little. "Oh dear, you really have lost your memories..." He heaves a heavy sigh.

"Do I have a sister?"

"I'm sorry. I thought..." He is silent for a moment and swallows laboriously. "You had a sister, but... She died when she was seven years old."

"Why? How? What happened?"

Lester looks at me for a moment. "Lilian had demons," he begins cautiously. "I think she had always had them, but when Ethan... when he changed... I believe Lilian was trying to protect you in her own way."

"Protect me from what?

He looks at me silently.

"What happened to my father?"

He slowly shakes his head. "Some things are best not remembered."

"Please tell me," I respond in a pleading tone. "She pushed him down the stairs, didn't she? I saw it, I was standing-" I gasp for breath. My hands are shaking. "I was at the top of the stairs and I saw her shove him. His blood..."

Lester looks down at his knees and then exchanges a telling glance with the caretaker. "Ethan," he begins, "was a sick man."

I look at him expectantly.

"It's probably a good thing that you remember nothing, or little, of that time. There's a reason why they kept it out of the papers."

I cast a glance out of the window and suddenly, for the first time in months, I think of Jack. I have been able to shut myself off from my memories so well, willy-nilly now, even during Lain's muttering. Until this moment, when the visions, he so desperately wanted me to believe were delusions, reappear before my mind's eye.

"Should I leave? I think you have enough to process right now."

I shake my head. "I have so many questions..."

He smiles. "I fully understand that and I want to answer them all for you, as far as I can. But we'd be stuck here for several hours."

I cast a questioning glance at the caretaker in the corner. "It's not like I ever get visitors. I suppose I have some hours to spare."

The man in the corner shrugs his shoulders indifferently. "I'm fine with it and I'm guessing Lain would only encourage this. At least you're talking now." He smiles subtly. "Now I finally know what your voice sounds like."

I turn my attention back to Lester. "I don't know... where do I start?"

"What do you want to know?"

"My sister... What is, or was..." I frantically search for words, but the fog in my head is thicker than ever. "What was she like?" I finally ask.

Lester smiles warmly and looks out of the window - his left eye, the glass eye, however, keeps staring at me, which reassures me in an

absurd way. "She was a very happy child. She always wore floral dresses," he begins.

"With flowers?"

He nods. "She loved flowers. Daisies, specifically. She called those the-
"

"Happy flowers," I complement him. The words leave my mouth
faster than they came to mind.

He raises his eyebrows. "Yes, the happy flowers... do you remember?"

I bite my lip.

"She thought those flowers always looked so happy. I don't know
how a flower can look happy, but it made me laugh every time. It's a
child's fantasy and that's so touching, so endearing. She was always
drawing flowers, too. She would even daub the walls in the corridor
if you weren't paying attention for a moment. Sia... ah, she was the
maid, had to scrub a lot of those drawings off the wall at the behest
of your father - er, of Ethan, I mean. But we all thought it looked
cheerful." He takes a breath in which he stares dreamily ahead. "It did
go with the lilies on the carpet," he adds, laughing. "Henry gave her
the wall in the shed. She was allowed to cover the whole thing with
drawings and she did, well... she nearly did. There was just one spot
left." He lets his head hang. "But she never got to finish it."

My heart pounds against my ribcage. "What was her name?" The
question formulate on my lips, but I already know the answer.

"Toke," the man with the hat replies.

My insides contract. "I've seen her," I whisper.

He nods slowly. "You were the one who found her, that day." He lets
his head hang.

"What?"

He looks up at me questioningly. "That's what you're talking about,
right?" he asks with an uncertain look in his one eye.

I shake my head for a moment. "No, I saw her, at the hotel. When I
was there in the summer."

His one eye turns away. "You mean you saw Toke there?"

I nod, "As a grown woman," I add. "With bright vintage floral dresses and bright red hair."

He frowns for a moment. "Toke was blonde, just like you."

I mirror his confused look.

Two bottles of water are placed on the table by Manny, the caretaker. I reach for one of the bottles and greedily drink from it. I didn't even realise he had left the room.

Lester looks at the bottle of water in front of him and gestures at it. "You drink it," he says softly in his warm voice.

"What caused her death?"

Lester folds his fingers together and looks at me with a fairly stern look. "Are you sure you want to hear this, now?"

I nod. "I've..." I fall silent as I bite my lip and search for the courage to finish my sentence, "tried for so long to retrieve my memories. Now I have all these blanks, of which I am not even sure if they are memories or delusions. I want the whole picture. I want to... finally know the whole story."

"I don't know the whole story either, I'm afraid, let me be clear about that. I can only tell you about what I remember myself. Those are only parts of the story."

"That doesn't matter. Tell me everything you know," I respond. "Maybe my memories will come back to me that way, even if it's only a few."

"Ignorance is bliss, Amber." He pauses and a profound silence follows as he pulls his chin to his chest. "I tried to protect you. You and Toke. I realised too late what was happening to... to you." He swallows wearily. "I didn't know until that day."

18 GOLDEN TEN

9th of July 1992

"Hahahahah!" Amber runs on her bare feet across the lilac lily carpet on the third floor of Lethalis. Her white dress flutters up and down, making the orange butterflies dance on the fabric.

Toke runs ahead of her down the corridor, on sallow green worn slippers, wearing a blue dress decorated with tiny daisies carefully embroidered on the fabric. She looks back at Amber and, as a result, bumps into the man walking down the corridor. He is wearing a shabby grey suit with a matching fedora.

"You girls be careful," Lester smiles. "Make sure you don't get hurt."

"Lessie, have you seen my markers?" Toke looks up at him questioningly with her big green eyes.

"No, I haven't seen them." He crouches down. "Did you ask Sia? She tidies everything."

"Sia is not here today. And she said I'm not allowed to draw on the wall!"

He chuckles. "That's because she always has to clean it up.

However..." he taps his chin, "...it's one week early, but we do have a present for you. Go and have a look in the shed, at Henry's."

Toke jumps in the air and runs down the corridor on her sandals, towards the stairwell.

"Me too," Amber says softly.

"Yeah, do you want to go see Henry too?"

She nods shyly.

"Come, we'll go together." He grabs her hand and walks with her towards the oak stairs.

"NO! How many times do I have to tell you!" a gruff voice shouts.

Lester looks aside and sees Lilian, in her finest red dress, appear around the corner.

"Crazy bitch!"

Lilian quickens her stride and stops just in front of Lester and Amber. She casts a glance at Amber, who is clinging to Lester's leg. "Get her out of here," she says with a fierce look.

"Come back, you hag! I'm not done with you yet!" Ethan appears around the corner, in one of his usual checkered blouses and tattered jeans, holding a half-empty liquor bottle.

Lester grabs Amber by her wrist and takes a few steps backwards, while Lilian slips past them and hurriedly dashes down the steps.

"You owe *everything* to me, you ungrateful cunt!"

Lilian runs, as fast as she can in stiletto heels, down the stairwell, haunted by Ethan's words. The sound of her heels still echoes through the stairwell when Ethan throws down the liquor bottle. The bottle shatters on one of the steps. Shards of glass spray in all directions and then remain motionless, glinting in the sunlight coming in through the high window. A moment later, there is complete silence.

Ethan turns around. He sees Lester standing in the doorway of room 301 and points at him. "Amber," he says in a commanding tone. He stumbles down the corridor and looks down at Amber's crown. She looks up at him with her big green eyes. "Come on, Amber," Ethan says soothingly, holding out his hand. "Come with daddy."

"We want to go to Henry's," Lester says gently. "We have an early birthday present for Toke in the shed."

"Give her to me."

"Ethan..."

"What did you say?" Ethan snaps at him with a piercing look.

"I mean, Mr. Price."

"Give Amber to me."

"This may not be the right mo-" begins Lester.

"Give. Her. To. Me," Ethan repeats in a sharp tone. "And don't contradict me ever again, understand? Because I will have you out of here and out of a job in a matter of seconds, no matter what the bitch says."

Lester looks at Amber and gently lets go of her hand. Not knowing that he will forever regret this moment, this choice.

Ethan grips her little hand tightly. "Make sure Lilian takes her pills. She's unbearable like this," he commands Lester. He drags Amber along towards room 399, which they have lived in as a family for years, while grumbling aloud about ingratitude and people not knowing their place.

Lester walks into the stairwell with his head bowed. He finds the shards of glass and sighs deeply. "Lethalis is losing its glory," he says aloud as he walks down the stairs to the cellar door. He grabs a cloth and a dustpan and brush and walks back upstairs to clean up the mess. He carefully picks up the large shards and wipes every nook and cranny, thinking only of the bare feet of the two girls who love running through the corridors here so much.

If only Sia were still here, he thinks wistfully. She really knows how to clean things. He sometimes called her a sorceress, because she knew how to get rid of the dirtiest stains with the simplest of means. And she had cleaned up broken glass so many times after Ethan's tantrums. Those tantrums have only become more frequent in the last few months, now that Lethalis has had to close its doors and a reopening has been delayed by the ongoing investigation. The staff and occasional underground guests, who quietly come and go, are the only living souls left wandering through Lethalis. Even though this month is supposed to mark the peak season of the hotel.

If only it had never been banned, the Golden Ten gambling. Lilian did a fantastic job as hostess, entertaining one party after another and emptying many a purse as if it were nothing more than a routine chore. And when the games were still legal and it was the main entertainment for most of the guests, they had been happy. That might have been their happiest time as a family, even. Ethan and Lilian and then Toke too, followed not much later by little Amber.

Back then, they were so busy that he had his hands full standing behind the front desk, checking in guests and helping bring their bags to their rooms. Sia had had a full-time job cleaning the hotel, and she had had plenty of help, although most of them were holiday workers who only worked during the peak season. And Henry, well... Henry always keeps himself busy. Both in summer, when the garden is thriving, and in winter, when he clears snow, repairs burst pipes and gathers firewood for the fireplace in the lobby.

Lost in thought, Lester lifts the dustpan full of glass to the nearest bin. With a cloth, he wipes the steps to dampen the smell of alcohol, which he rinses and hangs to dry. He goes back downstairs and walks out of the hotel through the back doors. His shoes crunch on the gravel, which Henry manages to keep cleanly white, as he walks to the shed - not knowing that in a few years' time, that shed will be razed to the ground because of the carnage that is about to take place. Not knowing that the only other survivor of that massacre will be taunted some 16 years later by his own mutilated appearance, a souvenir of this wretched day.

He walks into the shed and exchanges a glance with Henry before looking at Toke, who's drawing on the wall on the east side, which Henry has completely covered with blank paper, with her brand new markers. Butterflies, flowers, unicorns and rainbows already embellish nearly half the wall.

"She couldn't wait," Henry says with an apologetic look. "So I told her to give it a lash. I did tell her it's a gift from all of us, of course, including Sia."

Toke looks back for a moment and flashes a beaming smile.

Lester's hearty smile fills the room. "I don't blame her. It took a bit longer than expected. Ethan..."

"Yeah? It's that time again, isn't it?" Henry takes a few steps to the side and stands close to Lester. "Why are we still here, anyway?" he asks softly from the corner of his mouth.

Lester looks at him questioningly.

"Come on, Lester. There haven't been any guests for weeks. These days, the only visitors are those few poxy rats, as if they don't already have enough gambling debts, and the Garda and they only cost us money. Lethalis won't open anymore, believe me. It's over."

Lester continues to stare silently at Toke. "We are still getting paid, right?" he responds soothingly. "And besides..." he gives a nod in Toke's direction, "it's not just about us."

Henry shrugs. "They are not my responsibility, are they? I didn't become a father for a reason." He pulls out a packet of cigarettes and pops a cigarette in his mouth. "You know they aren't right in the head, yeah?" he continues softly as he looks intently at Lester. "Ethan is always on the lash and effin' and blindin' at everyone. And Lil? She'd better take her pills again with all her drivel of evil and what-ever else she comes up with. The lad's not who..."

Lester implores him to be quiet. He looks with mesmerisation at Toke's cheerful drawings on the wall. She has already covered almost two-thirds by now, though they are mostly lines and little is still coloured in. "We do what we can," he remarks.

Henry takes a deep puff and blows the smoke out through his nostrils. He wants to say a lot more, but decides to remain silent.

The shed door squeaks open and Lilian appears in the doorway with red cheeks and puffy eyes. She joins them.

Henry grabs his rake from the corner of the shed and walks out with his fag hanging halfway out of his mouth.

"Are you OK?" Lester asks softly.

Lilian bites her lip and nods. "I want to get out of here, Lester. I know I've said it before, but now... I really need to get out of here. Before he..."

"What's going on?"

She shakes her head. "I..." she begins. She buries her face in her hands and starts crying softly. "I can't do this anymore, Lester. I really can't do this any longer."

He casts a glance at Toke and then gently grabs Lilian's hand. "Should I get your medicine?"

She widens her eyes and yanks loose her hand. "NO!"

Toke looks back startled. The red marker she was drawing with falls to the ground and rolls to Lilians feet. The marker comes to a halt up against her red stiletto heel. "Keep drawing, love..." she says soothingly. She picks up the marker and puts it in Toke's hand. "Everything's alright." She feigns a smile and strokes Toke's head, who turns around again and, with some reluctance, finishes her latest flower on the wall.

She gets up and turns to Lester. "No," she hisses. "Those pills... I can't function with them..." She slowly shakes her head. "Jack says we should increase the dose," she whispers, "but I've told him so many times that they only make me feel worse. He doesn't listen to me. He acts like it's all in my head. But I know..." She bites her lip so hard that blood wells up from it. "It feels... it feels like they're trying to keep me small, Lester. Like I have to fit into a glass box and I can't take it anymore. I can't do this, Lester. They're trying to control me and I know... I know Ethan's sick..."

He takes his fedora off his head and clasps it between his hands. "Are you talking about his drinking?"

She shakes her head. "Help me, please, Lester. Toke and Amber... they need to get out of here. Away from him. Before he takes them away from me forever."

"What do you mean?" he asks with an agonised expression on his face. "What's going on, Lilian? I want to help you and I will help you, but what can I help you with?"

"Get us out of here," she whispers. "Today. Before it's too late. That man is evil." She bites her lip and looks deep into Lester's eyes with her big green eyes. "Please... get them out of here. At any cost. Don't worry about me. Get Toke and Amber and... run."

"What will they do without both their parents?" he sputters softly.

She shakes her head abruptly. "They're better off without us." She casts a glance at Toke and then looks around. Her eyes get big. "Where... where is Amber?"

He grimaces. "Ethan took her."

Her eyes bulge out of her sockets. "No... no..." She clutches her head with her hands, scratching deep furrows in her cheeks. "No... not Amber too..." She turns abruptly, sprints out of the shed and runs across the gravel at such a roaring pace that one of her heels breaks.

"Stay here, honey," Lester says, before following Lilian with a worried look. His heart races in his chest as he runs through the courtyard and sprints up the steps. He hears the screams on the third floor tremble between the walls of the stairwell.

THUD!

When he reaches the top of the stairs, he sees Lilian, throwing herself against the door of room 399. Just when Lilian is about to take another run-up, the door thrusts open. Ethan appears in the doorway with a malicious look in his eyes. He clenches his fist and punches Lilian hard in her face. "What did I tell you, you worthless piece of shit!"

"Devil!" screams Lilian back. "You filthy, vile devil! Give Amber back!"

Ethan retrieves a bottle of pills from behind his back, grabs her chin and forcefully pours half the contents down her throat.

"Ethan!" Lester shrieks. He yanks Lilian from his grip. She coughs and gags and spits out a few of the pills to the floor.

"*Mr. Price*," Ethan berates him.

Lester slaps her on the back and she gasps for air, nearly choking on the pills that are still stuck in her throat.

"Amber," she brings out in a weakened voice. "Amber..."

Ethan raises his hand once more, but Lester steps between him and Lilian. That's the moment he looks into the hotel room and sees it. The one image that will change him forever. Amber, lying silently on the bed, staring blankly ahead. Her dress lavishly dumped on the floor. Lester's legs feel like cement and for a moment he stands completely frozen. A thick fog wells up in his mind and that fog soon turns red. The world goes black before his eyes. He grabs Ethan by his collar and slams him to the ground. All the air squeezes out of Ethan's lungs as his back hits the lily carpet.

"Amber," Lilian repeats desperately. Her jaw and hands tremble. She crawls across the floor into room 399 as Lester throws another punch at Ethan. He punches him again and again and then is thrown backwards. Lester smacks down on the carpet.

Ethan quickly scrambles to his feet and runs down the corridor.

"Amber," Lilian wheezes.

Lester pulls himself up by the doorframe and silently looks down at the mother crawling across the carpet to her daughter.

"I need to clean her, Lester," Lilian says. "She needs to be cleaned."

"I know..." His voice breaks.

"I'm her mother. I can do it. I have to do it." She gently picks Amber up from the bed and holds her in her arms.

He turns away from them as she takes Amber into the bathroom, half swaying on her legs. With knees buckling, he walks to the stairwell and down a few steps. His legs give out and he collapses to the stairs. He rests his head in his hands. Defeated, he remains seated, partly on the lilac lily carpet and partly on the oak staircase. A tear rolls down his cheek and falls on the step below him.

Footsteps echo through the stairwell.

He remains seated with his head bowed until he sees two feet clad in work boots in front of him on the stairs. He raises his head slightly, without looking at the person in front of him.

"Jesus, Mary and Joseph, what's going on, Lester? Ethan is completely unhinged."

Silence.

"What did he do to you?"

Lester looks up slowly with a serious look in his eyes, his lips pressed together. "We need to get out of here, Henry."

"Yeah, I told you that, didn't I?"

"With Amber," he responds. "With Toke. With Lilian. As soon as... no, right now."

"Where are we going?"

"That doesn't matter. Away from here."

Henry looks at him for a long time and then nods. "Alright. Toke is in the shed. What's the plan, then?"

Lester slowly shakes his head. "There's no plan."

Henry casts another glance at him. "What about money? You know no one will hire me with my background. And you... well... I don't have to tell you that, do I?"

Lester looks at the backs of his hands. "That's not important now."

Henry stares silently down the third-floor corridor. "Alright then," he finally says. "Where do we meet?"

"At the shed. Within ten minutes."

Henry helps him up and walks down the stairs with a quick pace.

Lester walks over to room 399 and opens the wardrobe door. He snatches some clothes from the wardrobe and starts stuffing them into a bag. A few of Lilian's outfits and some of Amber's and Toke's outfits. The white dress with the orange butterflies should be burned, for all of our sakes.

There are groans and coughs in the bathroom.

He looks up and pricks up his ears. Then he hears Lilian laughing cheerfully.

"Well done, Amber," her voice sounds.

He refocuses on packing and crams the last remaining clothes into the bag, which he swings over his shoulder. He rummages in the desk and takes out the identification documents of Lilian, Toke and Amber. As he grabs the papers, the bag slips from his shoulder, almost knocking over a candle - one of the many candles Lilian uses to save electricity.

"You can't leave me," Lilian's voice sounds, sweet as honey.

"Lilian?" he asks. He hoists the bag back on his shoulder. "Are you... ready?"

"I can't get her clean, Lester."

He frowns deeply. "Can you dry her off and get her dressed? Henry and I... we're ready. We're leaving, along with you. He and Toke are waiting for us in the shed."

Silence.

"Can you go there? As quickly as you can. I already have your clothes and papers with me, you don't need to bring anything else." He glances at the bottle of pills lying half-open on the floor of the room and the few slimy pills sticking to the tufts of the lily carpet.

"Yes," sounds her voice dreamily.

"The sooner, the better," Lester responds. He walks out of the room and continues his way outside. As he walks between the hedges, he notices how quiet it is outside. On a day like this, with the sun burning in the sky, you wouldn't expect the horror that had just taken place in this hotel.

He walks into the shed. The bag promptly falls off his shoulder.

Henry lies on his back on the concrete floor with his eyes closed. Next to him lies his rake and at his feet lies the red marker, which Toke had been drawing with, with no cap on it. The cap lies a few metres further down under the lawnmower.

He kneels down beside him and takes his pulse, anxiously feeling for his heartbeat.

At that moment, Henry blinks his eyes languidly.

"Henry... Henry," he groans. "What happened? Where is Toke?"

He sits up wearily and rubs the back of his head.

"Are you all right?"

"I'm seeing double, man." He presses a hand to his forehead.

"Do you know where Toke is?"

He looks around dazedly. "Who?"

Lester squints his eyes. Henry attempts to get up, but he stops him. "Stay here," he cautions soothingly. "You shouldn't walk around now, you might have a concussion. Stay put for a while, I'll come and get you in a bit." He jumps up, runs through the courtyard and back into the hotel through the glass doors. He scours the ground floor, calling out her name. "Toke, Toke!" The lobby is empty. The dining room is empty. The basement is empty.

Ethan, meanwhile, walks curiously calmly up the stairs to the third floor. His eyes are fixated on Lilian, who is standing at the top of the stairs. Amber stands behind her in the white dress with orange butterflies. She is hiding behind her mother's legs.

He starts grinning. In his one hand he clasps a large chef's knife that belongs to Irvin. The blade gleams in the sunlight. "Where do you think you're going, Lily?" his voice whispers menacingly. "And you've got Amber with you, even. You know she's mine, don't you? They're both mine."

They are ten steps apart.

Lester runs across the first floor. Toke's name echoes through the long corridors. He busts open door after door, in a blind panic.

"Bastard," Lilian responds in a trembling voice. "You sullied her."

He shows a wicked grimace. "She is as she should be. Mine. And she always will be."

She gasps.

He is five steps away from her.

Amber steps back anxiously.

"Give her to me, Lil. After that you can do whatever you want. Disappear into thin air... I can make that happen, you know. I'll just leave you in the well and have it sealed. Then you'll stay here forever, where you belong. Together with my girls." He puts his foot on the second-to-last step. His knuckles turn white around the handle of the knife. His hand lifts in the air.

Lilian lets out a scream and shoves his shoulders hard.

Lester is about to run up the stairs to the second floor when the knife clatters between the steps and misses him by a hair. The knife stands straight up in the oak step. He sprints up the stairs with wide eyes and stumbles upon the bloody scene at the top of the stairwell. Ethan is lying with his neck buckled against the wall. The back of his head is cracked open against the wall and blood is seeping down the wall along the flat part of the stairs. He looks up and sees Lilian, who slowly turns around and disappears from sight. He walks cautiously further up the stairs. "Lilian?" His voice trembles. "Lilian, where is Amber? Where's Toke?" He is so fixated on the woman who has been pushed to the limit that he fails to notice the little blonde crown around the corner of room 301. He walks over to room 399.

Amber walks on her bare feet across the carpet and then down the first part of the stairs. She casts a glance at her father, who's lying open-eyed staring into nothingness, and runs on to room 299, the longstanding vacant room where she and Toke play together and hide from their father's tantrums and their mother's psychotic episodes, though Amber doesn't understand much of that at this point in time. She opens the door and walks in. "Toke?" she asks in a small voice. She looks around the empty room. She opens the big wardrobe doors, but the closet is empty. She looks under the bed, but there is nothing under the bed either. She walks to the bathroom door and lets it swing open.

She looks at her sister, whose birthday would be in a week. Whom was decorating the shed wall just a moment ago. Whom just this morning was running with her through the corridors of Lethalis, where they had always been together. Her blonde hair had danced up and down with every step. Now those same blonde hairs lay like a wreath around her head on the cold stone floor. She kneels down beside her. Her knees become wet and warm. She gently strokes her little hand over her sister's head. Her hair sticks to her scalp and is red in colour.

"Amber!?" echoes Lester's voice. His footsteps rumble across the second floor and slow down. He glances at the only room door on the floor that is open. Of course, he thinks to himself. Their play-room! He steps inside and his gaze is immediately drawn to the two sisters - one lying down and the other sitting up, both in a large pool of blood. He gasps for breath.

Lilian appears by his side. Her breath falters for a moment. She starts screaming so deafeningly that the windows shake in their frames. "Now look! Look what he has done! Look at that!" she screams.

Lester stumbles over to Amber and is about to grab her, but due to the look in her eyes, he can't touch her. "Get Amber out of here," he says softly to Lilian, whose voice is broken to the point where she cannot scream anymore.

She picks Amber up and takes her away.

Lester kneels in front of Toke's body and closes her eyes with his fingers. "I'm sorry... I'm sorry..." He starts sobbing. His back shakes. "I'm sorry..."

Meanwhile, Lilian lays Amber on the bed in room 399 and walks silently to the door. She locks it with the big brass room key and walks to the desk, where she lights the candles one by one.

Humming softly, she walks back and forth with the candles, scattering them around the room. A few under the desk, a few by the curtains, a few by the bedside table and a few beside the bed. The little flames playfully wiggle back and forth, grabbing the rim of the curtains and the tips of the duvet. "This is our last chance, Amber."

Amber sits up and looks at her mother, perched on the floor in the middle of the room.

"Honey," she chants sweetly. "I can clean you... I can purify you. But I need to hear you say it... I need to hear you say it, darling... Tell me he is evil. That he is the devil. Tell me you see it, because then maybe there is still hope. Tell me."

The flames crackle.

Amber looks around anxiously and jumps off the bed. She crawls into her mother's lap, who puts a hand on her crown. "Mommy," she sobs.

"Tell me, my darling. Otherwise all is lost."

The flames grow.

"Tell me, Amber," Lilian's voice sounds stern. She grabs Amber by her little shoulders and shakes her with a twisted expression on her face.

The heat is suffocating.

"Tell me!" she screams.

Amber's eardrums burst.

"I need to hear it from you!" Lilian's hands clench so hard around Amber's wrists that her nails split open the skin underneath.

"Daddy!" Amber's high-pitched voice moans.

She rattles her once more. "That man is evil," she hisses. "He took her from me and now he wants to take you away."

"Daddy!"

Flames whip around and engulf the bloodied sheet.

THUD. THUD. THUD.

"LILIAN!" Lester's voice sounds from the corridor. His fists pound on the door. "LILIAN, OPEN UP!"

"But no one will take you from me. I will purify you. Yes, I can purify you. Your soul must be cleansed! I can bring you back. You I can bring back. This time I will succeed."

THUD. THUD. THUD. THUD!

"LILIAN!"

Blood trickles down Amber's wrists and drips onto the lilac lily carpet, scorching all around them.

Lilian grips her wrists even tighter and pushes them towards the fire. "I will cleanse you."

The flames roll along her arm hair and the heat makes her skin bubble. She screams. And screams. And screams.

The door succumbs to Lester's torment and flies off its hinges. He rushes into the room, snatching Amber from Lilian's clutches and pulling her away from the fire.

Lilian wants to grab him, but he pound her in the face with a fist. Her head tilts back and the burning flames seize her hair. The fire rolls across her copper-coloured locks at the speed of lightning.

He lifts Amber out of the room and, coughing from the smoke, lays her down on the carpet in the corridor. Just as he has laid her down, he is struck on the back of his head. His head snaps to the side.

Amber whimpers, looking up at her mother towering over them with a half-shattered desk chair in her hands.

He scrambles to his feet and sends her flying into the room, desk chair and all. Back into the inferno.

The fire creeps steadily across the carpet tufts towards the corridor.

Footsteps hurtle through the stairwell.

Lilian's face emerges from the flames and her hands grab Lester just as he's about to turn to Amber to bring her to safety. She pulls him into the fire with her. The flames wrap around his face and he screams.

Henry comes running around the corner and sees Amber lying on the carpet with simmering forearms. He waves through the smoke with his hand, picks her up and runs down one floor. He runs into room 201 and puts her in the bathtub. He turns on the shower tap and feels the water before holding her little arms under it. "Stay put like this. I'll get back to you soon, promise," his voice sounds agitated. "Stay put!"

The smell of burnt flesh fills the corridors as sirens bellow outside.

Lester manages to free himself from Lilian's clutches, but not without losing half his face and one eye to the heated battle for life and death.

Henry finds him on the third floor and drags him to the room opposite 201. He turns on the shower tap and sprays it over Lester's face, shuddering. He squeals and howls like a little boy from the water, grabbing Henry by his shoulders. "I know," Henry begins softly. "It went arseways, but you did it. Amber's safe." He looks with an agonised expression on his face at the man whose half face has melted away. "You saved Amber."

Amber notices little of the firefighters and the extinguishing of the fire. She only sees the flakes of ash swirling into the bathroom. She only smells that particular pungent odour, which - even at her young age - she thought she would never forget. She hears the crackling flames reverberating in her ears and the sound of her name being repeated over and over, whispering and shouting. She sees only the flawless face of the young man with the narrow jaw, who helped calm the simmering flesh on her arms, and the battered face of the man who saved her life and whose life would never be the same after today.

19 SNOWFLAKES

I look into Lester's good eye, still barely comprehending what I've just been told. I avert my gaze silently and watch as the snowflakes merrily swirl down outside. "Henry," I begin. "What happened to him?"

Lester hangs his head. "He didn't survive the night, I'm afraid."

My breath falters.

"He suffered a skull fracture from the blow from the rake." He looks up at me with moist eyes. "But he passed away peacefully, Amber. He went to sleep and just didn't wake up again. That's one small fact we can take comfort from."

I put my palms together and support my face with it, with my nose between my fingers and my chin resting on my thumbs. "And Toke... How...?"

"I don't honestly know, sweetheart. I don't know whether Ethan did it on purpose or it was an accident. I have no idea what had happened there in that bathroom."

Tears well up in my eyes. How could I have ever forgotten Toke? I rock back and forth. My hands squeeze my upper arms. I lift my head and look at the faded scar on his face. I lean forward and reach for his cheek with my fingertips. I see his eyes snap open. I hear Manny's clothes rustle as he takes a more alert stance. Then I feel the ridged skin, both rough and smooth and at the same time soft and hardened. "You saved my life," I say softly.

A tear rolls down his cheek and slides down my fingers. I gently retract them.

"I didn't recognise you," he says smothered. "Then, in the newspaper. I had read the report, that morning, of you being missing, and I saw your picture." He smiles through his tears. "But I didn't recognise you. You've grown so tall. Such a beautiful lady, just like your mother. I'm so sorry you had to go through all this." His voice falters. "After what happened in Lethalis..." He touches his scar gently. "I didn't even know if you were alive. I never saw you again after that day. I did look for you, but there was no Amber Murphy with your features. I did find an Amber Price and I thought you might have taken on your father's name, however crude, but it wasn't her either." He dries his cheeks. "I really wanted to meet you again. I have always wanted to know how you were doing. Whether you had been adopted and by whom. Whether you had turned out well. Whether you'd been able to put the past behind you and... I'm so late..."

I grab the second bottle from the small table and take a sip. "You're here now," I say softly. I squeeze my eyes to hold back the tears. "You're the only one who's here."

"When I read you were here, I drove down here that same day. But..." he casts a glance at the caretaker, "...I could only see you by appointment. And that was only possible when you were stable. So I came back every week. And in the weeks when I couldn't come by, I sent letters."

"I didn't get anything," I respond with a sideways scowl at the caretaker. "But... why?" I wipe my own cheeks dry.

"I was hoping I could help. I thought I might be one of the few who could, though that might sound narcissistic."

I take another sip of water and shake my head thoughtfully. "I think so too, honestly."

"Your helping hand... Linda, was her name?"

"Lain," I respond.

"She said you hadn't spoken a word since you've been here..."

I nod affirmatively.

"I'm glad you're talking to me. And I consider myself a lucky man for being able to see you again." He beams. "How big you've grown. A grown-up, really." His smile fades. "Though you had to grow up all too fast."

I cast a glance at the snowflakes swirling towards the window and sticking to it. They will stay there until the sun melts them away. Their final resting place. I look at Lester again. "Can I ask you something?"

He makes an inviting gesture with his hand.

"You said you now introduce yourself as Frederick. Why is that?"

He opens his mouth and reflects. He turns his gaze to the window and I see his good eye tracking the falling snow. "The times were times, back then." He stares out the window gloomily. "After I pulled you out of the flames, I struggled to break free from your mother." He snorts. "She was extremely strong, almost indestructible. I don't know where she got the strength, but I finally managed to get her off me... into the inferno. She never got out of there." He casts a glance at me. "I had to come along to the police station and... well, they couldn't say for sure whether Lilian was the one who had started the fire. Despite Henry's statement and despite your statement. They weren't convinced that I wasn't the instigator."

My mouth jars open. "But that's absurd. I saw my mother do it!"

"And I'm one hundred per cent sure you told them that too. You were very articulate and straightforward, for how young you were, let alone what terrible things you had just gone through. But they didn't care about that." He brings his hands up and turns his palms towards me. Then he turns his hands over and shows the backs of his hands. "To them, I was a black man who played a part in the live burning of a white mother. I spent six years in jail for involvement in manslaughter, with no evidence." He puts a hand on his heart. "I knew the blows of the whip, so when I got out, I changed my name and built a new life for myself." He looks at me with a sad look in his eyes. "But Lethalis never let me go, so I stayed around nonetheless. In Midsberg, near Lethalis. Just a few bus rides away from you, apparently."

My diaphragm shocks. Tears flow down my cheeks again. Words fail me.

His hand closes around mine. "This should never have happened to you."

A wheezing sound escapes my throat. My lungs expand and contract uncontrollably under my pulsating diaphragm. Snot drips down my lips and mixes with my salty tears.

"We need to end here for today," Manny's voice sounds.

Through my hazy retinas, I can barely see what is happening. I feel a hand on my back and feel myself being pulled up from the chair. I am guided towards the door. With a jolt, I turn to face Lester.

He clasps his hat against his thighs with trembling hands.

I open my mouth and try to speak, but only frosty whimpers are heard.

He nods with a sad smile. "I will visit you again soon." He disappears from my sight as I am led out of the room. "I promise you that," he calls after me. The warmth of his voice echoes heartily down the corridor.

I struggle to hold myself up by Manny's shirt as he leads me back to my room. As soon as I am inside, I crash down on the bed. I feel his hand patting my shoulder for a moment. I perceive the sound of the squeaky water tap, the running water and the full cardboard cup being placed on the floor beside me. I hear the sound of his voice, trying to convey encouraging words despite them not reaching me. Then there is the sound of the door closing with a soft click and locking. His footsteps die away and silence overtakes everything.

Lester contrasts starkly with the swirling snowflakes as he walks slowly towards the car park in front of the institution. He stops and looks back at the building towering above him. His eyes are damp and a subtle smile marks his lips. "I'm glad you're still here," he whispers to the icy wind. A shiver runs down his spine. He turns and wants to walk on but he nearly bumps into another person. "Oh, pardon me," he says.

The other man meets his gaze with dull grey eyes. "That was my mistake. I wasn't paying attention, sorry." He swallows. His fingers circle the pale skin that draws a line around his ring finger.

"It's not as bad in there as it looks from out here," Lester encourages him in his warm voice.

The man runs his hand through his ash-blonde hair. "Thanks," he responds with a crooked smile.

They give each other a nod and walk on, until the blond man comes to a halt a few metres down the road. He turns around, his eyes squinting at the icy wind, and looks at the man with the scarred cheek.

Snowflakes swirl down, delicately coating the grey fedora.

www.ingramcontent.com/pod-product-compliance
Lightning Source LLC
LaVergne TN
LVHW020321200726
843507LV00012B/2192